"...Although the three-part story is set largely at a church and invokes faith, it's never sanctimonious in tone, and it can be enjoyed by community-minded non-Christians. The author clearly establishes and develops each character, which will compel readers to take a genuine interest in their lives. Madding's prose is clear and readable throughout without seeming overly informal. He also appears to be well acquainted with the city of Atlanta, as his descriptions are precise and easy to visualize. His overall approach to service is refreshing as he coaxes readers into examining their prejudices and selfishness..." - *Kirkus Reviews*

"A timely, heart-warming story of a church working through what it means to be the Church. Peachtree Street Church could very well be any congregation, and following their journey is both a joy and an exercise in introspection." - *Shawn Smucker, author of The Day the Angels Fell*

"Allen Madding reminds all of us that while we are playing checkers, God is playing chess. ShakenAwaken reminds all of us of the power of keeping our eyes and ears open to God's next move in our lives. Powerful!" - *Mike Kalapp, Pastor*

"This book is vital for our Christian culture right now. The plot draws us into the plight of homeless people and before it's over, you know exactly how you can work to end homelessness in your area. So helpful! This book is like nothing I've read before, and I cannot recommend it more. It's a well written, captivating, hope-filled story." - *Priska Jordan, Christian Faith Blogger, priskajordan.com*

"Allen Madding' s SHAKEN AWAKE is an effective and convincing (if sometimes overly optimistic) argument in novel form for a new method of helping the homeless by building community." - *Indie Reader*

SHAKEN AWAKE
THE COMPLETE TRILOGY

Allen Madding

Charm House Publishing

Saint Petersburg, FL

Publisher's Note: This is a work of fiction. Names, characters, places, and
incidents are a product of the author's imagination. Locales and public names
are sometimes used for atmospheric purposes. Any resemblance to actual
people, living or dead is completely coincidental.

Editors: Priska Jordan and Crystal Rowe
Book Layout ©2017 BookDesignTemplates.com
Cover Design ©2019 BookCoverDesign.Store

Ordering Information:
This book is distributed by Ingram, One Ingram Blvd., La Vergne, TN 37086.
www.ingramcontent.com

Shaken Awake - The Complete Trilogy / Allen Madding. -- 1st ed.
ISBN 978-0-578-65851-3
Library of Congress Control Number: 2020904422

Contents

Foreword

The single greatest cause to homelessness is a profound, catastrophic loss of family. When that happens, we don't turn over that problem to the government. It's up to the Kingdom, the metaphorical village, to continue to raise those children.

As long as we keep distance between us and them, it's easy for us to judge and stereotype the "thems," because they're out there. They're beyond the tinted windshield of our SUVs with SiriusXM® pouring into the deal. We need to get out of that environment and go connect with them one-on-one. Sit down with them and go, "Oh, you actually have a name. Really? Awesome. Tell me about yourself."

"Well, I was born in 19-whatever and my mom suffered from mental health issues." And we pause. "Well, my mom suffered from mental health issues, too." All of a sudden, there are these connecting points. These are our neighbors. We're not so different after all. We find we both need healing.

It's all about the community being inspired into a lifestyle of service, and that starts by diving into a relationship with individual human beings. So, roll the window down and say hello. Go break bread with your neighbors. When that happens, when relationships begin to form, we begin to experience the power of community.

Housing will never solve homelessness, but community will, because people desire to be fully and wholly loved and fully and wholly known. Stuffing someone into four walls and a roof doesn't answer that primal call for healing connection. That's the difference. These men and women coming into our community thrive once they reconnect to themselves, others, and God. It is up to us to live out our call of building human-to-human, heart-to-heart relationships.

Alan Graham,
Founder/President/CEO, Mobile Loaves & Fishes,
Author of *Welcome Homeless: One Man's Journey of Discovering the Meaning of Home*

Shaken Awake

Dedicated to my loving wife, Allison, who has constantly encouraged me to write and who has worked beside me hours on end launching and operating a nonprofit. You have quietly served beside me, going out in the middle of the night to pick up food and shuttle it to shelters, gotten up at the break of dawn to work canned good drives on Thanksgiving mornings, worked in the cold at fundraising events, and been a constant source of inspiration. Without your support I would have given up on writing a long time ago, and I never would have started a food rescue program. Thank you for your constant demonstration of grace in your everyday relationships that sets an example for me daily. I am humbled by your support and dedication, and I am confident that God has a crown adorned in jewels waiting for you just for living with me.

"Jesus comes to us in the poor, the sick, the dying, the prisoners, the lonely, the disabled, the rejected. There we meet him, and there the door to God's house is opened for us."

HENRI NOUWEN

CHAPTER 1

It was 4 o'clock in the morning when the phone rang. Bleary-eyed, Samuel Matthews reached for his wire-rimmed bifocals and his cell phone. Early morning phone calls had become regular over the last decade as the congregation of Peachtree Street Church grew older. The old pastor began to scroll through an invisible list in his mind of the elder members and wondered who it would be this time.

"Reverend Matthews," said a deep voice on the phone, "This is the Atlanta Police Department. One of our patrol officers has found a dead man on the front steps of your church. We were hoping you could help identify the body."

Sam ran his hands through his grey hair. When the phone rang, he certainly wasn't expecting the police. And while he had grown accustomed to reports of heart attacks, strokes, and broken hips, this call jarred him. A dead man on the front steps of the church?

After a brief pause, the old pastor responded, "Where do you need me to go?"

The dispatcher directed him to Grady Hospital. Sam was all too familiar with his route to the hospital – so much that he imagined his 15-year old Ford Crown Vic, a former police car he had bought at an auction, could drive itself there.

As the pastor quietly got dressed, different scenarios ran through his mind. Maybe the man was a victim of a shooting. There had been plenty in the neighborhood surrounding the old, historic church. Drug deals gone bad, carjackings, violent robberies, home invasions – the streets got mean at night.

After a short drive with very little traffic, Sam pulled into the parking lot of the E.R. and parked his car. A brisk wind chilled him as he made his way to the door. He pulled the collar of his wool coat tight around his neck and stepped up his pace across the parking lot. Although Georgia was in the sunny South, it could get icy-cold in the city at this time of year. Fourteen degrees, the thermometer by the Emergency Room entrance displayed. With the wind chill, Sam guessed it probably felt somewhere around zero.

He approached the counter and identified himself to the attendant. A few minutes later, a nurse appeared and walked him to a room with two Atlanta Police Department detectives. They were in street clothes, but Sam recognized them by their trademark fedoras. It was tradition in the Atlanta Police Department to award a detective with a fedora for solving a homicide case. A single white sheet covered a body lying on a table.

"Reverend Matthews," began one detective, "one of the patrol officers found this man dead on the front steps of your church. We couldn't find any ID on the body. No wallet. The Medical Examiner has not evaluated the body yet, but the E.R. physician says it looks like he froze to death."

"Good Heavens!" replied the old pastor.

The detective pulled back the sheet enough for Sam to see an old, tired face outlined by gray, stringy hair and a week-old beard. He did not recognize the man, but he did recognize the worn and weary look of his face. He had seen that look on hundreds of faces on the streets around the church over the last 15 to 20 years.

"Sorry, officers," Sam said. "I don't know him. He is not one of the church's regular attendees. We have a lot of homeless in the area around the church, but I don't really know any of them."

What a horrible way to die: alone, cold, helpless – and at the doors of a church. The one place where people should find comfort, help, and rest. Instead, this poor soul only found locked doors. Over the years, the administrative board had wrestled with vagrants, looters, and kids looking for places to get high. Many of the doors were both locked and chained. Lower level windows were covered with bars. In fact, if one walked by on the side street without looking up to see the tall steeple, they might mistake it for a prison.

What on earth was this man doing on the front steps of the church? Sure, on a night this cold, the shelters in Atlanta would be at capacity. But if he had been around the neighborhood, he had to know this church did not offer food or shelter for the homeless.

A sickening sense of sadness overcame the old pastor. He turned and walked out of the room, slowly down the corridor, and back to the lobby, lost in his thoughts.

Over the years, Sam had watched the congregation of Peachtree Street Church dwindle from over 500 to less than 100. Nothing the old pastor tried changed the decreasing attendance. There were no young families with children anymore. The average member was 55 years old. Along with the dwindling attendance was the dwindling offerings. A trust fund left from a late member's estate kept the light bill paid, but the operating budget was tight. More than half of the education wing was abandoned. As the congregation shrank in size, less space was needed for Sunday school classes. Nowadays, there were only four classes still meeting.

Every day Sam arrived at the church, he encountered homeless people. The shelters closed at sunrise to encourage the residents to look for jobs and to give the staff an opportunity to clean the facility. So, the homeless took to the streets every morning. Some made their way down to Chick-fil-A for coffee and free Wi-Fi. Others found a warm, comfortable seat at Starbucks. Sam wished that the church could do something to help these people – especially on these coldest of nights. He knew the shelter was forced to turn away people when it reached capacity, and on the colder nights it happened more often than not. But the church had no budget to operate any new ministries even on a short-term basis.

A weekly soup kitchen would be a great outreach to the homeless community, but it would require food and extra utility expenses. Temporary emergency shelter for the homeless during cold snaps was desperately needed, but there would be extra insurance requirements, building and occupancy code concerns with the city, and, once again, extra utility expenses.

He steered the old car back to his apartment building still thinking about the nameless man found on the steps of the church. How could this happen at a church? When he walked back into his apartment, it was 6:30 a.m. It was pointless to go back to bed, so he made coffee and oatmeal and sat down to read his morning devotional. After breakfast, Sam pulled out his cellphone and dialed the chairman of the board of trustees for the church, Phil Portman, and told him of the events of the morning.

"If the Atlanta Journal-Constitution runs a story about this man's death, I certainly hope they leave out the church's name," Phil said.

Sam had not even thought about the possible bad press that might be associated with the man's death.

"You probably need to prepare a brief statement for Sunday in case a reporter calls and wants to talk to you about the situation," Phil continued.

Sam drove to the church. He entered through the side door that entered the stairwell nearest his study, carefully locking the door behind himself. He settled into his high-back leather chair behind a large cherry desk and prepared a brief statement summarizing the story of the man found frozen to death on the steps of the church. Once he was satisfied with his prepared statement, he turned to the window of his study that looked out onto the street and stared off into space, lost again in his thoughts.

CHAPTER 2

A lvin Smith sipped a cup of hot tea while reading his morning copy of the AJC. After years of working at the General Motors plant in Doraville, this had become his daily routine over the last 10 years. As he read through the local news, his eyes stopped on a story about the death of a 73-year old man. "Two years younger than me," he thought to himself. He felt himself flinch when he read where the man was found. He forced himself to re-read the sentence again. The man had frozen to death on the steps of Alvin's church, the church where he had married his late wife Janet. Where his son had been baptized. The church that held Janet's funeral when she lost her struggle with breast cancer.

It shook Alvin to his core. He felt numb inside. It was as if someone had hollowed him out. Peachtree Street Church had always been a symbol of Alvin's faith. It was like a lighthouse on the shore of the storms in his life. When his son was born, members of their Sunday school class brought over meals for an entire week. When Janet was diagnosed with cancer, it was where Alvin quietly eased in and made petitions to God for her healing. When she died, church members again brought meals. How could someone in need die right on their doorstep? How could someone simply needing shelter from the cold die at a place that was supposed to represent safety? The lighthouse had failed.

"What if that had been me?" he thought to himself.

He had always considered himself blessed. He didn't take his pension check for granted. He remembered when GM filed bankruptcy and he feared his pension might disappear in the legal wrangling. Fortunately for him, the pension plan had been assumed by the Pension Benefit Guaranty Corporation. But he knew several men who had lost their retirement savings when former employers had gone bankrupt. He also knew that pension plans were a thing of days gone by. He talked with many men a few years younger than himself who had no pension. Many only had a few thousand dollars in retirement savings, if anything at all.

"Where would I be right now if I didn't have my pension check?" Alvin thought. "Right next to that man on the steps of our church."

The thought of it sent a shiver down his spine. He couldn't sit with his thoughts any longer. He pulled on his jacket and went for a walk to clear his head.

As he walked down Juniper Street, Alvin thought about how blessed he had been over his life. After graduating high school, he went to work at a gas station where he learned to become a mechanic. A few years later, a friend went to work at the GM plant in Doraville. His friend got Alvin an interview, and Alvin soon went to work there as well. Alvin spent 44 years working at the plant, receiving promotions and pay raises that enabled him to raise a family and send his son to college. Alvin didn't take any of it for granted. He had high school friends that enlisted in the Army. Some came home wounded and struggled to reintegrate back into day-to-day life stateside. Some struggled with alcohol, some with drug dependence, and most were in and out of the Veteran's Hospital.

One friend that Alvin kept in touch with – Bobby Carpenter – suffered with Post Traumatic Stress Disorder. Alvin remembered Bobby calling him one night to pick him up from the Atlanta City Detention Center. Bobby had walked into a drugstore to have a prescription refilled. While standing in line, he heard the label printer printing labels for prescription

SHAKEN AWAKE · THE COMPLETE TRILOGY | 19

bottles. The thump-thump-thump sound that the printer made sounded just like the machine guns Bobby heard when he was in combat. His mind did not identify the sound as a printer, but instead he heard machine guns. True to his training, Bobby leapt for the floor for cover, knocking over a display shelf. Other customers were frightened by his behavior. Someone called 9-1-1, and the Atlanta Police Department picked him up and carried him to the detention center. After being interviewed by the medical team there, Bobby was released, and Alvin picked up his old friend and drove him home.

Alvin thought about Bobby and wondered how many veterans had come home from serving their country and encountered difficulty. How many were homeless? How many were dependent on soup kitchens and shelters for their survival? How easy would it be for someone like Bobby to lose a job because of their struggles with the effects of PTSD, then have their utilities cut off, and then be evicted from their home? How many were sleeping on the streets of the city, in parks, or under overpasses? How humiliating would it feel to go from proudly serving your country to being homeless?

Alvin decided that a good southern-cooked lunch might raise his spirits. Returning home from his walk, he decided to drive to his favorite restaurant, Mary Mac's Tea Room, a 1945-era restaurant known for southern comfort food. As he pulled into the parking lot, he spotted a Mercedes that he was almost certain belonged to Phil Portman, the investment banker who chaired the board of trustees for the church. Alvin made his way around the block to the front door of the restaurant. When he walked in, he saw Phil, standing near the counter, waiting to be seated.

"Well, hello Alvin," Phil called. "Care to join me for lunch?"

Alvin always hated eating alone in public, so he quickly accepted the offer. Shortly, a middle-aged man in black slacks and a starched white shirt greeted them and led them to a table near the front of the building. The two men scribbled down their orders on the notepads provided to them and handed them over to the waiter. The waiter soon reappeared with two glasses of sweet tea and a basket with fresh baked cornbread, yeast rolls, and warm cinnamon rolls. Alvin lost himself for a moment as he enjoyed one of the delicious cinnamon rolls.

Phil brought Alvin back to reality when he asked, "Did you hear about the body they found on the church steps yesterday morning?"

Alvin's momentary bliss suddenly disappeared.

Alvin slowly responded, "Yes, I saw it in this morning's AJC."

"Damn," Phil replied, "I hoped the church would not get any bad press out of the whole situation."

Alvin was surprised by the response. "Bad press? All I can think about is how if it weren't for a couple of really good breaks in my life, that could have very well been me found dead on the steps."

Phil's face made it apparent that the thought had never entered his mind.

"You know," Alvin continued, "we kid ourselves thinking we are self-made men. We are blessed beyond measure. Instead of being grateful for how blessed we are, we often pat ourselves on the back for a job well done and poke our chest out like banty roosters. These kinds of events make me stop and consider how just one small incident could leave someone's life in shambles."

Suddenly, the conversation was interrupted by the reappearance of the waiter with two plates of golden fried chicken and abundant helpings of vegetables. Phil unfolded a napkin and draped it across his thigh.

"Do you think the church is somehow to blame?" Phil asked.

"You know," Alvin replied, "I've been sorting through my thoughts on all that most of the morning. I cannot say that Peachtree Street Church is to blame for the man's death. But I do believe that if there are people freezing to death on the church steps, the church needs to do something other than hope that the local news does not run the story. I believe the church has a responsibility to the neighborhood and the community. Peachtree Street Church once met the needs of the community, but when the offering started running low, it seems the ministry stopped and general preservation took over. Now we're busy maintaining a museum dedicated to the memory of what the church used to be."

Phil took a long sip of sweet tea and looked up at Alvin.

"I wish there was something we could do," Phil said. "but we barely have enough finances to pay the preacher, maintain the building, and pay the utilities. In the past 10 years, we dismissed the church secretary, associate pastor, and choir director. We have volunteers filling positions that were once full-time staff members. The only people still on the payroll are Reverend Matthews and two part-time janitors. We just do not have the budget to do anything else."

Alvin laid down his fork and looked at Phil.

"If we cannot afford to do the work of the church," he said, "we should close the doors and stop calling it a church. If we are maintaining a facility for one Sunday morning worship service, we would be better served to sell the property to a developer and meet in a hotel."

Phil shook his head. "We cannot shut down the church!" he replied.

Alvin sat quietly looking at Phil. Phil could feel his clenched jaw. Why was he suddenly so tense over this conversation? He looked down and realized he had balled both of his hands into fists. He relaxed his hands, drew his breath, and looked up at his friend.

Quietly, Alvin replied, "We have to do something. We cannot sit idly by while people needing our help die on our doorstep."

When the two men completed their lunch, Phil picked up the check and said, "Lunch is on me."

Alvin thanked him, and the two walked around the building to the parking lot. As they rounded the corner, an older man – Phil guessed in his 70's, with a half-grown beard, wearing three tattered coats and mismatched gloves – approached them.

"Excuse me, do y'all have any leftovers from your lunch you could spare?" the hoarse sounding voice asked.

Phil was dumbfounded. When he saw the man approaching, he expected another encounter with a homeless man wanting money. He rarely, if ever, gave any handouts when asked, because he assumed they would buy alcohol or drugs with the money.

Once on the MARTA heading to an Atlanta Braves game, Phil had witnessed a man asking for money for food. Several people on the subway had opened their lunch bags and pulled out a few items. Before the next stop, the man was holding a sandwich, an apple, and a banana. When Phil stepped off the train, he looked down on the platform and next to the train door was the sandwich, apple, and banana discarded. Ever since, Phil recalled the experience anytime he was approached for a handout.

Alvin answered the man before Phil could. "Sorry we don't, but stay right here a few minutes, and I'll be right back."

Before Phil knew what was happening, Alvin disappeared around the corner. Phil stood motionless trying not to make eye contact with the man. After a few awkward moments, the man spoke up.

"It wasn't always like this," he said as if answering a question. "I used to have a nice house overlooking Piedmont Park. But several years ago, my wife became ill. Our insurance company said that our health insurance policy didn't cover cancer and wouldn't pay a dime. So, I took a second mortgage against our house to pay her medical bills. After she died, I couldn't pay the two mortgages, and the bank foreclosed on the house. I've been on the street ever since."

Phil heard a noise and looked up to see Alvin reappear around the corner carrying a bag.

"Sorry for the wait," Alvin said. "Here are two plates. One for lunch and another for your dinner. There are four bottles of water as well."

The man seemed stunned by Alvin's gift.

"Thank you very much, sir. This is way better than what I had hoped for."

He took the bag and shuffled off out of sight. Alvin and Phil quietly walked to the parking lot. Phil stood by his car and watched Alvin drive away. He shook his head recalling their conversation at lunch and the encounter on the sidewalk.

CHAPTER 3

Phil awoke Saturday morning, dressed and drove to the gym. He went through his normal cardio workout, showered, dressed and stopped by Starbucks for a cup of coffee. He found a quiet table in the corner and sat down. He retrieved his tablet and opened up the Sunday school lesson material to prepare for Sunday. Phil began to read the scripture passage:

"When the Son of Man comes in his glory, and all the angels with him, he will sit on his glorious throne. All the nations will be gathered before him, and he will separate the people one from another as a shepherd separates the sheep from the goats. He will put the sheep on his right and the goats on his left.

"Then the King will say to those on his right, 'Come, you who are blessed by my Father; take your inheritance, the kingdom prepared for you since the creation of the world. For I was hungry and you gave me something to eat, I was thirsty and you gave me something to drink, I was a stranger and you invited me in, I needed clothes and you clothed me, I was sick and you looked after me, I was in prison and you came to visit me.'

"Then the righteous will answer him, 'Lord, when did we see you hungry and feed you, or thirsty and give you something to drink? When did we see you a stranger and invite you in, or needing clothes and clothe you? When did we see you sick or in prison and go to visit you?'

"The King will reply, 'Truly I tell you, whatever you did for one of the least of these brothers and sisters of mine, you did for me.'

"Then he will say to those on his left, 'Depart from me, you who are cursed, into the eternal fire prepared for the devil and his angels. For I was hungry and you gave me nothing to eat, I was thirsty and you gave me nothing to drink, I was a stranger and you did not invite me in, I needed clothes and you did not clothe me, I was sick and in prison and you did not look after me.'

"They also will answer, 'Lord, when did we see you hungry or thirsty or a stranger or needing clothes or sick or in prison, and did not help you?'

"He will reply, 'Truly I tell you, whatever you did not do for one of the least of these, you did not do for me.'

"Then they will go away to eternal punishment, but the righteous to eternal life."

-Matthew 25:31-46 [i]

Phil felt conflicted. He thought of the man he met yesterday on the sidewalk outside Mary Mac's and the circumstances that left him living on the street. He thought about the many faces he encountered over the years asking for money. How could he determine who really needed help and who was a con artist? How could he know they weren't going to use the money he gave them to buy drugs?

As he pondered those questions, he wondered about the odds that this Sunday school lesson would come up the Sunday after a man had frozen to death on the front steps of the church. Phil knew that this lesson guide was used by congregations all over the United States and tomorrow every one of those churches would be studying the same lesson material, but it certainly seemed like more than mere coincidence to him. He finished reading the lesson materials and made some notes.

"How big of a problem is homelessness in our city?" Phil wondered to himself. He knew Atlanta Mission did a lot of work to aid the homeless, so why were there still people sleeping on church steps? He started researching the issue on the internet. The first statistic he came across stunned him. "More than 10,000 people in metro Atlanta experience homelessness on any given night, with more than 40 percent being women and children," he read[ii]. He was shocked by the fact that a survey of Atlanta homeless shelters indicated a shortage of 1,700 beds. He continued searching and discovered: "The average two-bedroom apartment in Atlanta rents for $834/month. You would have to earn $16 per hour or $33,280 a year to afford that apartment"[iii]. The scale of the problem was becoming clearer the more he read. Atlanta Mission, one of the oldest and largest providers for the homeless was providing for over 950 individuals every day. It would take 11 organizations the size of Atlanta Mission to effectively solve the issue, Phil concluded.

Phil jotted notes from his research on the homelessness situation in Atlanta. He closed his tablet, threw away his empty coffee cup and headed to his car. He couldn't help but think about what Alvin had said at lunch on Friday and how quickly he had sprung into action. But how could Peachtree Street Church do anything with its thin budget and small congregation?

When Phil arrived at the church Sunday morning, he walked into the Sunday school classroom he had shared with seven other men for years. Alvin was already there and had made a pot of coffee.

"Bless your soul," Phil greeted Alvin.

Alvin smiled and poured Phil a cup.

"Did you happen to read today's Sunday school lesson?" Phil asked.

Alvin chuckled. "I did. Pretty timely, huh?" he replied.

Phil smiled. The rest of the group trickled in, making small talk and pouring coffee. At 10 a.m., Phil called for the group's attention and asked Alvin to open with prayer. Alvin and the rest of the men bowed their heads in silence, and he began praying. He first thanked God for each man present and their families. He then prayed for individuals who were ill and those dealing with the loss of loved ones. He closed the prayer asking for wisdom and guidance for all present to be positive influences in their community.

Phil read the scripture lesson for the morning: "*When the Son of Man comes in his glory, and all the angels with him, he will sit on his glorious throne. All the nations will be gathered before him, and he will separate the people one from another as a shepherd separates the sheep from the goats. He will put the sheep on his right and the goats on his left.*

"*Then the King will say to those on his right, 'Come, you who are blessed by my Father; take your inheritance, the kingdom prepared for you since the creation of the world. For I was hungry and you gave me something to eat, I was thirsty and you gave me something to drink, I was a stranger and you invited me in, I needed clothes and you clothed me, I was sick and you looked after me, I was in prison and you came to visit me.'*

"*Then the righteous will answer him, 'Lord, when did we see you hungry and feed you, or thirsty and give you something to drink? When did we see you a stranger and invite you in, or needing clothes and clothe you? When did we see you sick or in prison and go to visit you?'*

"The King will reply, 'Truly I tell you, whatever you did for one of the least of these brothers and sisters of mine, you did for me.'

"Then he will say to those on his left, 'Depart from me, you who are cursed, into the eternal fire prepared for the devil and his angels. For I was hungry and you gave me nothing to eat, I was thirsty and you gave me nothing to drink, I was a stranger and you did not invite me in, I needed clothes and you did not clothe me, I was sick and in prison and you did not look after me.'

"They also will answer, 'Lord, when did we see you hungry or thirsty or a stranger or needing clothes or sick or in prison, and did not help you?'

"He will reply, 'Truly I tell you, whatever you did not do for one of the least of these, you did not do for me.'

"Then they will go away to eternal punishment, but the righteous to eternal life."
- Matthew 25:31-46

Phil paused after reading the scripture again. He drew a breath and read aloud from the leader's guide: "The church is to be the hands and feet of Christ." As he read, he felt an inner conflict. He agreed with charity and helping, but wasn't there a point where helping could hurt? How could you provide a hand up instead of just a handout?

The leader's guide provided a list of questions to stimulate discussion, but Phil did not need them. He instead flipped to the notes he had made while researching homelessness in Atlanta.

"Guys, I was disturbed by this lesson material after the events of this week," he said. "I know all of you heard about the man who froze to death on the front steps of the church. And I'm sure that all of us have encountered someone begging for money on the streets. How do we respond in a way that helps long-term without creating dependency?"

He looked around the room to a few blank stares. A few others stared at the floor to avoid making eye contact.

Alvin spoke up, "I think we respond by doing what they cannot do for themselves and what those around them either cannot or have decided that they will not."

As Alvin spoke, Phil reflected on watching Alvin buy the homeless man lunch outside Mary Mac's earlier that week.

"I did a bit of research this week and made some rather startling discoveries," Phil continued. "For instance, did you know there are more than 10,000 homeless people in metro Atlanta and on any given night the shelters are at least 1,700 beds short of being able to accommodate everyone?"

Phil looked around the room. All eyes were on him.

"One-thousand and seven-hundred," Alvin repeated. "What do they do when it rains? How do they survive the cold?"

One of the other men spoke up, "Some of them have a tent community under the overpass at I-75 and I-85, but the Department of Transportation bulldozed a bunch of tents there last month."

Phil added, "Did you know at current rental rates you would have to earn $16 an hour to afford an apartment? If a man has a minimum wage job in Atlanta, he cannot afford a place to live."

Alvin responded, "What if you're a single mother working a minimum wage job trying to provide for your children? Where do you go?"

Phil looked at his tablet, "I don't know, but according to what I read this week, 40% of the homeless people in Atlanta are women and children."

Alvin spoke again, "We have to figure out some way we can help with this situation. People shouldn't die on the steps of a church because they have nowhere to seek shelter from the cold."

Phil glanced up at the clock and realized it was time to dismiss. "Guys, it's time to wrap up. Please give this some thought and let's talk some more. Knowing our church finances, I don't know how we can do anything, but I am shocked by the need." Phil said a short prayer and the men departed the classroom.

As Phil walked out of the room, he realized that he felt personally challenged by the entire situation, but he could not resolve within himself a course of action. Phil had spent years in the corporate world facing challenges, determining a course of action, and pursuing it with dogged determination. He realized that for the first time in a long time, he was facing a challenge where he did not know how to respond. It was a feeling of helplessness that he did not like. He felt like a ship lost in a fog without means of navigating a proper course.

Phil made his way into the sanctuary and assumed his regular position in his regular pew. As the worship service proceeded, he found himself automatically responding but not paying attention to the service or Reverend Matthews's message. He was still processing all the information he had learned over the week regarding the homeless situation in Atlanta. It seemed like an intricate puzzle that had no solution. Why was all of this coming to rest on his doorstep if there was no way for him to act in response? What was he missing?

He replayed his chance lunch with Alvin and the conversation they had. What would Alvin do? What was he suggesting Peachtree Street Church do?

CHAPTER 4

Reverend Matthews was in his study at the church when he noticed snow falling outside his office window. He laid his reading glasses down on his Bible and pushed himself back from the desk. He walked to the window to look out on the street below. The street was blocked with cars as far as his eyes could see. Snow in Atlanta was a seldom occurrence, and he knew the city was not well prepared for it.

Unfortunately in the South, ice usually accompanied any snow they got, which meant many of the streets and highways would be shut down. He pulled on his scarf and wool overcoat and walked out to look at Peachtree Street. A blast of cold air greeted him when he opened the door leading from the sanctuary onto the street. He was startled for a moment to see all four lanes of the street choked with bumper-to-bumper traffic. Peachtree looked like a parking lot. The snow was continuing to fall and the sidewalk and steps leading to the sanctuary were beginning to ice over. It suddenly occurred to him that he might have a difficult time getting home. If the sidewalk was icing, the streets could not be far behind.

The thought of sleeping at the church did not bother him much. He had slept in his office a time or two over the years for one reason or another. He had a few canned goods and some instant oatmeal in his desk. There were a couple of cases of bottled water and a small stock of coffee on hand for Sunday school classes and other church events. He even had a pillow and a wool blanket in the closet of his office for just this kind of occasion.

His thoughts turned to the people in the cars. Would they all get home? If Peachtree was jammed up like this, it had to mean that the interstate wasn't moving either. He carefully made his way back into the church, navigating past the ice patches developing on the concrete surfaces. He returned to his office and turned on his radio. The news staff was reporting that all four major highways were overwhelmed with traffic. The schools notified parents that they were closing for inclement weather at 1 p.m., so parents left work in a rush to pick their children up from school. Within minutes, over two million people were trying to leave work to drive to their children's school. It was simply more traffic than the Atlanta roads could support. Meanwhile, as the cars sat motionless on the streets and interstates, temperatures continued to fall, as did the snow. Initially, the roads were warm enough that the snow melted for the first couple of hours, but as the temperatures dropped, the melted snow became ice. Bridges began to freeze, and numerous hills became impassable.

As he thought about what was developing just a few blocks away on the highway and just outside the church on Peachtree Street, he wondered about the homeless. How many wouldn't find a bed in a shelter and would need a warm place for the night? He picked up his office phone and called Alvin Smith. Alvin answered on the third ring.

"Alvin, it's Reverend Matthews. I'm concerned about how many people will be seeking shelter tonight and how many will not find a bed in the local shelters," he said.

Alvin responded, "Preacher, I was thinking the same thing. There are people stuck out on the interstate that will run out of gas and be stuck in their cars before long. What do you think about opening up the fellowship hall tonight as an emergency shelter?"

The preacher paused and glanced out the window noticing that the cars had not moved since he walked outside.

"Opening the fellowship hall will not be a problem, but we are going to need blankets, water, food, and volunteers," Sam answered.

Alvin was already developing a plan in his mind. "Call the Salvation Army and see if they can help. I will call the men from my Sunday school class and see if we can get to the church."

Reverend Matthews dialed the Salvation Army and told them what they wanted to do. The person who answered provided some hope. Although the streets were blocked with traffic, they had some ATVs using the sidewalks to shuttle supplies to temporary shelters. Matthews then called Atlanta Mission to offer their facility as an overflow for the night, and he called the local news to get the word out. Once he was off the phone, he walked down to the fellowship hall and turned on the heat. On his way back to his office, he heard a pounding on the door that led to the street. He carefully opened it to find Alvin Smith.

"Hello, Preacher!" Alvin exclaimed. "The roads were blocked, so I walked it."

The two men hugged. Before long, the men of Alvin's Sunday school class started to arrive. Every one of them had walked to the church from their homes or offices. Alvin pulled out two large coffee urns and began brewing coffee. Some of the other men took inventory of what food was on hand.

A couple of the men arrived carrying grocery bags. A couple others arrived with a few blankets. Each had grabbed what they could before heading to the church. Before long, peanut butter and jelly sandwiches were being made and a pot of soup was cooking. Suddenly, the sound of ATVs was heard just outside, and Alvin met two young men delivering cases of water and boxes of military surplus blankets. While helping them carry the supplies into the church, Alvin slipped several times on ice. Conditions were worsening. It would be dark soon and temperatures were dropping. What was not already frozen would certainly be freezing in the next few hours.

CHAPTER 5

Joy Davidson listened carefully to the weather forecast for the day on the radio while she made lunches for her two children. "Snow in Atlanta? Yeah, OK," she thought.

She heard the forecast earlier in the week and noticed the grocery stores were completely out of bread, very low on milk, and all the rock salt was gone. However, the schools had not announced closings or early departures, and she assumed the weather changes would not amount to much.

She walked into the second bedroom to check the progress of the morning routine. Cheryl was dressed and putting on her boots. She could hear the sink running in the hall bathroom. She poked her head in the door to see Jeremy fully dressed and brushing his teeth.

"Get a move on, mister," she prodded him. "You don't want to miss the bus."

"Yessum," he replied while spitting toothpaste in the sink.

Missing the bus was not an option as Joy had little time between getting them on the bus and her commute to work. After a few minutes both children bounded into the living room gathering their book bags and lunches. Joy gave them both kisses and shooed them out the door to meet the bus. She walked out to the corner and stood with them, staying until the bus arrived and both of her children were safely on board. She walked back to their modest apartment to finish her own preparations for the day before beginning her commute to the office.

She packed her lunch, straightened up the kids' rooms, and pulled on her heavy, hooded coat. With one last glance around the apartment, she dialed the heat back in an effort to keep the power bill in check. She pulled on a pair of gloves, turned off the lights, locked the door, and headed to her car. The faded old Honda cranked up, and Joy coaxed the heater.

"Come on warm air," she said.

She dug out an ice scraper from the glove box and cleared the frost from the windshield. When she crawled back in the driver's seat, she felt the lukewarm air blowing.

"Thank you, heat," she muttered to herself.

She pulled the shifter into gear and headed out. Some thirty minutes later, Joy pulled into the parking deck below the office building where she worked, parked the old Honda, and took the elevator up to her office. As she entered the office, she saw the cityscape for several miles. She paused to gaze at the horizon and saw nothing that indicated rain or snow. "Silly weather guessers," she thought. She hung her coat in her cubicle and walked to the break room for some much-needed coffee. One of her coworkers was there stirring a cup of coffee when she walked in the doorway.

"Good morning, Joy," she said. "Think we'll get any of that snow they're talking about?"

Joy shrugged as she poured a cup of coffee.

"The last time they predicted snow we saw a handful of flakes and nothing stuck," she replied, "but my kids would love to see some."

Her co-worker chuckled, "Yeah, they have a 50/50 chance of being right. Last year, my husband listened to the weather before leaving for work. They said 20% chance of rain, and he elected to ride his Harley. Five miles into his commute, the bottom fell out, and he rode the rest of the 40 miles in pouring rain."

Joy walked back to her cubicle, logged into her computer, and immersed herself in processing insurance claims.

Around 10 a.m., the guy in the next cubicle joked, "The weather folks predicted snow to start at 10 a.m. Hmm. I see nothing for miles."

Joy stood up and walked over to the window and looked out across the city. It was a grey overcast morning but no rain or snow in site. She returned to her cubicle and resumed her work.

CHAPTER 6

Ron Barlow smiled as he walked into the garage and saw his new Dodge Charger. It was the car of his dreams when he was in high school. Now that his kids were grown and on their own, he finally had the opportunity to buy one. For the first time in several years, he looked forward to his commute, as it gave him a chance to drive the Charger. As he slid in and hit the ignition, the V-8 rumbled to life. It was music to his ears. His morning schedule was a little different today as his district manager was flying in from Boston, so Ron offered to pick him up from the airport. It got him out of the office for a few hours and provided more opportunity to drive the Charger. He merged into the southbound traffic to begin his journey. The airport was only 26 miles from his house in Dunwoody, but during the morning commute Ron estimated an hour's worth of driving. To be safe, he allowed an hour and a half. If traffic was manageable, he would grab some breakfast at the airport.

An hour later, Ron was on the airport perimeter road, negotiating his way into the hourly parking deck. If it did snow, the parking deck would provide cover. Ron found a spot hundreds of feet from any other cars to avoid door dings and parked the Charger. He ambled his way to the terminal, pulling the collar of his wool coat tightly around his neck. Still, he felt the biting wind as it blew through the parking deck. When he entered the terminal near baggage claim, he headed toward the display board that reported incoming arrivals. When he located the proper flight number, he found a surprise. Under the column "Arrival Time", he saw the word "delayed" in red.

"Well, I guess breakfast is in order," he said to no one in particular as he headed to the main terminal restaurants. He found an empty table, placed his order, and pulled up the USA Today app on his tablet.

After a filling breakfast and consuming all the day's news, Ron checked the status of the incoming flight again. The airport website was showing a new arrival time of 12:20 p.m. "Well, I did want out of the office," Ron thought. He pulled up a book on his tablet and got a coffee refill.

Finally, the Boston flight arrived, but it was 12:45 p.m. when Jeff, his district manager, texted him to say they were at the gate waiting to deplane. Ron texted him back, saying he would meet him at the South Terminal baggage area. He paid his tab, tucked his tablet into his coat, and headed to baggage.

Ron was surprised when he arrived at the baggage claim. Through the floor-to-ceiling windows, he saw it was snowing, and it appeared to be sticking to the roofs and benches. After a few minutes he heard a familiar voice.

"Loafing around all day at the airport, huh?" Ron spun around to see Jeff. "I thought they would never get us out of Boston. We waited two hours for the plane to arrive," he said.

Ron shook his head and the two men walked to the baggage carousel. He kept looking out the window. He thought it odd that it was snowing in Atlanta midday. Snow had been a rare occurrence for as long as Ron had lived in the city. When it did snow, it usually happened overnight. Jeff caught Ron looking out the window as he walked back up with his luggage.

"I take it you don't see much of that here?" he said.

Ron laughed, "We didn't get a single flake last winter."

As the two headed out of the terminal, Ron slipped on ice on the sidewalk but managed to right himself.

"Easy there, big guy," Jeff hollered. "They need to get these sidewalks treated before they get themselves into a liability suit."

The two men made it to the car, and Ron stowed Jeff's luggage in the Charger's trunk.

"This is where the bonus check went!" Jeff joked.

"Yeah, that and about $35,000," Ron replied.

They climbed in the Charger, and Ron hit the starter. The big V-8 rumbled to life, and Jeff smiled.

"Now, that's what I'm talking about!" he exclaimed.

As they exited the parking deck, Ron saw the airport perimeter road was bumper to bumper and at a crawl.

"I hate Atlanta traffic," he stated.

Once they reached the ramp for I-75/I-85 North, traffic seemed to improve.

"At least it's moving," Ron thought.

As Ron concentrated on navigating the traffic, Jeff noticed the Southbound traffic just over the concrete divider wall. It looked like traffic leaving the city was at a complete standstill.

As they approached the curve just south of Turner Field, traffic backed up in all lanes going north. Instinctually, Ron turned on the radio to find out what was happening. They continued to inch along, but they could see the southbound side was completely stopped. Soon they heard that a tractor trailer had slid sideways on the southbound side south of the airport and had all lanes blocked. As they continued the slow crawl north, the snow continued to fall.

"The D.O.T. is never gonna be able to treat these roads from with all this traffic," Jeff noted. "Why is traffic so heavy?"

Hardly before Jeff had finished the question, the radio news was reporting all metro school systems had decided to close at 1 p.m. for inclement weather.

"And of course, they called all the parents about noon to pick up their kids," Ron said, "Boom. Instant gridlock. Just add snow."

"And ice," Jeff added.

After almost two hours, Ron could see Georgia Tech and the Varsity Drive-in sign marking his approach to midtown Atlanta. A typical 15-minute drive had taken hours.

"I'm gonna try to sneak off here," he said. "We'll have better luck on surface streets than this mess on the interstate."

Jeff agreed. "Heck, it's already almost 3 p.m. At this rate, there's no point in trying to get to the office. We should just try to get to my hotel."

It took some work, but Ron maneuvered toward the off ramp. Concerned about the possibility of ice, he made sure he had considerable room ahead of him before he started up the incline and leaned on the accelerator to gain some velocity. The Charger's V-8 rumbled, and up the ramp they went. Ron had his hands full as the back of the Charger danced on patches of ice, but he managed to make it to the top of the ramp and to North Avenue. Ron's plan was simple. He would turn onto Peachtree, take it up to Jeff's hotel on 17th, drop Jeff off, and head up Roswell Road, a four-lane surface street, the rest of the way home.

That plan was going well until everything stopped at 10th Street. A MARTA bus had slid on a patch of ice and crashed into a delivery truck on the other side of the street. Peachtree Street was blocked both directions. The wreck broke a fire hydrant, which was now shooting water twenty feet in the air and freezing on the street. When Ron tried to turn around, the Charger would not budge. It was spinning tires on ice. Soon there were a dozen or more cars behind them in the same predicament. And now the sun was beginning to go down. The men sat quietly for a few minutes with the Charger idling to provide heat as they listened to the radio reports. I-285 was blocked both directions with multiple wrecks. GA-400 was completely stopped where it passed under I-285. I-75 was blocked both directions on both ends of the city. I-85 South was blocked with wrecks. In fact, the only place any interstate was moving was I-85 north of Buford. Then, the reporter recited a list of city streets blocked with ice followed by a list of wrecks.

Finally, the news broadcast began listing emergency shelters for homeless and people stuck out in the weather. Ron recognized the name of Peachtree Street Church.

"That's only about a few blocks away, if you feel like walking," he said. "That, or we can sit here until this thing runs out of gas."

He glanced at the fuel gauge which showed a little less than an eighth of a tank.

"And that will happen before sunrise," he concluded.

"OK," Jeff replied, "I can walk a couple of blocks."

CHAPTER 7

J oy's cellphone rang just before noon. When she looked at the display, the caller ID showed the call was from her children's school. She answered the call and listened to the recorded message. The school was closing at 1 p.m. due to inclement weather and deteriorating road conditions. She picked up her desk phone and called her supervisor and told her that she needed to leave to pick her children up from school. As she ended the call, Joy could hear other cellphones ringing throughout the office, and she realized many of her officemates would be leaving to pick up children. She pulled on her coat and scarf, gathered her other belongings and headed to the elevator. When she got to the elevator lobby, there were almost a dozen people waiting for the elevator. The doors drifted open to reveal an elevator car that was already half-full. Everyone was courteous and half of the waiting crowd got on the elevator. Soon, another partially full elevator stopped, and Joy managed to squeeze in. The elevator stopped at every floor on the way down to the parking garage. At the last five floors, the doors opened, and the waiting crowd recognized there was no more room in the elevator car. Finally, at the parking deck, Joy noticed a lot of moving cars and walked carefully to her tired old Honda. She crawled in, cranked the car, and followed the conga line of cars headed out of the parking deck. When she arrived at the exit, there were 20 to 30 cars in a line in front of her waiting to get out onto the street. She noticed the street seemed unusually busy and quickly recognized that most of the working public had gotten off work at almost the same time.

"Wow. I wonder how many schools decided to close at 1 p.m.," she said to herself. She sat for another 20 minutes trying to get out onto the street and answered herself, "Apparently all of them!" She became concerned that she was not going to get to the school by 1 p.m., so she called the main number. A recorded greeting announced that school officials and teachers would remain with students in the gymnasium as long as necessary as buses were unable to reach the school due to ice at the exit of the bus parking lot. An hour passed before Joy was able to drive the half of a mile from her office to the on-ramp for I-75 North that would carry her home. Traffic was inching down the ramp at a snail's pace. Joy turned on the radio and flipped over to the local news where the traffic report was a steady listing of traffic jams. The traffic on the ramp quit moving. She stared out the windshield as the snow continued to fall. After another couple of hours, she saw people walking up the ramp from the interstate. "What in the world?" she thought. As they got closer, she was almost certain that she recognized them. She squinted her eyes and suddenly realized four of the people walking toward her were from her office. She rolled the window down and asked what was happening.

David, an actuary from her office recognized her, "Hey Joy. Bad news. There is a huge wreck out there, and six or seven semis have slid across the interstate. All of the lanes are blocked."

As they were talking, Joy could hear tires spinning in the distance. Cars were trying to climb the off-ramp from the interstate to 17th Street. Apparently, the combination of the ice and the grade of the ramp was more than the cars could handle. They were sliding out of control. Joy realized she would run out of gas if she did not get moving soon. She decided to be creative. She maneuvered to the shoulder of the ramp, turned the car around and drove slowly back the wrong way to 17th Street. After another hour, she was crossing the bridge over the interstate. Looking down she could see cars sitting in both directions on the interstate. After a couple of turns on side streets, she made her way to the gas station at the corner of 14th Street and Spring Street. To her dismay, the station lights were out. They had closed early due to the weather. She looked at the gas gauge on the tired old Honda. It was sitting on "E". She only knew of one other station further north on Peachtree Street, so she headed up 14th to Peachtree. It was getting dark, she was tired, and she wanted to get to her children. One block from the stop light at Peachtree Street, the Honda quit. She was out of gas.

"I am done," she said to herself as tears rolled down her cheek. She heard her cellphone ringing. She answered it and recognized the voice of her children's principal.

"Joy?" Principal Smith started.

"Yes, this is Joy," she replied.

"I wanted to call and tell you not to try to drive up the hill to the school. Several parents have slid off the road, and it's a mess. We have all the children in the Gym. They are warm. A couple of the coaches managed to walk out to Dominos, so we fed pizza to all of the children for dinner. We have staff on hand to spend the night. We can try again after the sun comes up tomorrow," he said.

Joy cried even harder.

"Thank you," she said. "I didn't know what I was going to do. I ran out of gas, and I'm stuck in Midtown. I don't know what I'm going to do tonight."

As they were talking, Joy's radio was still on and the news team was reading emergency shelters. She heard them say that Peachtree Street Church at 12th and Peachtree was open.

"Principal Smith, thanks for calling. I'm going to walk to a nearby church for the night. I will talk to you in the morning," she said.

Joy hung up the phone, buttoned up her coat, stepped out of the old Honda, and started walking toward the church.

CHAPTER 8

F red sat at Starbucks, staring out the window at the falling snow. He had learned to ignore the dismissive looks he received by the patrons in their expensive suits as they impatiently waited for their soy lattes. The camouflage pants he wore always got their attention, but they were warm and sturdy, and something just felt right about wearing camouflage. Maybe it had something to do with his two tours of duty in Iraq, or maybe it was because it made him less noticeable when he slept in the bushes alongside parking decks and apartment buildings. Either way, they were free and clean.

He was grateful that Starbucks opened at 6 a.m., and that as long as he was drinking coffee and not bothering anyone, they would let him sit in one of the leather chairs in their warm shop all day. He always managed to have the $1.45 to buy one cup of coffee each morning, and that allowed for free refills. A couple of the regulars knew him and said "Hello" each morning, but not the suits.

As he watched the snow falling, he wondered how he would stay warm when night fell. He had been sleeping in a tent and sleeping bag the last six weeks thanks to a gift from a local church. He set it up under the interstate overpass along with about two dozen others. It was warm and dry and made life a lot better. But a week ago – right before the cold snap – he had come back to his tent from Starbucks and found everything gone. He asked around and learned that the D.O.T. came with bulldozers and leveled all the tents. Then, a couple of front-end loaders scooped up the resulting mess, dumped it in dump trucks, and hauled it all off. So, tonight there would be no sleeping bag or tent – just his blue bomber jacket, long sleeve T-shirt, camouflage pants, and work boots.

He knew the shelters would be full. He had given up his spot in one when he got his tent so that someone else could have a warm and dry place to sleep. Now he was one of a thousand or so "odd men out" as he called it.

"Maybe it will quit snowing and it will melt before dark," he thought.

He ran through a mental list of places to sleep. "It's a shame the security folks get so pissed about someone sleeping in a parking deck," he thought. There were lots of them in Midtown, and all of them were empty at night. They were not very warm, but they were better than sleeping outside. At least he had the temporary reprieve from the elements until Starbucks closed at 8 p.m.

Around 11 a.m., Fred started to get hungry. That was almost a constant thing these days. He rummaged through his pockets and found the Chick-fil-A gift card someone had given him a couple days before and rubbed it as if it might bring good luck. He hoped there was enough on the card for a sandwich. He carefully stood up from the comfortable leather chair and waited for all the painful pops in his ankles, knees, and hips that always seemed to follow. After the pain subsided, he straightened up and walked next door to Chick-fil-A. He purposely aimed to get there before noon when the office workers all arrived in addition to the occasional busload of school kids visiting the High Art Museum. The place was often packed at noon, and he tried to avoid crowds at all costs. Crowds made him uncomfortable with all the pushing and shoving, not to mention the disapproving stares. He walked in the front door and was instantly greeted by Mike, a Chick-fil-A employee he had come to know.

"Fred! Freddie! Freddie Mac! The Fredster! What's up, Fred!" Mike said.

Fred could not help but chuckle. Mike had a way of doing that with him. "My stomach's a growling," Fred said.

"We can help with that!" Mike said as he gestured toward the ordering counter.

He walked to the counter and was greeted by a young girl who looked up, smiled and said, "Hi! Welcome to Chick-fil-A. How may I help you?"

Fred handed her the gift card and said, "Could you check and see if I have enough for a sandwich?"

"Sure," she replied, taking the card and swiping it through the register. "Sir, you have a remaining balance of eleven dollars. That is enough for any complete meal combination or sandwich."

Fred thought about a bowl of soup and a sandwich, but he wanted to make the balance on the gift card last as long as possible. "Just a sandwich," he said.

"OK, that's one Chick-fil-A sandwich. Would you like a drink or anything else?" she asked.

"Nope. Just the sandwich," Fred replied.

"Is that for here or to go?" she asked.

Fred looked around the dining room. It had several unoccupied tables, and it was not busy yet. It seemed safe.

"I'll eat here," he replied.

She entered his order, swiped the gift card, and handed it back to him. Another employee approached the counter with a sandwich on a tray and handed it to him.

"Thanks," Fred said.

"My pleasure," replied the girl.

Fred walked to a table in the back corner and sat with his back to the wall, facing the doorway. It was something he did instinctually these days. In fact, he did not even realize he was selecting this seating choice anymore. In the Army, he learned to protect his back or "cover his 6". Now, he did it automatically. He sat quietly, watching the snowfall increase and accumulate on the outside awnings, and he noticed the traffic picking up. He slowly ate the warm sandwich, savoring every bite, and sipping on the coffee that he had wisely refilled before leaving Starbucks.

Once he had polished off the sandwich, he picked up his coffee and headed back to Starbucks.

"Have a good day, Fred," Mike called out to him. "Stay warm."

Fred gave Mike a peace sign in response. As he walked back to Starbucks, Fred sensed a drop in the temperature and noticed the wind had picked up. When he walked into Starbucks, the manager came over.

"What now?" Fred thought, "Another customer complaint?"

"Hey Fred," she said. "We are closing in an hour due to inclement weather so our employees can get home before the roads get bad."

"Crap!" Fred thought.

He contemplated his options. He sat down in one of the comfortable leather chairs. Chick-fil-A would probably close early too. Then it hit him. He could go out into the building's main mall area. The security guards would not bother him if he sat in one of the out-of-the-way areas – especially if he did not go to sleep on one of the tables.

Precisely at 1300 hours, the Starbucks manager flipped the open signs to closed and locked the doors. She unlocked the door for each customer as they left. Fred followed the last one to the door.

"Need a refill to go, Fred?" she asked.

"Sure," he replied, handing her the cup.

She quickly returned with a fresh, hot cup of coffee and walked him to the door. "Have a good night," she said.

"You, too," Fred replied before waving his customary peace sign.

He walked to the mall area of the building. All the other businesses were closed, and it was uncommonly dark for early afternoon. He saw a security guard watching him from the concierge desk. He silently nodded and walked to the far end of the food court past a vacant restaurant suite and settled at a corner table to watch the snow.

Fred was not exactly sure what time it was when the security guard shook him awake, but it was dark outside.

"Hey, buddy. I'm sorry, but you can't sleep here. You're gonna have to leave," the guard said.

Fred did not feel like arguing and he knew if he did, it would cause problems when he came back. He nodded and stood up cautiously, waiting for all the painful pops to subside. Once the pain relented, he straightened himself and walked toward the exit. He had no plan or destination and was still groggy from his nap.

When he got outside, he was met with a gust of biting, cold wind. He zipped up his bomber jacket and pulled out the gloves the shelter had given him. He walked out to Peachtree Street and looked around, trying to decide where he should go. He walked to the corner of Peachtree and 14th and paused to think. He saw a woman get out of her car and start walking toward the intersection.

"Car trouble?" he asked.

She nervously looked at him and back at the tired old Honda. "I ran out of gas," she said.

"There's a gas station about two blocks behind you," Fred volunteered.

"Yeah, but they're closed," she told him.

He sighed. "I guess we're both seeking shelter then," he said.

"I heard on the radio that Peachtree Street Church is open as an emergency shelter," she replied.

Fred's face lit up. "Really?" he said. "That's just two blocks this way! I'm sorry. My name is Fred." He held out his right hand.

"Hi, Fred. I'm Joy," she replied, shaking his hand.

"Well Joy, let's get you to the church and out of this cold," he said.

Quietly, the two walked down the sidewalk, carefully trying to navigate through the patches of ice.

CHAPTER 9

J eremy Davidson was just finishing lunch when he heard the school TV system broadcasting a special announcement.

"Good afternoon, students," said Principal Smith. "We have a special weather announcement. A winter storm is approaching, and it is snowing. We are closing school for the remainder of the day. Buses will begin loading at 1 p.m. We have notified your parents. Outside temperatures have been dropping since you arrived this morning. Please be sure to put on your gloves and zip up your coats before going out to the bus line. We will keep the gym open for car riders waiting for their parents to arrive."

Jeremy quickly got up, tossed his trash and put his tray on the dishwasher conveyor belt. He walked to his teacher's table.

"Mr. Albert," he said, "I am going to go get my sister."

Mr. Albert nodded, "Good deal, Jeremy. If there is a long wait for the buses or any problems, I will be hanging out in the gym with the car riders. Just come down there and find me."

Jeremy headed to the wing of the school where his sister's class was. As he rounded the corner, he saw the door open. Her class was quietly watching a movie. He poked his head in the door and quietly called out, "Cheryl."

His little sister's head popped up from the corner of the room. She grabbed her backpack and scrambled for the door. Her teacher, standing by the doorway, knelt and gave her a tight hug.

"You stay warm tonight. Get Jeremy to help you build a snowman," said Ms. George.

Cheryl smiled. She walked out to Jeremy and took his hand, and the two headed toward the bus line. When they arrived at the doors leading to the bus line, Jeremy slowed his pace. He looked up at the clock on the wall that showed 1:30 p.m. He looked back out the windows.

"Where are the buses?" he asked.

Cheryl looked out the window. She could see a couple of teachers but not a single bus.

"Maybe they're driving slow to be safe," she said.

"Maybe," Jeremy said, "or maybe they can't get up the hill. Let's walk down to the gym. They will make an announcement when the buses get here."

They walked over to the gym and Jeremy saw Mr. Albert. They walked over to where he was standing.

"Mr. Albert, are the buses having problems?" Jeremy asked.

"Hey, Jeremy!" Mr. Albert said. "We're waiting to hear what's going on. We've got popcorn and hot chocolate while we wait."

Jeremy led Cheryl over to the bleachers. They took off their backpacks and sat down.

"Want some hot chocolate and popcorn?" he asked.

"Sure!" Cheryl exclaimed. "I just had lunch, but I love popcorn!"

He smiled and walked across the gym to get two hot chocolates and a small bag of popcorn. He walked back to where she was sitting and handed them to her. Cheryl smiled back and started munching on popcorn.

More students wandered into the gym and soon the large video screens on the walls lit up. Jeremy grinned when he recognized the movie that was beginning: Despicable Me 2.

"Hey, Cheryl. How many times have you seen this now?" he asked.

She stopped stuffing popcorn in her mouth for a minute and thought about her response.

"Um. Six times, I think," she said with a giggle.

Jeremy smiled.

"Yeah. That's about what I was thinkin'," he replied.

Halfway through the movie, it suddenly stopped, and the principal appeared on the screen.

"Good afternoon, students," he said. "It seems the weather has taken its toll on the roads outside. The buses are not able to get up the hill from the bus lot. We have notified your parents. We will keep the building open until everyone has been picked up. In the meantime, settle in and enjoy your movie."

"Great," Jeremy said. "Early release and we're gonna be staying at school."

Cheryl   looked up at him.

"But watching Despicable Me is a lot more fun than school-work!" she pointed out.

"True," Jeremy replied.

CHAPTER 10

G ladys sat patiently at a table in the mall area outside the covered entrance to Chick-fil-A dutifully every morning. It was out of the weather, and she knew around 6:30 a.m. they would open the gate and she could get a complimentary cup of coffee. Last night had been bitter cold and the damp and cold was a bad combination for the arthritis in her lower back. Her hefty backpack that contained all her earthly possessions just aggravated the issue on days like today. She found a copy of the morning's Atlanta Journal Constitution that someone had left on a table and browsed through the headlines. As she glanced past stories of violence and crime, she recalled a line from a song: "I don't read those daily news 'cause it ain't hard to figure how people get the blues. They can't dig what they can't use. Stick to the simple, and be much less abused."[iv]

"True!" she said to herself out loud.

She folded the paper and stuffed it into her backpack. If she had to sleep outside tonight, it would make good insulation inside her coat. After a few more minutes, she heard whistling. That would be Mike coming to open the gate.

"Gooooooood morning, Gladys!" he said.

For the love of all that is good and holy, how could one five-foot-tall bald guy be so happy at 6:30 in the morning? She smiled without a word, gently stood up, picked up her backpack, walked into Chick-fil-A and up to the counter.

Mike smiled at her. "Could I interest you in one of our delicious hand-spun peach milkshakes?" he asked.

Gladys stared at him like he had five heads.

"Son, did you fall and hurt your squash? It's 28 degrees out-side. Nobody wants a milkshake in this weather," she snapped.

Mike chuckled. "That's good, because they aren't available at breakfast and the peach shake doesn't come back until spring," he replied.

Gladys shook her head of silver hair, which was held in place by her signature head scarf.

"Your mama dropped you a lot, didn't she?" Gladys asked.

Mike chuckled again before pouring her coffee. He grabbed four french vanilla creamers and set them on the counter in front of her.

"Would you like anything else?" he asked.

Gladys pulled out a clasped coin purse and set down a hand-ful of change.

"I want a chicken biscuit too, please," she said.

Mike rang up the order, counted out the cost from the coins she had laid on the counter, and slid the rest back to her. She picked up the coins, put them back in the change purse, latched the clasp, and stuck it in her bra. When Mike returned with the biscuit, she took it and her coffee back out to a table in the mall area so she could enjoy it in the quiet. Once she had finished her biscuit, Gladys reached in her backpack, dug out a book of crossword puzzles and a pencil, put on her reading glasses, and started working on solutions. She liked crossword puzzles, because they kept her mind sharp. She much pre-ferred sitting on a bench in Grant Park when working on her crossword puzzles, but the cold weather eliminated that option from her consideration.

CHAPTER 11

When Mary shut off the vacuum cleaner, she faintly heard her cellphone ringing over the sound of the children playing in the den. She sprinted to the kitchen counter to grab her phone and swiped across it with her finger.

"Hello," she said breathlessly.

"Hey, sweetie," her husband, John, said. "I'm stuck on 75 in downtown. Traffic is at a standstill. Don't hold dinner for me."

Mary did not like the sound of that. It had been snowing for five hours, and it was getting dark.

"Call me in an hour and let me know how you are doing, OK?" she asked.

"Sure, sweetie. Don't sweat it. I'll be fine. I've got a large coffee I poured when I left the office, and I snagged a couple granola bars. Even if it takes me 7 or 8 hours, I'll be fine," he reassured her.

She knew she should not worry. John had grown up in the country fishing, hunting, and camping most of his life. She was certain that if he had a sharp knife, two matches, a roll of duct tape, and a pair of vise-grips, he could survive a zombie apocalypse. In their ten years of marriage, he had never taken either of their automobiles to a mechanic for service. He repaired the washing machine, the dryer, the refrigerator and the heater, and he remodeled the upstairs bathroom. The neighbors constantly came over when they needed help with an appliance or plumbing. And she had seen him cook complete meals over a campfire – including peach cobbler. If anyone could survive a cold night in a car, John would be the man for the job, but it still did not keep her from worrying about him.

John tilted his seat back. The heater was keeping the cab of his truck plenty warm. Traffic had not moved an inch in the last hour, so he might as well try to take a nap. He pulled up the emergency brake for added safety. He figured if traffic began moving, someone would honk. The people in Atlanta loved to honk. John closed his eyes.

It hardly seemed an hour had passed when someone was knocking on his window. John sat up and rubbed his eyes. When his eyes focused, he saw a flashlight outside his window. He partially rolled down the window to see what was happening.

"Sir, my name is Private Henderson with the National Guard. Is there anything you need? We have food and water. If you are low on fuel, we can transport you to an emergency shelter," the man said.

"Thank you very much," John said, "but I am good. I've still got more than half a tank of fuel."

"OK, sir," said Private Henderson. "Hang in there. We have several folks out of fuel, so we will keep moving. Stay warm."

John looked at the clock on the radio display. It was 10 p.m. He had been sitting here for five hours, and traffic had not moved. He punched a button on the steering wheel.

"Call Mary," he said.

"Dialing Mary using OnStar," the system responded.

Mary picked up on the second ring.

"John! Are you OK? Where are you?" she asked.

"I'm sitting exactly where I was the last time I called you. I took a little nap, and a nice National Guardsman woke me up checking car-to-car."

"I wish there was something we could do," Mary replied.

"It's OK, hun," John replied, "but I'm getting bored. Get some sleep, and I will talk to you in the morning."

"I love you, dear," Mary said.

"I love you, too," he replied. "Sweet dreams."

John punched the button, and the call ended. He settled back into the seat and closed his eyes again.

"I might as well sleep," he thought.

The second time he woke, John heard what sounded like a woman's voice, but he could not make out what she was saying. He raised the back of his seat up and looked around but could not make out where the voice was coming. He reached under the seat and got his flashlight, stepped out of the truck, and looked around. He saw a woman about four cars behind him standing outside a car. He walked back to where she was.

"Ma'am, are you OK?" John asked.

"My car ran out of gas, and my baby is getting cold," she replied.

"Get your baby, and come sit in my truck," John offered. "Y'all can stay warm until we can figure something out."

The woman reached in her car and pulled out a baby seat covered in blankets. They walked back to John's truck, and he opened the passenger side door and helped her into the truck. John crawled back in the driver seat. He turned on the radio and tuned in to WSB for news.

"Have y'all had anything to eat?" he asked.

"Not since lunch," she answered.

John figured that the woman and child needed water and something to eat. He had one granola bar and half a cup of coffee. He knew that was not going to meet their needs. While he was contemplating the situation, he heard a listing of emergency shelters being read on the radio. He turned up the volume. "Peachtree Street Church at 12th and Peachtree" was one of the shelters that stuck out to him. He picked up his phone and punched in the address in Google Maps. It showed they were about six blocks from that shelter. He debated with himself whether it would be safe to carry the child that far in this weather.

CHAPTER 12

Reverend Matthews was amazed at the number of people coming through the door of the church. They had not been prepared for serving as a shelter, and they were certainly not prepared for what they were seeing. All the blankets sent from the Salvation Army had been distributed, but people were still filing into the fellowship hall. He walked into the kitchen where Phil and Alvin were working.

"How's it going, guys?" he asked.

Alvin looked up. "I think we have about one case of water left. We are completely out of bread so the tray of peanut butter and jelly sandwiches they are working on right now is the last of it. We've handed out six pots of soup. We've found enough can goods in the pantry to make up two more pots, which we are cooking now. After that, we are out of food."

Phil looked up from stirring a pot of soup at the stove.

"I figure we can sleep 250 to 300 here in the fellowship hall," Phil said. "At my best guesstimation, I think we are already at that number. Should we open up the educational wing?"

Reverend Matthews grimaced and replied, "Most of those rooms are completely empty. Does the heat work over there?"

"Empty rooms are perfect for sleeping. The last I checked, the heat worked. It was just dialed really low to prevent frozen pipes. I think all of the bathrooms are still functional."

"OK," the old pastor replied, "I'll go over and turn on the lights and turn up the thermostats."

Phil looked over at Alvin. "Two days ago, I was overwhelmed with the sense that we needed to respond to the homelessness in this city, but I had no idea what to do. Today, it seems logical and apparent. Though for the life of me, I don't know how we are going to pay the power bill once this is over."

Alvin smiled. "I guess we're going to have to trust that God will provide. Seeing the number of cold and hungry people coming through those doors tells me that we are doing what we're supposed to be doing."

One of the other volunteers walked into the kitchen. "Guys, the National Guard is here."

Alvin wiped his hands on the apron he was wearing, pulled it off, and tossed it on the counter. He rushed out to the fellowship hall to see two men in army fatigues carrying boxes.

"Where would you like these blankets?" the man asked.

Alvin directed him to four empty tables where they had been distributing blankets earlier. Six volunteers came scurrying to resume their duties.

When Alvin turned around, there were eight more soldiers carrying boxes of blankets. Stunned, he walked back toward the kitchen where another soldier asked him where they wanted the food. He directed him to the kitchen, and four soldiers started carrying in containers of sandwiches, soup, coffee, and water.

Alvin stepped to one side of the kitchen and began weeping.

Reverend Matthews walked into the kitchen visibly shaken.

"Manna from heaven is falling. We have food and blankets, and there is another truck bringing cots," he said.

Alvin stood speechless shaking his head.

"The National Guard is picking up people from the interstate and carrying them to emergency shelters. We may have arrivals all night," he continued.

Alvin smiled. "Turn up the thermostats in the sanctuary. They can sleep in the pews if necessary."

"Great idea," replied the pastor, and out the door he flew.

CHAPTER 13

No one knew Lewis Edward Davis by his given name. His long, solid-white hair and beard had earned him the nickname "Santa", and he was good with it. Many of the people walking on the streets of downtown Atlanta would not look a homeless man in the face as they passed, but Lewis was regularly greeted with a smile that he attributed to his resemblance to the jolly, fat man. Children were drawn to him, and parents did not object when they wanted to speak to him. Lewis considered himself blessed to be accepted and adored despite his daily struggle to find food and shelter.

Many passers-by wondered why he didn't sleep at one of the homeless shelters, but Lewis had been beaten and robbed of his few possessions several years ago while sleeping in a shelter and vowed to never put himself in that situation again. He would gladly accept a meal in a shelter, but he felt safer sleeping on the streets. He had found several doorways of buildings on side streets where he was sheltered by the cover of darkness and not easily seen by potential robbers.

He regularly sat at a table in the food court of one of the office buildings each morning with his rucksack, patiently waiting for a complimentary cup of coffee. The rucksack holding extra clothes and blankets was the only remaining hint of his military service. Every time he threw it over his shoulder, he briefly recalled the long marches he took on mud roads of foreign jungles when he was in his 20s.

Lewis managed to sit unmolested in the corner of the warm food court for the better part of the day. He snacked on some cookies he received from "The Cookie Lady". He did not know her real name, but he had come to recognize her from her weekly trips to the city park to hand out homemade cookies to the homeless people who frequented the area. The city of Atlanta had passed a law making it a crime to pass out food to the homeless, but the cookie lady was undeterred. He had seen the beat cops order her to move on, but she would simply walk around the corner until the cops were gone and continue distributing her weekly load of encouragement. Once Lewis saw a drunk get in her face and threaten her with a knife. Lewis and three other men charged to her aid. While two of the men took the drunk to the ground and disposed of the knife he had wielded, Lewis and another safely escorted her away. The cookie lady fondly remembered her rescuers from that day and always looked for them each week.

Lewis saw the security guard wake the woman with her hair wrapped in a scarf and knew it was time to return to the street. He hoisted the rucksack onto his shoulder and made his way out into the cold.

CHAPTER 14

Jeff and Ron gradually walked up the edge of the on-ramp toward Peachtree Street. Jeff thought to himself that if he had known he would have been hiking in the snow and ice, he would have packed better shoes. Ron said little and just continued pressing on toward the top of the ramp. Walking up the grade of the ramp would wind most people on a typical Georgia day, but the cold air combined with the snow and ice patches made it considerably more exhausting. They stuck to the edge of the ramp, finding the climb easier in the snow-covered grass than the slick, icy asphalt. After several minutes, they reached the top of the 10th Street bridge. They stopped and looked out at the downtown connector. It was a solid parking lot of cars as far as they could see in either direction.

"How in the world will the D.O.T. clear the interstate with all of those cars blocking it?" Ron asked.

Jeff shook his head. "I don't see how they could. There is no way a salt truck could get through and certainly no way a plow is getting through that mess of cars."

The two men pressed on, making their way across Spring Street and West Peachtree.

"This seems a lot shorter when you're driving it," Ron noted.

Jeff laughed and replied, "Yeah, I don't think I have ever walked this much in Atlanta in my whole life!"

They finally reached the corner of Peachtree Street and made a left. Ron checked his watch – they had been walking for almost an hour. He could feel ice forming in the hairs of his nose. He thought about the homeless that he had read about that slept in doorways and under bridges.

"How could they survive a night like this?" he thought.

Ron looked over at Jeff. He could see that he was growing tired and cold.

"You OK, bud?" he asked.

"Yeah, I'm t We're about there, right?" Jeff asked.

"Yeah, man. See that steeple up ahead on the right? That's it," Ron pointed out.

The sight of the church seemed to bring new life to Jeff's pace through the snow. Finally, they found themselves in front of the tall sanctuary doors. Ron could see several people entering a side door just a short distance down the street beside the church. He followed them into the door and down a hallway to a large dining hall filled with people. The warmth of the building hugged them as they walked further inside. They could feel their feet and faces beginning to thaw. A short, gray-haired lady approached them holding a small tray of Styrofoam coffee cups with steam rising off them.

"Would you boys like a hot cup of coffee?" she asked.

Ron and Jeff both smiled. "I can't think of anything that sounds better," Jeff said as both men took cups and cradled them in their hands.

CHAPTER 15

Gladys did not mind that the security guard told her she would have to leave the building. She wasn't angry or put out; she realized he was doing his job and simply following his boss's orders.

"You can't fault a man for doing what he is told," she said to herself.

Her feet ached as she shuffled out of the warm building into the cold. The wind was howling between the buildings along Peachtree Street, making it feel even colder than what the mercury would show on a thermometer. She adjusted the collar on her coat and kept her head down as she slowly made her way up the sidewalk to keep the freezing wind out of her face. She adjusted the straps of her backpack on her shoulders to try and alleviate some of the pain in her back, but it seemed to make little difference. The sidewalk was a couple inches thick in snow and slick with ice. Gladys struggled to keep her footing, occasionally slipping on ice patches. The weather, coupled with the pain in her feet and back, were hampering her slow progress up the street.

After a couple of blocks, she stopped to catch her breath and consider her options. It was quickly getting dark, and she had not found a good place to settle for the night. She pushed on up the street. She hadn't gone a few steps when she slipped on a patch of ice. She jerked to right herself. She fell and heard a loud pop in her left hip. A sharp pain pierced her hip. She fell, striking her head on a fire hydrant, and everything went dark.

CHAPTER 16

John woke to the sound of voices. He rubbed his eyes and tried to focus. His truck was still running. The fuel gauge showed just under half a tank. The woman was quietly holding her child and looking around for the source of the voices. John stepped out into the roadway to see people pulling sleds with glow sticks attached to them. As they came closer, he could see boxes on the sleds. A young man, whom John judged to be about 19 years old, approached him.

"Sir, could you use some water, a sandwich, or a piece of fruit?" the young man asked.

John was mute with surprise for a moment, but quickly regained his senses.

"Um, sure," he started. "There's a lady in my truck with a baby that needs food more than I do, though."

The young man smiled and said, "We can help with that, too."

The young man dug into one of the boxes. He quickly retrieved a bag and handed it to John.

"Here are a couple of jars of baby food," he said as he put them in the bag. "And here's a six pack of water, a couple of sandwiches, and two apples," still packing the bag. "How's that?" he asked with a smile.

"Great! Thank you!" John replied.

"Don't mention it," said the young man. "We're just helping our neighbors. Welcome to Midtown," he added.

As John walked back to his truck to share the food and water with the woman and her baby, he could see another five or six people with sleds passing out food.

CHAPTER 17

They were less than a block from the church when Fred saw something on the sidewalk just ahead of him. He squinted his eyes to make out what it was. A few steps closer, he realized it was a person covered in a light dusting of snow. He rushed to see if they were alive. He quickly recognized it was Gladys, the lady who always had her hair tied in a scarf. He put his ear to her face and heard her breathing and felt warm air against his face. He rubbed her arm. Joy knelt on the other side of her, taking off a glove and putting the back of her hand to Gladys's cheek.

"She's pretty cold. I wonder how long she's been lying here," Joy said.

Fred continued rubbing her arm, "Gladys! Gladys! Wake Up, Gladys!" he yelled.

Joy could hear the desperation in his voice. After a couple minutes, Gladys's eyes fluttered, and she groaned.

"Gladys, can you hear me?" Fred asked.

Gladys continued to groan as she opened her eyes and looked directly into Fred's face.

"I've died and gone to hell," she said, "and I'm stuck looking at your mug."

Fred smiled. "Not exactly. You're in the snow on the side of Peachtree Street," he replied.

"My head is aching like it's been cracked with a bat, and my hip is killing me," she said. "I think it's broken."

As Fred tried to think of the best way to get help for Gladys, he heard a noise and looked up to see Santa coming down the street – not Santa Claus, but the homeless guy he knew as "Santa".

Lewis quietly surveyed the scene as he approached.

"Is she alright?" Lewis asked.

Fred replied, "She thinks her hip is broken, she's hit her head pretty hard, and I'm worried about how cold she is."

Lewis sat down his rucksack and knelt beside Gladys.

"We need an ambulance, but I bet 9-1-1 is busy. I don't know that an ambulance can get here anyhow," Lewis said.

Fred retrieved his cellphone and dialed 9-1-1, but the call dropped. He tried again in vain.

"I can't get a call to go through," he said.

Lewis looked up at Fred.

"Why don't you two walk to that church up there? I see lights. Maybe someone there can help," Lewis suggested.

Lewis dug through his rucksack, pulled out a wool blanket and a tarp, and covered Gladys to keep her warm.

Fred and Joy headed for the church. They could still hear Gladys moaning as they walked away. Finally, they found themselves in front of Peachtree Street Church. They turned down the street alongside the sanctuary and followed the noise of a crowd. As they approached the side door, Fred saw two men in military camouflage. He approached them.

"We're trying to get some help for a lady that's fallen back there," he said.

The two national guardsmen looked up quickly at him, giving their full attention.

"Where is she?" one asked.

"About half a block south of here on Peachtree Street," Fred replied.

"We're on it," the soldier responded.

He grabbed his radio and barked an order. A Humvee came around the corner from the church parking lot, followed by two ATVs. The two soldiers climbed into the Humvee and proceeded down Peachtree Street.

Fred opened the door to the church and held it for Joy. The two squinted at the light and bathed in the warmth of the building. They made their way down the corridor to a large room filled with people.

A volunteer greeted them at the doorway and led them to the food line.

"We'll get you something to eat here. Want a cup of coffee while you're waiting?" she asked.

Almost in unison, Joy and Fred both responded, "Yes."

She returned with two Styrofoam cups of coffee with steam rising off them.

"Here ya go," she said. "Y'all get something warm to eat, and then we'll get you some blankets."

CHAPTER 18

Lewis kept Gladys talking while they waited. He was afraid she might have a concussion and knew it was important to keep her awake. He kept her as warm as he could and continued searching the darkness for headlights.

Suddenly he heard a sound. He looked up to see headlights coming down Peachtree Street and heard what sounded like dirt bikes. He wrinkled his brows and squinted his eyes toward the source. Soon he could make out a Humvee followed by two four-wheel ATVs.

"Here comes the cavalry," he told Gladys.

Within moments, four soldiers surrounded Gladys. One began a physical assessment while another unwrapped a survival blanket. A third soldier pulled a backboard out of the Humvee.

"You're probably not gonna like this much," started one soldier, "but we're gonna have to roll you onto your side to get you on this backboard."

Gladys nodded without a word. She groaned loudly as they log-rolled her onto her side and on top of the backboard. Then then wrapped her cocoon-style in the survival blanket and strapped her in.

"Ma'am," said one of the soldiers, "I'm gonna give you some oxygen to keep you comfortable." As he slid a mask over her nose and mouth, he said, "Just breathe normally."

Looking toward the other soldiers, he ordered, "Let's get her out of the cold. Ready? 1-2-3."

Suddenly, the four soldiers lifted Gladys on the backboard and carefully slid her into the Humvee. Two climbed in the cab and took off for Emory Hospital. The other two helped Lewis collect his blanket and tarp.

"Can we give you a ride?" one soldier asked.

Lewis smiled. "Sure," he said.

"Alright," the soldier responded. "How about coffee and hot soup?"

Lewis quickly replied, "Sounds good to me!"

Lewis climbed on the back of one of the ATVs, and they headed back to the church.

Awakened

Dedicated to my loving daughter, Lindsey.
You have been my biggest fan and cheerleader since the day you
were born. Through some of the darkest and loneliest days in my
life, you chose to stand beside me and encourage me. For that I
will always be grateful. I love you with every fiber of my being.
- Daddy

"If the local church wants to be the hope of the world, it needs to step into places in which people find themselves hopeless."

JARRID WILSON

CHAPTER 19

S amuel Matthews awoke with his back aching. He careful- ly lifted himself to a seated position on the edge of the sofa and retrieved his wire-rimmed glasses from the nearby shelf. The ticking clock over the study door showed 7 a.m. He slowly rose to his feet and shuffled to the window. The street below was silent – in stark contrast to the day before, when it was packed with cars trying to leave the city. The ris- ing sun shone on the sheet of ice covering the sidewalk and street below. The grass bordering the sidewalk lay hidden be- low a few inches of snow. He stood at the window, peering at the tranquil scenery for several moments, lost in his thoughts. He refocused his tired eyes and shuffled for the door to the hallway.

Stepping into the hallway, he gradually made his way to the educational wing that just days before sat empty and unused. He stopped at the first classroom and quietly opened the door just enough to look upon the sleeping refugees from the bitter winter storm. Army cots lined the walls and the center of the room. Through the dim morning light, he could make out the faint images of mothers and children huddled under wool blankets. He quietly closed the door, making every effort not to disturb the tired souls who had survived a frightful after- noon. When he found the door to the next room unlatched and partially open, he poked his head through the opening and took a peek. Another ten to twelve cots filled the room along with tattered backpacks and plastic grocery bags stuffed with dirty clothing. The nearest sleeping body had a head full of tangled hair that framed a weathered face. Directly under the cot was a pair of work boots that showed signs of age and disrepair. His nose burned as he peered in the door from the musk of a dozen bodies that had not showered in what he estimated to be at least a month.

He quietly backed into the hallway, paused for a moment, and drew a breath of the cleaner air. He proceeded to the next classroom and then the next, repeating the process 30 more times over all three floors of classrooms before reaching the end of the hall that led to the gymnasium. As he rounded the corner, his nose detected a different scent – that of fresh, hot coffee. He pushed open a door and stepped into the darkened gym, carefully moving around the perimeter of the gym floor in fear of stepping on a sleeping soul lying on a thin mat. He found his way to the door to the kitchen by the dim light peeking out from under the door. As he pushed the door open and stepped into the kitchen, he squinted at the brightness of the room.

His eyes adjusted from the darkened gym, and he lifted his glance to see six volunteers huddled over the stoves. He recognized Phil and Alvin as he made his way toward four large coffee urns and filled a Styrofoam cup. Phil looked up from his work to catch the old pastor's eye.

"Morning, Reverend Sam," he said.

"Good morning, Phil," Sam replied. "Did you get any sleep?"

"Yeah, we managed to put a few cots up on the stage area. I slept on and off for about 4 hours or so. Figured we'd have 500 hungry faces greeting us soon, so we started scrambling some eggs and frying some bacon and sausage."

Alvin looked up, and Sam quickly realized he was wearing an apron covered in flour.

"Biscuit maker, I presume?" Sam inquired.

"You betcha!" Alvin replied with a smile.

Sam returned a tired smile and headed back to the gymnasium, nursing the cup of coffee. As he stepped back into the gym, he noticed the lights were slowly flickering on. The gym lights took several minutes from when they were first powered on until they were fully light. He looked across the gym to see what seemed like hundreds of mats dotting the floor – some still had sleeping bodies, some were covered in a pile of pillows, blankets, and clothing. People were walking in and out of the gym locker rooms. Some were headed for the showers, while others were walking out with toothbrushes sticking out the corner of their mouths.

The amount of supplies that had been provided by the Red Cross, the National Guard, and the Atlanta Mission staggered his mind. But there they were, hundreds of people from varied walks of life quietly living inside the church building that had laid silent for several years. He returned to the hallway where a half dozen volunteers were organizing a table by the door to meet any additional walk-ins who had weathered the night and might be seeking shelter this morning.

Sam walked back into his office and turned on his radio to catch the local news and an update on the weather. He sat motionless as he listened, occasionally taking a long sip of coffee as the news report continued.

The highways and interstates were still shut down, but State of Georgia and county employees had worked through the night sanding bridges, moving stuck tractor-trailers, and clearing wrecked vehicles. The Governor's office and the Mayor's office had both released statements requesting everyone stay off the roads for 24 hours to allow crews to clear wrecked and stalled vehicles. Grocery stores reported outages of milk, bread, and water. Utility companies were reporting over 650,000 residents without power. The airport had been another shelter, with stranded travelers sleeping in concourse aisles, at airline gates, and in the main terminal. Hundreds of flights had been cancelled or delayed while crews worked to clear runways and de-ice aircraft.

As Sam listened to the news, he began to wonder. This storm had stranded a lot of office workers from the office buildings and skyscrapers around the church, but it had also proven too much to withstand for the homeless who typically slept in parks, under bridges, and in doorways around the city. But Atlanta had many freezing nights in the winter. What did those who were homeless do on those nights? The Atlanta Mission was a huge building, but it couldn't house the entire homeless community on one night. His mind went back to the man who was found frozen on the steps of the sanctuary just a few weeks ago.

What Sam had witnessed over the last 24 hours was a great and wonderful thing, but it was obvious to him there was a great deal more that needed to be done. Where could he start? Where would he get the money? He removed the wire-rimmed glasses and rubbed his tired eyes.

CHAPTER 20

Fred opened his eyes to the burning pain in his lower back. He shuffled around on the military cot that had been his bed for the night trying to find some relief and a semblance of comfort. He reached below the cot and patted his backpack and boots. He always worried about sleeping in shelters because of the theft of his limited belongings, but hard times can sometimes cause a man to make difficult decisions that he might otherwise not choose. Last night's storm had been one of those times. He had awakened several times during the night scared someone had stolen his boots when he realized his feet were not heavy, but after a couple minutes he would realize where he was and pat the boots under his cot to comfort his mind.

As he laid in the dark staring at the ceiling, he wondered about Gladys. The military boys seemed to have been taking good care of her, but he had to wonder if she had gotten to the hospital OK. He wondered how the emergency room had treated her. Hospitals could be pretty heartless toward homeless folk, he thought. And on a night as bad as this one, he wondered how packed the emergency rooms were.

Silently, he started praying, "So yeah, um, God. Miss Gladys has had a tough go of it with this storm. I know I prolly ain't in too good a standing to be asking for favors and such, but she's always seemed like good people. Please pull on the hearts of the nurses and folks over at Grady Emergency Room to have some mercy on her and help her. I know she was hurting pretty bad, and she had been in that snow for a while. Please have 'em to warm her up, do whatever surgery she needs, and make her comfortable. I won't bother you with anything else. I imagine you're busy with all the folks in this storm worried about their kids and families. I'll let you get back to all that, but please look out for Gladys. I'm pretty sure she is one of yours."

He rolled over on his side which seemed to give him a smattering of relief and tried to go back to sleep. He lay there for a few minutes and then silently prayed again.

"Um, God, sorry to interrupt you again, but I just thought it was rude to be asking a favor without saying a thank you. It sure is nice to be lying on a cot instead of on a concrete step, and the heat in this building sure is nice on a night like tonight. Thank you for the folks downstairs that made all them sandwiches and soup and gave us all blankets. I don't know much about this church, but they must be pretty decent folks to let some stinking street vagrant like me sleep in their place and feed me. Anyhow. Thanks. This night is a might better than I had thought it was gonna be."

He reached under the cot, patted his backpack and boots, and settled back in to sleep.

CHAPTER 21

Gladys looked around the exam room and wondered what was going to happen next. She was grateful for the stack of heated blankets they had piled on her and for the pain medications they were giving her for her hip. The nurses and staff had rumbled her up and down the hall to x-Ray rooms and every kind of scan she had ever imagined and a few more. Just as she was mid-thought, in popped that little redheaded nurse that had been working with her.

"Miss Gladys," the little redhead said, "the doctor is going to be in to see you in just a few minutes. We have got all your lab work, scans, and x-Rays back, so he should be able to tell you what our treatment plan is going to be. How are those pain meds working? On a scale of 1 to 10, with 10 being the worse pain you have ever experienced in your life, what would you rate your current pain?"

Gladys twitched her nose, "I'd say a solid 7."

"Well, that is a definite improvement over the 10 score you gave me when they brought you in, so I'd say we're making some progress," said the little redhead.

Gladys smiled, "Yeah, and I'm not shivering anymore so there's that," she replied.

"Well, Miss Gladys, if you need any more of those heated blankets, you just let me know."

Gladys closed her eyes and tried to think of something to take her mind off the pain. Her mind quickly drifted back to the office building where Starbucks and Chick-Fil-A were. She was just fine sitting there until they kicked her out in the cold. If they had left her alone, she probably would not have fallen and she wouldn't be in this blasted hospital, she thought to herself. But what is done is done. She sighed a quiet sigh and folded her hands across her belly.

"Dang, the lights in this room are bright," Gladys thought. "If they shut the dang things off, I might be able to sleep with these meds."

As she lay there quietly, she could hear the steady tick of a clock in the room.

"Yeah, that would make it hard to sleep, too, I imagine," she thought.

A machine to her left made a purring sound, and the cuff on her arm began to tighten. After a minute or two, the cuff gradually deflated, and the machine beeped a couple of times.

"They sure don't want you sleeping around here," Gladys thought.

With sleep seeming to not be a ready option, Gladys started silently praying, "God, thank you for not letting me freeze to death out there on that sidewalk. Thank you for those military folks that got me out of the snow and to the hospital in that rough riding overgrown Jeep looking thing they had. Thank you for the sweet little redheaded gal that's been helping me. I can't remember her name for the life of me, but she sure is sweet and trying to take care of me best as she can. Bless whatever intern they give me to have enough sense to figure out what to do, 'cause this pain is a bit more than I can live with on a regular basis. I'm a tough ol' bat, but this is a bit much. Please bless all the other homeless folks out there on the streets tonight that they might get some shelter from this storm, and if you could find a way to let me sleep a little, I'd be mighty grateful. Amen."

Gladys lay still with her eyes closed and tried to sleep. The next thing she knew, she was hearing a voice calling her name.

"Gladys, Gladys," the voice called.

Confused for a second, she tried to clear the fogginess of her mind. Who was calling her? It was a man's voice. Was it God? Had she died and the creator was now calling her name? With her eyes still closed, she tried to turn her head toward the voice.

"Gladys!" the voice called again, this time with a little more enthusiasm.

She wrinkled her brow as she tried to understand what was happening. "Yes?" she replied faintly.

"Gladys, I am an orthopedic surgeon," said the voice. "The Emergency Room staff called me in to review your x-rays and your injuries. You have a broken hip. This is a common injury for senior adults. We find the hip weakens as many adults get older, and at some time, they take a step or slip a little, and the hip breaks and they fall. From reviewing your x-rays, I believe that is exactly the case with your injury. I understand you were out in the storm, walking to a shelter and fell. I believe your hip gave way causing you to fall. This is a straight-forward procedure. I am going to take you to surgery and insert a couple of pins in your hip to strengthen it and allow it to mend. You'll spend a week or so recovering, and we will have you up and walking around in no time. An anesthesiologist will be along shortly and will become your new best friend. She will give you a medicine in your IV that will help you relax, and then we will get you to the Operating Room where she will get you to a nice peaceful sleep for the surgery. Do you have any questions or concerns?"

Gladys squinted her eyes toward the direction of the voice. How long had she slept? She continued to squint until she could make out the face of a young, sandy blonde-headed kid in a lab coat that did not look old enough to shave, in her opinion.

"Doc," she started, "if y'all can help me sleep and ease this pain, I'd be mighty obliged," she said.

"Don't you worry, Gladys. We are going to help you with both of those requests. I'll see you in a few minutes. Try to relax."

The young doctor disappeared out of her line of sight. She could hear a few voices in the distance but could not make out what they were saying. She closed her eyes again.

"Gladys," another voice soon was calling.

"That's me," she replied.

"Gladys, I am the anesthesiologist. Are you allergic to any medications?"

"Not that I know of," Gladys replied to the middle-aged lady looking over the top of a pair of glasses.

"Ever had any surgeries? Ever had any problems with any kinds of anesthesia?

"Twenty years ago, I had my appendix out," Gladys answered, "but I don't remember having any problems."

"Ok. That's great," said the woman. "I'm gonna start a medication to help you relax and take some of the edge off your pain. It may even make you a little drowsy. Then, once they get you into the Operating Room, I will give you another medication that will help you go into a really nice deep sleep."

"That sounds wonderful," Gladys responded, "I'm worn out and haven't been able to sleep since I fell."

The woman gently patted Gladys on the shoulder.

"Don't you worry, sweetie," she said, "we will get you some sleep very shortly."

The woman injected a medication into the IV bag hanging on the pole just to the left of Gladys shoulder. She stood silently watching Gladys and then the IV. After several minutes, she stepped back closer to the side of the bed.

"How are you doing now, Gladys?" she asked.

"Well, I'm a little foggy and kinda feel like I could sleep," Gladys replied.

"Alrighty then," the woman responded, "don't struggle with it. Relax and get some rest."

The woman disappeared out of Gladys' sight, and Gladys closed her eyes and soon fell asleep.

CHAPTER 22

A s Sam sat in his office listening to the news, a thought popped into his head. A homeless man had been brought in last night talking about a homeless lady that he had found lying covered in snow as he was making his way to their shelter. His mind began to process the situation. The man had told him that she was a lady he regularly encountered, so Sam knew there would be no family or friends checking on her. She would be just another face being processed through Grady's Emergency and Surgery Centers. If her hip was broken as the man had seemed to believe, she would be in the hospital for a couple of weeks and then would need therapy to return to walking. He knew this was a painful recovery for an elderly person, as he had visited several of his church members who had been through the procedure and recovery. The fact she was homeless added to the difficulties that lie ahead for her. Where would she convalesce after being released from the hospital? How would she get to follow-up appointments?

All the big picture things that had burdened Sam's mind several minutes ago were now completely out of his mind. He needed to find this woman and be the family for her that she currently did not have. Fortunately for him, he was on the pastoral care team at Grady and received a daily listing of patients who sought clergy. But if she did not check that box on the admitting paperwork, she would not be in the email he received every morning. Sam was very familiar with the Health Insurance Portability and Accountability Act (HIPAA) and the protection of patient privacy, so he knew it might take some maneuvering for him to locate her and assist her. But Sam was determined. He needed to locate the homeless guy from the night before and get a few details.

With the sound of some popping and cracking in his joints, Sam stood up from his desk and headed to the fellowship hall. He knew breakfast was cooking and the people sheltered in his church would begin to trickle in to eat.

When he walked into the fellowship hall, it was alive with commotion. There was already a line of approximately 100 people waiting for a plate of breakfast. The smell of eggs and bacon filled the air, and his old nose caught the delightful aroma of coffee. He smiled and made his way toward two tables hosting a dozen insulated containers of coffee with the words "U.S. National Guard" stenciled on the side. He filled another Styrofoam cup with the hot nectar and bypassed the sugar and creamer containers. Black coffee had been a constant source of comfort and strength years ago in college and seminary for him, and now he never gave sugar or creamer a second thought.

As he drew his first sip from the steaming cup, he noticed a couple of the Guardsman standing near the door to the alley. He walked to them and greeted them.

"Good morning," he started.

Two young men and a young woman he estimated to be in their mid-20s looked up and smiled.

"Good morning, Pastor," one replied. "How are you this brisk morning?"

Sam smiled, "I can't complain, and who would want to listen to it if I did?"

The three chuckled.

"Pretty brutal night last night," said the young lady. "These folks are really appreciative that you opened the church to provide them shelter."

"Glad we could help," Sam said. "I have a question for you. One of the homeless guys I spoke with last night was telling me he had discovered a lady covered in snow right before he came inside. Did any of you hear anything about her?"

The Guardsman on the end looked up quickly.

"Yes, sir," he responded. "Gladys. Her name is Gladys. She had a broken hip and had fallen and lost consciousness. My squad transported her to Grady E.R. last night."

Sam smiled again, "I wanted to visit her and see if I could help her in any way. Since she is homeless, I know she won't have a family to lean on for help."

"Let me get my squad leader for you, sir," the young Guardsman replied.

He quickly disappeared out the door. After a few minutes, he walked back in the door with a captain in tow.

"Captain Miller, this is the pastor of this church. He was hoping to visit the homeless lady we transported to the E.R. last night with the broken hip," the young Guardsman said.

Captain Miller extended his hand and shook hands with Sam.

"Samuel Matthews, sir," Sam said as he shook the Captain's hand.

"Good to meet you, Pastor," the Captain responded. "Since the lady had no next of kin for us to notify, I sat at the hospital until about an hour ago. They were taking her to surgery when I left."

"Do you think you could get me over there in the mess the streets are in today?" Sam asked.

"Without a doubt, sir," the Captain said. "My squad has been maneuvering the city pretty well."

"Corporal," the Captain called to one of the Guardsman, "the pastor and I need transportation to Grady."

"Yes, sir," the young lady replied, "I will ready a Hummer."

She scrambled out the door. Within a few minutes she re-appeared and walked directly to them.

"Pastor, it is still very cold outside. You probably ought to put on this parka," she said, handing him a heavy, dark green parka with a fur-lined hood.

"And here are a pair of our arctic mittens," she said as she handed him the gloves.

Sam pulled the heavy parka on and the mittens. He looked at the odd gloves without individual fingers in amazement. He had never worn any gloves so thick in his life. The Corporal escorted Sam and the Captain to a Hummer waiting just out-side the door. He pulled himself up into the giant truck and settled into a seat.

"Buckle up, Pastor," said the Captain. "This will be a bumpy ride avoiding stalled cars and other obstacles."

Sam quietly complied, pulling on a seat belt and buckling it around himself. The Hummer proceeded down the street and at the first intersection, he saw four or five cars blocking the street. Without a word, the driver jumped the curb with one set of wheels and maneuvered around the mess. They pro-ceeded down the street, jumping the curb on a frequent basis. Sam was shocked at the number of abandoned and wrecked cars they encountered on the way. He had made the drive to Grady so many times over the years, he had hardly paid any attention to landmarks and sites along the way. But today, ma-neuvering the streets was so difficult that they were traveling around 15 miles an hour. Everything was going by so slowly, so the old pastor had a great deal of time to look at everything along the way. Everything was covered in snow or a layer of ice. Tree limbs bowed under the weight of the ice and occa-sionally, he would hear a loud crack when a limb would snap under the weight of the ice. It was an eerie experience for Sam. Normally, he would encounter a great deal of traffic along the route and would see numerous pedestrians. But today, the city seemed lifeless. He saw no other cars moving on the streets. There were no pedestrians on the sidewalks. It was almost depressing to see the empty streets and abandoned cars.

The short trip took the group an hour to complete. When they arrived at Grady Hospital, Sam noticed a change in its normal appearance. The Emergency Ambulance entrance was double stacked with ambulances and military Hummers. He could see a dozen or so people wrapped in parkas, pushing stretchers into the Emergency entrance.

When the Hummer pulled up to the main Emergency entrance, a Guardsman rushed to the rear door of the Hummer and assisted Sam and the Captain in exiting the vehicle.

"Watch your step, sirs," the young Guardsman said. "We have been salting the drive and sidewalk, but ice is continuing to form."

They made their way into the Emergency entrance, and Sam could see approximately 50 people in the waiting room. He unzipped the heavy parka and retrieved his Clergy identification badge form his coat pocket. He signed in as he had done a hundred times before and picked up the clipboard marked "Patients seeking clergy." He scanned the list but did not see any listing that he thought would be Gladys. He looked at the Captain.

"I don't see her on the visitation list," Sam said.

The Captain looked up and grinned. "She signed me in as her legal guardian, so I can get you in to see her."

The Captain had a brief discussion at the admitting desk and then pointed to the hallway door.

"She went to surgery two hours ago, so we have to go up to the surgery center," he reported.

As they made their way down the hallway toward the elevators, Sam held up his hand. He punched a code into a door lock and opened the door to reveal a small kitchenette.

"Coffee, Captain?"

"Absolutely!"

Sam poured two cups of coffee, handed one to the Captain, and then proceeded down the hallway.

When they reached the elevator, Sam instinctually punched the up button. When the elevator doors opened, a middle-aged, redheaded nurse stepped out and smiled a huge smile.

"Pastor Sam!" she exclaimed excitedly, giving him a huge hug. "So good to see you!"

Sam smiled and looked at the Captain.

"Perks of the job," he said jokingly.

They stepped into the elevator car and, without giving it much thought, Sam punched the button for the fifth floor. He had been to the Surgery Suite so many times, it was almost automatic. When they stepped off the elevator, he led them directly to the patient advisory desk. The man behind the desk looked up and recognized the Captain.

"Hey, you made it back," he said, seeming surprised. "They completed the surgery, and she is in the Recovery Room now. You should be able to see her in a few minutes."

The two men found a couple open seats in the surgery waiting area and quietly sipped their coffees. Sam began thinking of how Peachtree Church could continue to minister to the families they had sheltered during this storm after things resumed to normal. He wondered how they would pay the power bill after heating the Education Wing for more than just enough to keep pipes from freezing for the first time in five years. Granted, there were many people sheltered at the church who had homes to return to after the roads cleared, but there were many who were homeless when they walked in the door and would return to homelessness.

It was a complex problem that could not be solved by handing out one meal or providing one sleeping bag. There were numerous situations that resulted in each homeless person's journey. How could those paths be altered? Sam had been around the streets of Atlanta long enough. He knew it was not a problem that could be solved overnight. And it would not be solved by the next person to win the Mayor's race. Many had tried over the years with various initiatives, but the problem remained.

Sam looked around the waiting area for something to distract his thoughts. As his eyes surveyed the room, he saw a magazine rack on the wall. He walked over and perused the collection – most of which was at least six months out of date. He shook his head and returned to his seat.

"So, Captain," he said, "what part of the area do you live in?"

The Captain raised his head and replied, "Down near the Speedway."

Sam looked confused.

The Captain recognized the look and quickly attempted to clarify: "Atlanta Motor Speedway. Hampton."

"Oh," Sam replied. "And what do you do fulltime?"

"Well, I am going to college and working security at the Atlanta airport," the Captain answered. "It keeps me busy balancing all of the time commitments, but I have my goals in sight."

"Do you have a lot of homeless in the Hampton area?" Sam inquired.

"Some," the Captain replied, "but a drop in the bucket to what you guys have in the inner city. How do you address such a large homeless community?"

Sam shook his head, "Many have tried different programs and such, but the problem has not been effectively addressed. I am sitting here trying to figure out the answer myself. When we opened the church doors for the storm, I expected we would see lots of stranded commuters and a handful of homeless. But what I noticed last night and this morning walking the halls is that we really saw a mix of demographics and a lot more homeless than I expected. I really think it is a huge need, and the Church should be actively seeking to serve and solve the need. Our struggle is that our church has withered and barely pays the light bill. In fact, this is the first time in over five years that we have had anyone in the education wing, gym and fellowship hall. The more I think about it, it is almost like as a church, we have fallen into serving ourselves and maintaining instead of servicing the community."

The Captain nodded.

"That's a shame," he said. "That's a really nice facility y'all have there, and it's in a prominent location."

"Expensive real estate is what it is," Sam responded, "and expensive to maintain and operate."

"I always wondered if the homeless in the city would be willing to locate to another area of the town if they had a comfortable place to live. You know, some kind of community," the Captain said.

A lady sitting to the right of the Captain suddenly spoke up, "Sorry to eavesdrop on your conversation, but I couldn't help but hear your discussion."

Both men looked up at a short, grey-haired lady that Sam guessed was 65 or more.

"I have a son-in-law who lives in Austin, Texas, and he was telling me about an organization he volunteers with out there. For years, they ran food trucks, delivering food to homeless and struggling families. About a year or so ago, they started a master planned community just outside Austin for the homeless. They have old, restored travel trailers and tiny houses where each person has a clean, comfortable, safe place to live. They have doctors and counselors who volunteer there at an onsite community clinic, and they provide job training. I bet something like that would work in a city like Atlanta. You would just have to find a big enough plot of land to house it."

Sam felt a chill run down his spine as the woman talked.

"What is the name of the organization?" he asked.

"Mobile Loaves and Fishes," she replied.

Sam pulled out his notebook and jotted down the name.

"I'm going to have to research that one," he said with a smile.

After a few more quiet minutes, the man from the desk approached them.

"Captain," he started, "Miss Boatwright is ready to be moved to a room."

The Captain looked confused.

"Miss Boatwright, um, Gladys?" the man responded.

"Oh!" the Captain exclaimed. "Don't know that I have heard her last name until now."

"If you gentlemen will follow me, I will take you over to meet her on the way."

They proceeded thru a set of double doors, down a corridor, and around a corner where they met an orderly pushing a hospital bed out of another room.

"Josh," the man said, "this is the family for Miss Boatwright."

The orderly looked up at the two men, down at the patient, and then back up, a bit bewildered.

"Not natural family," said the Captain.

"Community family," interjected Sam.

"Ah, OK," the orderly responded. "I'm Josh. She seems to be doing well. She's a little bit groggy, but surgery went well, and she has not had any complications in recovery."

"Thank you for updating us," Sam replied. "If it's alright with you, we will follow you to her room and wait there until she wakes up."

The orderly nodded his approval and started pushing Gladys' bed toward the elevator.

CHAPTER 23

A lvin sat quietly in the kitchen at the end of the large prep table, eating a plate of breakfast and revisiting the events of the last 24 hours in his mind. Peachtree Church had sheltered some 500 people over the night. That was more people than the church had under its roof in any one month over the last year. He figured that at least 200 of them were homeless. He began calculating numbers in his head. If 50 shelters opened in the city, and they each sheltered around 200 people, and a third of those were homeless, then that would mean over 3,000 homeless had been sheltered overnight. He shook his head at the thought. That was the equivalent of a small town. How could a community that size be adequately served? Not just housed and fed, but served? How could an organization meet medical needs, counseling needs, drug and alcohol rehabilitation needs, and physical therapy needs? How could a ministry provide job placement services, resume writing services, and job training for a community that size? It seemed overwhelming.

As he ate the plate of food, he remembered a video he had watched several months back of Andy Stanley, the son of First Baptist Pastor Charles Stanley. He could not recall Andy's whole message, but he remembered one phrase that had caught his attention: "Do for one what you wish you could do for all."

"OK," Alvin said, seemingly to no one, "what could I do for one?"

Alvin gave the question careful consideration. His work at the GM plant was not a direct skill that would be marketable anymore, with the closing of assembly plants and such.

"What is it that I have to offer?"

As he sat sorting through the questions running through his mind, he heard a rustling noise that demanded his attention. He adjusted his focus to see that Phil had walked into the kitchen and was putting serving trays into the sink.

Alvin thought for a second and then spoke up.

"Phil, we have worked almost 24 hours now. Reckon some of the folks out there would be willing to lend a hand with some of this cleanup?"

Phil paused and lifted an eyebrow.

"You know, I hadn't even thought of that," Phil said, "but I am a bit tired. Maybe it wouldn't hurt to ask."

Alvin wiped his hands on the apron he was still wearing and walked out into the fellowship hall. He stepped into the center of the room and in a loud voice asked, "Excuse me, folks, but would anyone be willing to volunteer to wash a few dishes?"

A couple of hands went up. and two people approached him.

"I'd be more than glad to help wash some dishes," the first man said.

"Great," said Alvin. He extended his hand to the man and shook his hand. "I'm Alvin. What's your name?"

"Howdy, Mister Alvin," the man replied. "My name is Fred."

A second man standing next to Fred spoke up.

"Mister Alvin," he said, "my name is Jose. Y'all have been mighty generous with the food and shelter. I'd be more than glad to help out with those dishes."

Alvin shook the man's hand and said, "Thank you, buddy. I really appreciate the help."

He led the two men back into the kitchen where Phil was scrubbing a large pot.

"Phil," he said, "I've brought in reinforcements."

Phil looked up and smiled. "Alrighty! Thank you, gentle-men, for your help."

"No problem," Fred said. "I have a few years of experience at this task."

Fred and Jose began washing, rinsing, and drying pots, pans, and serving trays. Phil walked back out into the fellowship hall to check on what else needed to be done. He was surprised to see people he did not know bagging up garbage, wiping down tables, and sweeping the floor. Alvin was a few steps behind him and stopped when he noticed the same thing. Several of the National Guardsman were assisting with the cleanup work.

Alvin looked at Phil. "Let's go see what needs attention in the Educational wing," he suggested.

Phil nodded, and the two headed down the hall, passing more people carrying out large bags of garbage. When they arrived at the first classroom, Alvin opened the door to see an elderly lady folding a blanket. The room was spotless.

"Anything we can do to help?" Phil asked.

"No, thank you," she said with a smile. "I believe I have this under control. A little slow, maybe, but under control."

The two men walked to the next classroom and saw a young mother putting socks on a little girl while her little brother sat on the floor, holding a sock.

Alvin knelt down.

"Son, can I help you with that?"

"Oh! Thank you," said the mother.

The little boy looked up at Alvin for a moment and then cautiously handed them the sock.

"Here we go," Alvin said as he helped the boy with the socks and a pair of tennis shoes. "Looky there, all laced up and ready to go!"

The little boy giggled and pushed himself up from the floor.

Alvin laughed and started to push himself up from the floor much slower than the little boy had done. Phil stepped over to him.

"How about a hand?" he said, offering Alvin assistance.

Alvin took his hand, and Phil helped him to his feet.

"Not as easy as it once was," Alvin noted.

"Tell me about it," Phil replied. "Tell me about it."

Phil and Alvin continued moving down the hall, room by room. Some rooms they found empty. Other rooms they found needing a little clean up. By the time they had proceeded through all the rooms on all three floors, it was almost lunchtime. They hustled back to the kitchen to prepare whatever was on hand for lunch.

When they arrived back in the fellowship hall, Phil quickly noticed there was a significantly smaller crowd than was there earlier when they were cleaning up from breakfast.

"The weather must be improving," Phil noted.

Alvin stopped and opened an exit door and stepped outside. It was still very cold, but some of the ice on the sidewalk had melted from the salt that had been spread on it. He stepped out and noted that the street alongside the church was still covered in snow. But at the intersection just ahead, he could see that Peachtree Street appeared to have been cleared. He returned to the fellowship hall to find Phil chatting with Fred, who had volunteered to wash dishes earlier. Alvin noted Fred had a heavy backpack leaned against his leg.

"Well, the side streets are still covered, but Peachtree looks like they have at least cleared one lane from what I could see," Alvin reported to the two men.

"Yeah," Phil replied, "Fred is contemplating heading out."

"What?" Alvin asked. "You've got to be kidding. You've got about four and a half hours of sunlight, and then it's gonna be miserable."

Fred shrugged, "I figure the regular spots will be back open, and I don't wanna be a burden."

"Nonsense!" Alvin said. "Plus, we need your help with lunch prep."

Fred cocked his eyebrow. "Well, if you need some help, I reckon I could hang around a bit longer."

The three men walked to the kitchen where two men and four ladies were gathered around the prep table.

"What are we working on, folks?" Alvin asked.

"We're making four different kinds of sandwiches," one lady responded. "Peanut butter and jelly, ham sandwiches with mayo, turkey sandwiches with sliced cheese, and bologna sandwiches with mustard."

"Alright," said Fred, "let me wash up, then I'll help."

The three men washed and dried their hands, donned serving gloves, and joined the crew making sandwiches. By the time they had a serving tray of each kind of sandwich ready, a line was forming in the fellowship hall.

Alvin carried a tray out to the serving line to see around 150 people still in the shelter ready to eat. Like Fred, many of the homeless had already headed out to return to their normal day-to-day life. Several stranded commuters had left to find their cars and find a way home. Alvin thought it was prudent for those who had stayed for lunch to stay the night. After setting the tray down on the serving table, he stepped toward the center of the room.

"Folks," he said in a loud voice, "the weather is still pretty rough out there, and most of the roads are still a mess. We will be open for anyone wanting to stay another night in the warm. Let's bless this meal so y'all can eat."

The room got extremely quiet as Alvin bowed his head.

He began to pray, "Lord, please bless this meal to nourish our bodies. Bless everyone here and their families and keep them all safe. Thank you for this meal and for a warm place to sleep. Amen."

As the people walked through the line, it occurred to him that he had never prayed in front of a crowd this size. It kind of startled him when he realized it. He looked around and then returned to the kitchen.

"I'd say there's probably 150 or so out there," Alvin told the kitchen crew. "I told them we'd have a place for all of them to sleep another night."

Phil looked at Fred and said, "Well, guess we will be needing some help with dinner tonight and breakfast again."

Fred looked directly at Phil but gave no response. He continued preparing sandwiches silently.

Alvin looked over at Fred, "What about it, Fred?" Alvin said, "You up for hanging out with us one more day? We sure could use your help."

Fred looked up at Alvin.

"Sure," he said.

Fred was not sure what to make of the current situation. In the last 10 years living on the streets of Atlanta, no one had expected anything out of him. He had not been asked to help with anything, and he certainly had not been included in anything. But now, here he was helping in this emergency shelter. He could not quite put his finger on why, but he kind of liked it. He did not mind the work. He had been used to hard work in the military, and this paled in comparison to any of that kind of labor. The more he thought about it, the part he liked the most was he could see other people benefiting from what he was doing. And heck, he had always preferred to make his own way and earn his keep over just being handed things. That had been the hardest part of being homeless for him. Adjusting to having to swallow his pride as a man and accept the charity of strangers.

Besides, no one had bothered his backpack or boots during the night. This was a different crowd than the regular shelters he had experienced. There was something different about the people that were serving here. Heck, he could not remember anyone sitting down and just having a conversation with him in other shelters. In the last 24 hours, four or five of the people volunteering here had sat down next to him and just chit-chatted. Yeah, he would stick around tonight and in the morning. Not having to seek shelter from the cold was a fringe benefit, the way he saw it – icing on the cupcake.

CHAPTER 24

J oy Davidson looked around the classroom where she had slept the night before and tried to tidy things up. When she was satisfied that the room looked as good as it did when she walked into it the night before, she pulled on her coat and gloves and stepped out into the hallway. An older lady with a cheerful grin greeted her just outside the classroom door.

"Good morning, sugar," the lady said. "Did you sleep well?"

"Yes," Joy replied. "It took a bit for me to shut my mind down and finally go to sleep, thinking about my children sleeping in their school gym, but once I got to sleep, I slept well. Thank you."

The lady smiled and nodded, "I'm so glad, dear. We are serving breakfast and coffee down in the fellowship hall. Head on down there and get a bite to eat before you try to head out."

Joy paused. She felt a sense of urgency to get out. She needed to get gas in her car and had to find roads that were open so she could get to her children's school. Who knew if she could get to that side of town or if you could get up the hill to the school, and she was not going to sit idly by wondering. But considering the conditions of the roads, she was sure if she could get to the school, it was going to take more than the usual 30-40 minutes. It might be a good idea to get something to eat before setting out on this trek.

"I guess that isn't a bad idea," she finally said.

Joy pulled her gloves off and stuffed them into the pockets of her jacket.

The lady smiled, "Well, I have always said breakfast is the most important meal of the day."

Joy laughed, "I tell my kids that all the time!"

Joy walked down the stairs to the hallway that led to the fellowship hall. Three-quarters of the floor was covered in cots like she had slept on, and one corner had rows of tables and chairs. A line of tables just beyond them made a serving line where she could see 50 or so people lined up, filling plates. She looked at her cellphone to see what time it was, but it was dead. She walked to the end of the line and waited her turn to get a plate. The smell of eggs and bacon mixed with brewed coffee reminded her of her grandmother's kitchen when she was younger. Just the memory put her in a good mood.

Joy fixed a plate of breakfast, got a cup of coffee, and stirred in some creamer and a couple packets of sugar. Then she found a table with an available seat and sat down to eat. She closed her eyes, quietly bowed her head, and offered up a silent prayer.

"Jesus, thank you for a warm place to sleep on a miserable night and the kindness of strangers to help me find this shelter. Thank you for this warm plate of food. Thank you for keeping Cheryl and Jeremy safe and warm at their school. Thank you for the teachers at the school who spent the night looking out for them. Please make a way for me to get the car running and a path for me to get to the school and get them home. Amen."

When she opened her eyes, she picked up a plastic fork and scooped a serving of eggs. When she lifted her eyes, she saw a smiling face across from her, a young woman in military fatigues sipping a cup of coffee.

"Good morning," the young woman greeted her. "I'm Beth. How are you this morning?"

Joy smiled, "I'm doing well. I'm Joy. Nice to meet you, Beth."

As Joy ate, Beth continued the conversation, "Were you one of the folks stranded out on I-75 last night?"

Joy shook her head, "I work on the other side of the interstate. The ramps were backed up, and I started running out of gas while I was just sitting there. I came across the bridge to a gas station on Spring Street, but it was closed. I ran out of gas before I could find another station."

"Well, that sucks," Beth replied.

Joy nodded, "Yeah, I was trying to go pick my kids up from school, but I never made it."

"Where's your car?"

Joy swallowed a fork of food and said, "The corner of 14th and Peachtree. Right in front of Colony Square."

Beth nodded and said, "Just down the street, a couple blocks here. Alright. Let me see if we can't help you with that. Finish your breakfast, and I'll talk to my PL."

Beth pushed herself back from the table, collected her plate and utensils, and carried them to a nearby trashcan. She walked to the corner of the room by an outside door and spoke with a small group of men and women in military uniforms. After a few minutes, she walked back over to where Joy was sitting. Joy had finished eating and was picking up her napkin, utensils and Styrofoam plate to toss in the trash when Beth walked up.

"Good news, Joy!" she said with a sly smile. "Or should I say: 'Behold! I bring glad tidings of joy!'"

Joy laughed.

"We have a couple of four-wheeler ATVs, jerry jugs of gas and battery jump boxes sitting outside ready to go," Beth reported. "If you think you are up for a ride, I'll take you to your car and see if we can't get you moving to check on your children."

Joy dropped everything in her hands on the table and gave Beth a huge hug.

"That's awesome!" she squealed.

Joy caught herself, stepped back and looked a bit sheepish.

"Oh sorry. Are you going to get into trouble for a civilian hugging you?"

Beth laughed. "No, no. I think we're good."

Joy picked up the trash she had dropped on the table and threw it in a trash can near the kitchen. She zipped up her coat, pulled on her gloves, and looked at Beth.

"OK," she said, "let's get off on this adventure."

Beth led her outside where four ATVs set parked on the sidewalk and three young men in military parkas stood by.

"Sergeant Smith," Beth said, "this lady needs help getting a car started at 14th and Peachtree. She says she ran out of gas there last night."

Sgt. Smith looked up at the two and asked, "Do you want a couple of us to go with you?"

"No, Sergeant," she replied, pulling on a heavy parka. "I've got this."

"Roger that," he responded. "If you have any problems, hit us up on the radio, and I'll send the cavalry."

"Will do," Beth replied.

Beth threw a leg over the nearest ATV, turned the key and pushed the starter button. The ATV roared to life almost instantly.

"Hop on, Joy," she said. "I promise not to give you a rough ride."

Joy carefully crawled on the ATV behind Beth.

"Wow, this thing is kinda roomy," she noted.

"Yeah," Beth said, "On both sides of you, there are hand holds. See 'em?"

"Yep," Joy said. "Ready to roll."

Beth pushed down on the shifter with her foot and rolled in the throttle grip with a turn of her wrist. The two eased off the curb and onto the frozen side street. They eased their way up to the corner of Peachtree where Joy could see several military vehicles parked in a line along the curb. Peachtree Street appeared to have been cleared at some point overnight. There was still snow against the curbs and small piles in the center lane, but the street looked maneuverable. Beth eased the machine north on Peachtree where there were half a dozen cars sitting motionless in the far lane.

Beth turned her head where Joy could hear her and shouted, "Which one is yours?"

Joy leaned forward and shouted back, "See that Honda up at the intersection?"

Beth replied, "Gotcha."

She drove to the rear of Joy's car and activated the four-way flashers on the ATV.

"Joy," she said, "we are in a dangerous position with cars coming down the street on 14th and Peachtree. I am going to need you to watch out for me while I get some gas in your car. If a car starts sliding toward us or something, you holler and get to the sidewalk."

Joy replied. "Gotcha!"

Beth unstrapped a jerry jug from the ATV and a funnel and walked to the rear of the car, cautiously looking every direction for oncoming cars. When she was confident it was safe, she flipped open the fuel door on the side of the Honda, unscrewed the gas cap, stuck the funnel in, and removed the cap on the jerry jug. She hoisted the jug up to the funnel and began pouring gas into the car.

"Car coming," Joy called out.

Beth looked up to see a car coming south on Peachtree. It changed lanes to go around them, slowed, and went by without incident. Beth watched as she continued to slowly pour gas into Joy's car. Beth patiently continued until she had as much gas in the car as she could coax out of the jug.

"OK, Joy," she said, "see if it'll crank."

Joy unlocked the door and tugged. The door was frozen shut. She gave it a hard tug – nothing. She gave it another hard tug – no movement. She gave it one more hard tug, and the door opened to the sound of breaking ice. She crawled into the seat, put her key in the ignition, and turned the key. All the lights on the dash came on. She waited for a couple of minutes for the fuel pump to pump gas back up to the engine and gave it another crank. The motor turned over but did not fire. She released it and waited another minute and tried again. Again, the motor turned over but did not fire. She released it and waited again. Once again, she twisted the key, this time the motor sputtered a few times and started.

"Yes!" Joy exclaimed.

She reached toward the floor and grabbed her ice scraper and crawled back out of the car. When she looked up, Beth had secured the jerry jug and funnel back on the ATV and was walking back with a small whisk broom. While Joy scraped at the windshield, Beth swept snow off the hood, side windows, and rear window. As the Honda started to warm up, the defroster began to make Joy's work a little easier.

"Ok, Joy," Beth said, "Sarge said the gas station north of here on Peachtree is open this morning. Do you have enough money to fill it up?"

Joy finished scraping off the windshield. "Yes. I sure do. I think I am good to go here. Thank you so much for all you have done to help me."

"No problem! A service of the National Guard!" Beth declared.

Joy crawled in the Honda and buckled her seat belt. Beth crawled on the ATV, kicked it into neutral, and started it. She stood on the foot pegs of the ATV looking all directions for traffic. She motioned for Joy to go ahead. Joy put the car in drive and made a U-turn in the middle of Peachtree to head north.

"You'd never do that on a normal day in Atlanta," she thought to herself.

Beth stood motionless until Joy was headed out of sight heading north to the gas station. She then sat down on the ATV, put it in gear, and headed back to the church.

Less than five miles away, Joy was cautiously making her way up Peachtree Street. Her commute was 25 miles each way. A trip that typically took 30-45 minutes, depending on when she left in the morning or afternoon, could stretch to an hour and a half if she hit rush hour. Today, with the interstates shut down, the drive would probably take over two hours. As she rounded a curve in the street, she saw the gas station on the right that Beth had told her was open. Sure enough, the lights were all on, and she could see a Jeep sitting at one of the pumps. She carefully pulled into an available pump and got out to fill the car.

As Joy filled the tank on the old Honda, she watched the occasional cars go by on Peachtree Street.

"Boy, I wish traffic was this light on normal days around here," she said to herself.

As soon as the nozzle on the gas pump hose clicked off, Joy put it back in the side of the pump, got the receipt from the pump, and hurried back to the warmth of the car. It was not a day to causally stand around outside. She cranked the car and prepared herself for what she expected might be a two- to three-hour drive. She navigated her way north on Peachtree until she reached the ramp for Highway 13, which ran parallel to the interstate, and hoped that the highway was open and maneuverable. As the ramp descended to the highway, she could see that the right lane had been completely cleared and about one-half of the left lane was cleared. As she began driving north on the highway, she passed abandoned cars on the right shoulder of the roadway. A little bit further and there was an abandoned bus on the left side, partially sitting in the left lane of the highway. After about a mile, she could see a pick-up in front of her. She slowed her speed and maintained about a four-car gap behind the truck. Normally anything more than a car and a half gap in Atlanta traffic would have someone trying to pass. Today, however, it seemed that everyone out on the road had opted to exercise caution, and Joy was good with that approach.

Joy looked down at the speedometer and chuckled. "30 miles an hour," she said out loud. "I can't remember the last time I drove 30 miles an hour on this highway when there wasn't a traffic jam."

Almost 30 minutes later, Joy could see where the highway crossed under I-285. She looked up as she approached the area and was shocked to see what looked like a wall of tractor-trailer rigs in both directions as far as she could see, sitting stationary on the interstate. As she passed under the interstate, she slowed for abandoned vehicles on both sides of the roadway, leaving a narrow path just big enough for her to maneuver. A mile or two later, she noticed the truck in front of her slowing. She moved the car a little to the left to get a look around the truck and see what was ahead. She could see five or six more cars in front of them. They crept along at a slower pace, and at one point there was enough of a hill that Joy could see about eight cars in front of her was a large, yellow dump truck with flashing yellow lights.

"Snowplow and salt spread truck," Joy guessed out loud. "At least I will have a freshly cleared route home," she said, staying positive.

Another 30 minutes went by as they crept along until they came to the intersection for Jimmy Carter Boulevard. The traffic light separated the line of cars behind the plow. When Joy crossed the intersection, the plow was long out of her sight. She drove along, still amazed by the amount of snow on the sides of the roadway and by the number of abandoned cars on the shoulder and the occasional car that had slid off into a ditch.

When Joy saw that she was approaching Pleasant Hill Road, she was almost certain she had been driving for over an hour and a half. She carefully turned off the highway onto the road and headed for her children's school. Another 20 minutes went by as she slowly made her way to the school and to the base of the long hill that had prevented the buses reaching the school just yesterday. Joy stopped the Honda at the bottom of the hill and looked up the roadway. The road was not plowed, but she could see a set of tire tracks leading up the hill that appeared to be all the way through the layer of snow. She figured that if the tire tracks had worn down to the pavement, the Honda should have enough traction to get up the hill. She looked to both sides at the snow-filled ditches. A Lexus sat at the bottom of the ditch on one side, a Dodge Minivan sat halfway down toward the ditch on the other side. Those two abandoned cars did not boost her confidence, but she was determined to reach her children. She rationalized that a little head of steam would help her climb the hill, so she got a little speed before starting the incline. The old Honda started up the hill. Joy had both hands tightly gripping the wheel. She reminded herself that the brake pedal would not be an option, so she regulated all her speed solely with the gas pedal. Every time the car wiggled a bit, she would lightly lift off the throttle but not completely. After a few more nervous minutes, Joy reached the top of the hill and turned into the driveway of the school. As she cautiously made her way along the driveway to the gym, she could see a handful of SUVs, pickup trucks, and Jeeps lined along the sidewalk along the gym. As she looked at the line of parked cars, she made a startling discovery. There were no other cars around the gym – just SUVs, pickup trucks, and Jeeps. There had been several cars sitting in the teachers' parking lot, but there were none surrounding the gym. Apparently, none of the parents had thought it safe to brave that icy hill in anything that was not four-wheel drive. As she parked her car along the sidewalk around the gym, Joy chuckled as she thought about what she had just done.

CHAPTER 25

Gladys struggled to open her eyes. Her vision was blurry, and she couldn't seem to focus her sight. She moved her head around a little and tried opening her eyes again, but things were still blurry, and the light hurt her eyes. So, she closed her eyes and elected to sleep a bit more.

"Gladys," said a voice.

Gladys wrinkled her brow and tried to place the voice, but for the life of her, she couldn't recognize it.

"Gladys," the voice called again.

"Yes?" she answered feebly.

She felt a hand pat the top of her left hand.

"Gladys, I am Reverend Samuel Matthews from Peachtree Street Church. I came to check on you and see how you were doing after your surgery to repair your broken hip."

"Oh," she replied, "Well that's mighty kind of you pastor. I've kinda been on my own for the last few years, so it's a nice surprise to have someone checking on me. Do you work for the hospital?"

"No," Sam said, "some of the folks that found you spent the night at our church last night and told me your story. I live by myself and couldn't imagine waking from surgery with no one to be around to help care for me. These hospitals can get pretty lonely at times."

Gladys turned her head toward his voice and squinted her eyes. She could make out a fuzzy image of a grey-haired man with wire-rimmed glasses.

"Pastor, I sure appreciate you coming out in this weather to check on my tired old soul. I don't know what's gonna happen with me now."

"Don't you fret, Gladys," Sam said. "You have become a defacto member of our community, and I am going to see to it you have company and help through the recovery process. The Captain of the National Guard unit that transported you here last night has been keeping a pretty good watch on you and was nice enough to drive me over in one of their huge, four-wheel drive vehicles."

Gladys managed a slight smile, "Those military folks sure were nice getting me out of that snow and to the hospital. That one young fella was barking orders about how to splint my leg, how to get me on a stretcher, and all. Honestly, I remember falling and being in a world of pain. The funny part about it was I felt the pain and then started falling. It seemed back-wards. I hit my head hard on the way down and passed out. I came back to, and I couldn't get back up to save my life. Liter-ally! I thought to myself if I didn't get back up that I'd freeze to death right there. But I couldn't manage to get up. I remember getting really cold and closing my eyes. I don't mean to get all out-of-body experience and sappy, but I made my peace with God and closed my eyes. When I woke to someone calling my name, I figured it was Saint Peter, but it was Fred. My head was aching like I had been hit with a bat, and my hip was scream-ing, so I figured this was definitely not Heaven."

A male nurse walked into the room and began checking her vital signs.

"Miss Gladys," he said, "how we doing?"

Gladys turned her head toward his voice, squinted her eyes and replied, "I'm guessing you are doing a bit better than I am, but I'd say I'm a sight better than laying out there on that side-walk."

The nurse chuckled.

"Alright, well we are gonna move you to a room where you can rest and recover," he said as he began moving an IV bag over to a pole on the bed and disconnecting the machine that was monitoring her pulse and blood pressure.

"You ready for a little ride?"

"I guess so," Gladys replied, "'cause I don't think I'm in any shape for a walk at the moment."

"Yeah, probably not today," he replied.

The nurse looked at Sam and said, "Are you going with us, sir?"

"You bet," Sam quickly replied. "Primary caregiver."

"Alrighty then," the nurse said, "let's get this show on the road."

He kicked a pedal under the bed to disengage the brakes and began rolling the bed toward the doorway. Sam followed the nurse as he pushed Gladys and her bed down the hallway toward a set of double doors. The nurse pushed a large metal button on the wall, and both doors opened for them. They proceeded down the hallway to an elevator lobby. He pushed the button, and the three waited quietly. After a few silent minutes the elevator dinged, and the arrow pointing up on the doorframe beside the elevator door lit up.

"Elevator up," said the nurse. "Ladies wear, shoes, handbags, and accessories."

He maneuvered Gladys' bed into the elevator and Sam followed them. The nurse pushed a button, and the doors closed. The elevator made a little rumble under their feet and began rising. After a few more minutes, the elevator dinged again, and the doors opened. The nurse rolled Gladys' bed out of the elevator and down the hallway stopping at a nurse's station.

"Morning, morning," he said. "I have a special delivery for you."

An older lady rose from a seat behind the counter and said, "Who ya got for me there?"

The nurse looked at the clipboard hanging on the bedrail.

"Miss Gladys Boatwright," he reported. "She just had a hip fracture repaired and is looking forward to a relaxing vacation at the Orthopedic Villas and Spa. She has requested comfortable accommodations overlooking the pool."

The older lady nurse grinned, "I think we have the garden room ready for her: Room 7023."

"Ya hear that Miss Gladys? They are giving you the garden room."

He rolled Gladys' bed to Room 7023 and maneuvered it beside the bed in the room. He lowered the rails on the bed in the room and on the bed on which Gladys had been transported. The older lady nurse from the nurse's station walked in the door as he readied things to move Gladys from one bed to the other.

"Miss Gladys," the woman said, "let us do the work. You probably aren't gonna like us for a few minutes for this, but once we get you moved onto the other bed, I have a pain med prescription for you that should win you back over."

Once they had the beds perfectly aligned, the male nurse locked the brakes on the bed where Gladys lay. Both nurses walked to the far side of the empty bed and positioned themselves.

"OK, Gladys," the older woman said, "you get a double handful of those covers and clench your teeth. We are going to pull the mat your lying on and slide you to your new bed."

Gladys grabbed two fists of the blanket that covered her.

The older woman looked at the male nurse and said, "Alright, 1, 2, 3."

They pulled in unison and carefully slid Gladys from one bed to the other. Gladys let out a groan and relaxed both hands.

"Alrighty, dear," the older woman said, "let's get you comfortable."

She gradually raised the head of Gladys' bed a few inches and slightly lowered the foot of her bed so that her knees were ever-so-slightly bent.

"Is that better than flat on your back, dear?"

Gladys responded, "Yeah."

"OK, dear," she said, "here is the remote. It has controls to raise and lower your head and feet to whatever is better for you. It also has the big red Nurse Call button on it. It also controls your television, the room lights, the window shades, and the heat. You can set the room any way that makes you comfortable."

The male nurse unlocked the brakes on the transport bed and maneuvered it carefully toward the door.

"Miss Gladys," he said, "I hope you have a pleasant recovery. Get to feeling better."

He rolled the bed out the doorway and out of sight.

The older woman walked to a whiteboard on the wall under the television across the room from Gladys' bed. She began writing on the board as she talked.

"My name is Christy. I am the head nurse on duty today. My nursing assistant is Katherine. We are glad you are on our wing, and we are going to do everything we can to make you comfortable and get you up and getting around as soon as possible. Don't you worry about a thing. We have been through this adventure with a couple hundred or so folks in the last couple of years, so we will get you through this smoothly."

Christy walked over to the IV pole and made an adjustment on the IV controller. She put a pulse oximeter on Gladys's finger and put a blood pressure cuff around her upper arm. She pushed a few buttons on the controller on the IV pole and the blood pressure cuff began to inflate. When the controller beeped twice, she noted the readings on the controller and pushed a button to record the readings. She pulled a small electronic tablet up and made a few swipes on it.

"As promised, I am going to get you that pain med."

Christy walked out the door of the room. Sam walked over to the edge of the bed.

"Gladys," he said, "I'm still here. If you need or want anything, you just tell me, and we will make it happen."

"Oh," Gladys said, "I thought you would have eased out when they rolled me up here. Thank you for staying, Pastor."

Sam smiled, "Like I said earlier, we are your family through this Gladys. We are here for you."

Sam walked over and sat down in a recliner that sat next to the head of the bed.

After a few minutes, Christy walked back in the door with a small bag in her hand.

"OK, Gladys," she said, "I have a cocktail for you to help you rest a little. In a couple of hours, a rehab nurse is going to come visit and help you get ready to get back to walking."

Christy spiked the smaller bag and ran a line from it to the main IV line and hung the smaller bag on the IV pole. She poked a couple of buttons on the IV controller and looked back at Gladys.

"Let that pain medicine get in your system, and you try to rest a bit. Maybe even sleep a little if you like. We will be in and out if you need us."

She walked over to Sam who rose to his feet.

"Hi, and what is your name?" she asked.

He smiled and replied, "I'm Reverend Samuel Matthews. Gladys doesn't have any local family, so I am here for her."

"Very nice," Christy said, "I see your Grady Clergy badge, so you have been here a time or two. If we can do anything to make you comfortable, let us know. We have coffee, juices, sodas, and snacks for you at the nurse's station if you want anything."

"Thank you," Sam replied, "That's very kind."

He sat back down in the recliner. Christy walked to the doorway.

"Alright, Gladys," she said, "you rest a bit, and one of us will be back by to check on you."

Within a few minutes, the pain medications began to work, and Gladys fell asleep.

CHAPTER 26

Ron Barlow had walked Jeff, his district manager, to his hotel on 17th Street after the two had eaten breakfast with the others who had sheltered the night at Peachtree Street Church. He was anxious to get back to 10th Street to check on his Charger. When they had abandoned it the night before, it still had gas, but it simply would not move due to the frozen street. He could see his breath in the cold air as he walked down the partially cleared sidewalk on the side of Peachtree Street. Seven blocks did not seem like much of a walk for him normally, but today's hike required his full attention to avoid ice patches and tree branches that had snapped under the weight of ice. Ron had always thought the Bradford Pear trees along Peachtree Street were beautiful, but today they were the worst of the casualties, having lost most of their limbs, filling parts of the sidewalk, forcing him to walk in the street at times.

When Ron finally reached 10th Street, there were many of the abandoned cars that had forced him to seek shelter. But some of the cars were gone. The wrecked MARTA bus and delivery truck that had caused the street blockage had been removed, and city workers had repaired the damaged fire hydrant water supply, or at least had it shut down. The weight of the vehicles used to tow the MARTA bus and delivery truck had done a lot to clear some significant ruts in the snow and ice for lighter cars like his to take advantage. As he got closer, he could see several people pushing a car toward the ruts while the driver spun tires anxiously seeking traction. When the car dropped into the ruts and started moving on its own, everyone let out a cheer.

When he reached the waiting Charger, it took a couple of firm tugs to separate the car's door from the frozen seals. He crawled in and cranked the car and turned on the defrosters. He opened the trunk and retrieved an ice scraper and looked at Jeff's luggage still in his trunk.

"Bet he would like to have that at some point," Ron said to himself.

As the car's engine warmed up, Ron set about scraping the windshield, side windows, and rear windows as well as brushing snow off the cowl area and hood. As he worked, he could hear the group pushing another car from its snowy would-be-grave over to the ever-developing ruts, and then the predicable cheers of success when one more was free and on its way. Ron wondered how long they had been freeing cars along the street and if anyone was having comparable success on the inter-states.

After getting all the ice scraped off, the car windows were still pretty fogged up, so Ron had no choice but to wait for the car's defroster to clear the windshield. A small clear oval was beginning to form at the center of the base of the windshield, so at least progress was occurring, albeit slow. Ron looked up and took stock of the situation on the street. There were four cars directly in front of the Charger. The group was presently working on the first of the four, trying to get it moving toward the ruts. Since he had to wait before his car would be ready to even attempt to be moved, he figured he might as well lend a hand.

He walked up to the group as they were pushing on an '80s model Mustang. Without a word, Ron stepped in next to one of the volunteers, braced against the car's trunk deck with both hands, steadied his feet as best as he could for traction, and began pushing. The driver spun the tires, desperately trying to gain traction as the group continued to struggle for footing and pushed. Finally, the old car began moving slowly. As the driver struggled to steer the car toward the ruts, the group assembled around it continued to struggle for footing while doing their best to push it. After several more minutes, the car finally fell into the tracks that had been worn into the frozen surface, and the old Mustang began to pull off. One of the people who had been pushing ran along the passenger side, managed to open the car door, and jumped inside. As the Mustang gradually drove out of sight, what had previously been a loud cheer was now expressed as a group sigh of exhaustion. Ron looked at the remaining group: two men in their early-20s and a lady he guessed to be late-20s, maybe early-30s. He looked at the next car in line in front of his.

"Does this Lexus belong to any of you?" Ron asked.

The woman quickly responded, "That would be mine. I thought we would never get to it," she said, sounding exhausted.

She reached in the car and cranked it. The windows had already been scraped, so it seemed ready to be the next one freed from the icy grips of 10th Street.

"OK," Ron said, "turn the wheels toward the ruts, but don't turn them completely that way until we get you rolling. If you turn too quickly, we won't be able to get it moving."

"Gotcha," the woman said.

He looked at the other two men who looked physically spent.

"How long you guys been at this?"

A tall guy wearing a Georgia Tech hooded sweatshirt responded, "A couple of hours or so, I guess. We've been trying to work our way back to our car," he said, pointing at a Honda Prius between them and Ron's Charger.

Ron nodded in response.

"Ready to get this one out of your way?"

They both chuckled.

"Yeah man," the second one said.

The three men assumed positions behind the car and stomped their feet into the snow-covered street to try and find traction so they could push the Lexus. As they began to push, one of them banged on the quarter panel.

"OK," he shouted, "try it!"

The woman began spinning the wheels, but the car was not moving. The men pushed harder as she continued to spin the tires, which only threw a spray of ice and slush covering their pants legs. Their feet were constantly slipping as they tried to push the Lexus, and they struggled to stay upright at the same time. The car just did not seem to want to move.

"Stop!" Ron shouted.

The woman stopped spinning the car's tires and the three men relaxed for a second. Ron walked to the front of the car to look at how the front tires were pointed. He knocked on the passenger window and the woman rolled it down.

"Straighten your wheels up, and let's see if that helps," he suggested.

He walked to the rear of the car and assumed a position pushing on the trunk lid.

"Alright," hollered the guy in the Georgia Tech sweatshirt, "hit it!"

The tires on the Lexus began spinning again, and the three men began pushing once more. Ron was certain he could feel the car gradually beginning to move. They pushed it a couple of feet and the woman began cautiously steering toward the ruts. After a few more minutes, the Lexus slowly approached the rutted area of the street, and the front tires fell into the ruts. The three men shifted to the driver's side quarter panel and gave the car one more good shove, and the rear tires fell into the tracks in the snow. The woman stepped on the accelerator again, and this time the Lexus began moving under its own power. She rolled the driver's side window down enough to stick a hand out and wave as she shouted a thank you. The Lexus gradually crawled out of sight. A cheer did not go up from the three tired men who stood motionlessly in the snow. In almost unison, the three turned and looked at the Prius sitting motionless and dark.

The guy in the Georgia Tech sweatshirt trudged his way to the driver's door and tugged it a few times to gain entry. He started the car, flipped on the defroster, and began rummaging around the interior looking for an ice scraper. After a few minutes of frantic motion inside the car, he popped his head out of the driver's side doorway and called to Ron.

"Any chance I could use your ice scraper?" he asked sheepishly.

"I got ya," Ron replied and walked back to the Charger, which now set idling with perfectly clear windows. Ron retrieved his ice scraper and walked to the Prius.

"You guys look spent," he said. "Y'all crawl in and thaw out for a minute. I'll get the windows for you."

The two men crawled into the car without putting up a fuss. Ron set about scraping windows. When he reached the rear of the car, he heard a noise and turned to locate the source. He could see a small headlight coming toward them from Peachtree Street. Four-wheeler ATV, Ron figured. He began scraping the back window and continued to watch the approaching headlight. As he finished scraping ice, a four-wheeled ATV pulled up in front of them. A tall figure wearing a heavy green parka stepped off the ATV and approached him.

"Hello, sir," said a male voice from under a fur-lined hood. "National Guard. Would you like some help getting this car moving?"

"You bet we would," Ron replied.

The man pulled up the seat on the ATV and retrieved a tow strap. As he walked to the front of the car, the two men stepped out of the car. They began to dig in the snow in front of the Prius to try and locate a place to connect the tow strap.

"I'm going to let y'all hook that up since it's your car," said the National Guardsman. "I am not assuming any responsibility for any damage yanking on it."

"No problem," shouted one of the two men from under the front of the car.

After a few minutes, they both stood up and began brushing snow off their clothes.

The young man in the Georgia Tech sweatshirt breathlessly spoke up, "I think we got it. Let's give it a try."

He crawled back into the driver seat while Ron and the other young man took positions at the back of the car. Again, they stomped their feet into the snow seeking to find firm footing. The ATV pulled the tow strap tight, and the Prius spun its tiny front tires. The two men began pushing as the ATV revved its engine. Against its will, the snow and ice released its grip on the Prius to the forces of the tugging ATV and the pushing of two tired men. The ATV gained the advantage, and the two men stopped pushing as it pulled the Prius into the ruts plowed into the slush by all the previous traffic. The young man that had been pushing with Ron scrambled to the front of the Prius and lay down in the street to disconnect the tow strap. Once he had it disconnected from the car, he carried it to the ATV and coiled it on the rear luggage rack.

"Thanks for y'alls help," the young man said as he crawled into the passenger side of the car.

He closed his door, and Ron watched the Prius pull out of sight. He turned and looked at the Charger and then back at the National Guardsman on the ATV.

"Guess it's just us now," Ron said.

He began walking back to the Charger as the ATV made a U-turn in the street and began driving toward him. Ron was not terribly enthused by the prospect of crawling under the front of the car in the snow to try and find a point of attachment for the tow strap, but he certainly preferred to sleep in his own bed tonight as opposed to another night on a military cot. He began digging into the snow. The ATV pulled up in front of the car and began idling. Ron dug a hole in the snow enough to expose the center of the car. He took the end of the tow strap and hooked it to a point on the lower front suspension.

"Alright," he said, standing up and beating the snow and slush off his clothes. "Let's see what we've got."

He crawled in the car, put it in gear, and gently stepped on the accelerator. The back tires spun, and the rear of the car danced side-to-side a bit, trying to find traction. He could hear the engine on the ATV begin to rev as it pulled. He continued to spin the rear tires of the Charger and moved the steering wheel back and forth, trying to help the car find any minute amount of traction. Finally, it began to move. The rear tires continued to spin, but the car was slowly moving forward. After a few more minutes of slow progress, Ron could feel the front wheels fall into the ruts in the street. The ATV continued to pull. Ron stepped on the accelerator a little harder spinning the wheels and steered the car enough to make the rear-end spin sideway and over into the ruts. He honked the horn to let the soldier on the ATV know he could stop. Ron crawled out of the car, knelt in the snow, and disconnected the tow strap. He pulled the glove off his right hand and extended it to the soldier on the ATV. The soldier quickly removed his glove and shook his hand.

"I greatly appreciate the help," Ron said. "I'd have been out here on my own without your help."

"Glad I could help, sir," the soldier replied. "Be safe out there."

The young soldier disconnected the tow strap from the back of the ATV, stowed it beneath the seat, and remounted the machine. He dropped it in gear and headed further down 10th Street. Ron returned to the warm Charger, closed the door, removed his gloves, and slowly headed to Peachtree Street.

"I'll drop off Jeff's bags at his hotel, and then I'm going home," he thought to himself.

CHAPTER 27

Jeff brushed snow off his pants legs and stomped his feet to get as much of the slush off his shoes before walking into the hotel lobby. He walked through the automatic double sliding doors that opened as he approached them. He walked across the tile-floored lobby to the check-in counter. A young man sporting a shirt and tie greeted him as he approached.

"Checking in?"

"Yes, sir," Jeff responded. "I was supposed to check in yesterday afternoon but got stuck in traffic and spent the night in an emergency shelter. Is my room still available?"

"Let me check for you, sir," the young man replied. "What name is the reservation under?"

"Jeff Treadwell," Jeff replied.

The young man punched away at the keyboard on the computer behind the counter.

"Yes, sir," the young man replied after a few minutes. "Your room was guaranteed for late arrival, and we held it for you. Would you like to charge the room against the credit card that it was reserved against?"

"Yes, please," Jeff replied almost automatically.

The young man pulled out a pair of door swipe cards, inserted them into a piece of equipment on the countertop, and punched a code on a keypad on the front of the machine. Jeff heard a distinct "thunk" sound, and the machine ejected both cards.

"Here you go, sir," the young man said.

He slid the key cards in a small bi-fold pamphlet. He wrote the room number on the back of the pamphlet.

"Your room number is 786. Elevator is down the hall and on the right. You are on the seventh floor. We serve a complimentary breakfast from 6 a.m. until 10 a.m. across the way in the lobby. Complimentary coffee, cappuccinos, and juices are available 24 hours. If you have forgotten any toiletry items, we have complimentary spares available here at the front desk."

Jeff took the bi-fold pamphlet and proceeded down the hall to the elevator. He pushed the call button on the wall next to the elevator door and patiently waited. After a few minutes, he heard the ding of the elevator and the up indicator next to the elevator door lit up. The doors opened and he stepped into the elevator. He pushed the number seven, and a circle lit up around the button. The doors closed, and he felt a slight rumble under his feet as the elevator began to ascend. After a few more minutes, the elevator dinged again and an LCD panel next to the door displayed the number seven. The doors opened and Jeff looked around. He located a sign indicating room number ranges and headed to the right toward his room. After a brief stroll down the hallway, he was at his room door. He slid the door swipe card into the door lock and then pulled it out. He heard a click and a green light on the door lock illuminated. He pushed down on the handle and opened the door. He walked into the room, flipped on a light switch. He walked over to a comfortable-looking upholstered wingback chair and flopped his tired frame into it. He reached into his coat pocket and retrieved his cell phone. He pushed a button.

"Siri," he said, "dial Jan."

The phone dialed the number, and his wife answered on the third ring.

"Jeff?"

"Hey honey," Jeff replied, "I finally got to my hotel. Ron is going to be bringing my bags shortly."

"Thank heavens! We've been watching the news, and it looks like the whole town is shutdown."

"Yeah," he continued, "I bet there were over 500 people in that shelter last night. Atlanta apparently has a pretty large homeless population. In addition to all the stranded travelers there last night, I talked to several homeless. From what they told me, there are more homeless on any given night than there are beds in homeless shelters. The individuals I met last night forego trying to get into a shelter on normal nights, but the weather forced them to seek shelter last night."

"That's terrible," Jan replied, "I can't imagine having nowhere to sleep at night and being subjected to the elements."

"Exactly," Jeff continued. "Something needs to be done. It got me thinking. Corporate does a lot of sponsorships and a lot of community involvement projects. I think they need to look into how we, as a company, could get involved in a solution to homelessness in Atlanta."

"That would be a terrific idea," his wife replied.

"Well," he said, "I wanted to check in and let you and the kids know I am alright. After I get my bags, I am going to get a hot shower and see if I can find some dinner."

"Alright," she said, "I love you, honey. Stay safe."

"I love you too, sweetie," he replied. "Good night."

He hung up the phone, slid it in his coat pocket, and closed his eyes for a minute.

CHAPTER 28

Ron cautiously drove north on Peachtree Street, ever thankful for the heat coming out under the dash of the Charger. When he reached 17th Street, he pulled into the circular driveway in front of the hotel. He put the car in park and dialed Jeff's number on his cellphone.

Jeff answered on the second ring, "Hey buddy."

Ron replied, "I'm downstairs in the driveway with your bags."

"Awesome," Jeff replied, "I'll be down in a second."

Ron hung up his phone and tucked it back in his coat pocket. In a few minutes, he saw Jeff appear through the automatic sliding doors of the hotel lobby. He punched the trunk release button and crawled out of the car. He walked around to the trunk and retrieved Jeff's bags, setting them on the brick pavers just behind the Charger.

"Thanks for this," Jeff said as he extended the handles on both bags.

"No problem," Ron replied. "Get some rest and have a good night."

"You, too," Jeff responded.

Ron watched him as he walked back to the lobby with the bags rolling along behind him. Once Jeff was inside the lobby, Ron walked back to the driver's side of the Charger, opened the door and crawled back under the steering wheel. He closed the door, pulled his seatbelt across his chest and latched it, and slid the shifter into drive.

"Let's go home," he said to himself. "Finally."

He pulled the Charger out of the hotel drive, maneuvered back to Peachtree Street and headed north to continue a trip that he had started the prior afternoon. He flipped on the radio to WSB and began listening to the news of continued power outages, downed trees, fallen limbs in roadways, and the mess that was the interstates. Captain Herb Emory gave a report from the WSB traffic helicopter as he flew over Atlanta's interstates. Slowly but surely, wrecks were being cleared, and plows were beginning to clear lanes.

The drive was oddly eerie to Ron. He had made this trip a few thousand times and had always enjoyed the city lights as he drove through town, but tonight was different. The buildings were all dark, very few lights were shining, and many of the traffic signals were out. It was almost like a completely different city that he had never seen. Every intersection was an adventure. Many of those out and about were not familiar with how to handle an intersection without operational traffic lights. Ron remembered that in those cases, you treated the intersection as a four way stop. The first car that stopped had the right of way. If two cars stopped at the same time, the one to the right had the right of way. It seemed simple to Ron, but it was perplexing to many of the other drivers who stopped, looked at each other, and began waving.

"Where did these people learn to drive?" he said out loud.

After almost an hour, Ron completed the short drive from 17th Street to his townhouse.

"I bet I know a little dog that is about to burst," he thought.

He pulled the Charger into the townhouse's single car garage and closed the garage door. He opened the stairway door and began climbing the stairs to the main level.

"Buzz! Where are you buddy?"

He heard a jingle of tags on a dog collar and the familiar thump of paws galloping on a hardwood floor. A Bassett hound appeared out of the darkness with his tail wagging violently.

"I bet you need to go out, don't you, buddy?" Ron said to the dog.

He reached for a leash hanging on the wall just outside the kitchen and knelt down. He rubbed Buzz's head, and the tail-wagging increased in speed. He clipped the leash onto Buzz's collar and led him down the stairs to the front door. Once outside, Buzz's paws stopped at the edge of the porch, and he inquisitively sniffed at the snow lying on the ground in front of him. He cautiously stepped into the snow, one paw then the other, until he was standing on the snow-covered lawn. Buzz sniffed around before finding the perfect spot, the lamppost at the edge of the curbing. He hiked his hind leg and began to empty the contents of his bladder. Ron thought it would never end.

"You been holding that for a while, ain't ya, buddy?"

Buzz looked back at him over his shoulder still holding his hind leg in the air. Finally completing the task, Buzz dropped his leg and snorted almost in disgust. He turned and bounded for the door. Once on the porch, he shook himself from head to tail as hard as he could to rid himself of the cold snow and slush. He stopped with his nose on the door to the townhouse and looked at Ron over his shoulder. Ron quickly opened the door, unclipped the leash, and Buzz ran up the stairs. When Ron reached the top of the stairs, Buzz was sitting in front of the cabinet under the kitchen sink with one front paw held up in a begging position. Ron chuckled.

"Yeah, that was a good boy," he said.

Ron opened the cabinet door, reached into a box, retrieved a dog treat, and gave it to Buzz. Buzz's tail wagged with delight as he munched away on his treat. Ron patted him on the head. He unlaced his snow and slosh-stained shoes and set them by the door to the garage. He hung his coat in the hallway closet and headed up the stairs to the master bedroom. He walked into the bathroom, reached into the shower, and turned on the hot water. He peeled off his cold, damp socks, stripped off the rest of his clothes, and tossed them into a hamper by the bedroom door. He stepped into the shower and stood motionless as the hot water ran across his cold and tired muscles. He wondered how long he could stand there before the hot water gave out. He shrugged off the thought, shampooed his hair, lathered his body, and rinsed, pausing to let the hot water run across his tired muscles one more time before shutting the water off. He grabbed a huge fluffy towel and dried himself off.

"Man, it feels good to get a hot shower again," he thought to himself.

He had only been a day without the convenience. He thought about some of the homeless people he and Jeff had met at the emergency shelter. One of the guys told him that sometimes it was a month before he had the opportunity to take a shower. He pulled on a pair of fleece pajama bottoms and a long-sleeved Atlanta Falcons t-shirt and flipped out all the lights. He crawled into his bed, thankful to be home, safe, and warm. He heard a jingle as Buzz climbed the carpeted ramp at the end of the bed and crawled up and lay down at his feet. Within a matter of minutes, Ron was asleep, with Buzz slightly snoring at the food of the bed.

CHAPTER 29

Joy put the car in park and shut off the old Honda's engine. She opened the car door, carefully stepped out, and searched for secure footing. Steadying herself against the car, she locked the door and carefully began walking toward the gym's main entrance. Fortunately, someone had cleared the sidewalk and salted it to prevent it from refreezing. When she opened the lobby door to the gym, she was instantly greeted with the roar of several hundred children. She secretly pitied the teachers and coaches who listened to that level of ambient noise daily for a living. As she approached the doors leading into the gym from the lobby, she was greeted by two ladies seated at a folding table.

"Good afternoon," said the first lady. "Name?"

"Hi," Joy replied. "Joy Davidson. Here to pick up Cheryl and Jeremy Davidson."

The woman looked down a clipboard for a moment, moving her lips silently as she read names.

"Ah," she remarked. "Here you are. Can I see a driver's license or another form of photo ID, please?"

Joy was already prepared for the request and had retrieved her driver's license from her purse.

"Here you go," Joy said.

The woman looked at the license, ran her finger across it, and looked back at the clipboard.

"OK, sign right here, please," she said, handing the clipboard to Joy.

Joy signed next to both children's names and handed the clipboard back to the woman who handed Joy her driver's license back. Joy stowed her driver's license back in her purse and pulled the strap up on her shoulder.

"This way, please," the woman said.

She led Joy into the gym and over to where one of the coaches was sitting on the edge of the bleachers.

"Coach Johnson, Ms. Davidson to pick up Cheryl and Jeremy Davidson, please."

The man stood to his feet.

"Alrighty," he said.

The woman turned and headed back to the lobby. The coach picked up a cordless megaphone, turned it upside down, and flipped a switch. He turned it right side up and spoke into the megaphone in a booming voice.

"Cheryl and Jeremy Davidson, your mother is here to pick you up," he announced.

He turned the megaphone back upside down and flipped the switch off. Joy wondered why he needed a megaphone with that booming voice but said nothing. Out of the corner of her eye, she saw some bustling. She turned toward the commotion to see Cheryl scrambling to put her jacket on and Jeremy walking toward his little sister, carrying his jacket and book bag. Joy began walking toward Cheryl.

"MAMA!" Cheryl exclaimed, running to greet her with a hug while dragging her jacket with one arm in one sleeve and the other out.

Joy reached down and hugged her and helped her finish putting on her jacket. Jeremy walked up.

"Hey Mom, how is it outside?"

Joy shook her head.

"It was an adventure getting up the hill in our Honda," she said with a smile.

"Yeah," Jeremy replied, "Coach said earlier you couldn't get up it without a four-wheel drive."

Joy laughed, "Somebody forgot to tell me that! Put on your jacket and let's get ready to roll."

"Sounds good," Jeremy replied, "My bed is a lot more comfortable than this gym."

The children collected their belongings and followed Joy out to the lobby.

"Thank you, ladies," Joy said as she passed the ladies seated at the folding table who were checking in another pair of parents.

"Y'all be safe," one of the ladies called out.

The three walked to the Honda dutifully waiting at the curb like a tired, old friend. Joy unlocked the car, and the children crawled in the back seat. Joy crawled in under the steering wheel and started the car and the heater.

"So, Mom," Jeremy started like so many times before, "I learned something interesting last night."

"Oh really," Joy said, "and what was that?"

"Well, I said something how I wish I was sleeping in my bed at home last night, and a couple of the kids told me they don't have beds at home."

"What?" Joy replied.

She could not imagine it. She had struggled providing for the children as a single parent at times, sometimes doing without things herself to ensure their needs were provided. She could not imagine them not having a bed in which to sleep.

"Yeah," he continued. "One kid's parents separated, and he's been sleeping in the floor in his bedroom of their apartment ever since. The other kid said his dad lost a job and they had to move in with his granny. His dad has a bed, his sister has the sofa, and he is sleeping on the floor."

Cheryl perked up at the conversation.

"My friend, Carlese, doesn't have a bed," she volunteered.

Joy looked in the mirror. "Carlese that lives downstairs from our apartment?"

"Yes, ma'am," Cheryl replied. "She was having a hard time staying awake in class one day, so I asked her what was wrong. She said she doesn't sleep well at night, because she is sleeping on the floor. She has a sister and two brothers, and they don't have beds either. I asked her why she didn't sleep on the sofa. She said they don't have one. She said they don't have any furniture. I asked her where they sit to eat, and she said they sit on the floor of the living room."

Joy shook her head and looked back up in the mirror.

"When you say your prayers tonight, I think you both should say a thank you for your warm beds."

Jeremy smiled, "Already on my list. Those gym mats weren't much to brag about."

Joy quietly wondered if the people at Peachtree Street Church might be able to help with some children's beds. The preacher had given his card to her and said to call if they ever needed anything.

"How about if the neighboring kids needed anything," she thought.

She decided to give him a call when things got back to normal and see what he could recommend. After safely navigating back down the hill, she drove the short route back to their apartment complex and up to their building.

"Boy, am I glad to see this place," Cheryl said, looking up.

"Yeah," said Jeremy, "me too."

"You aren't the only ones," Joy added. "I slept on an Army cot in a Sunday School classroom last night."

"Neat!" said Cheryl.

Joy laughed.

"It wasn't quite the adventure you might imagine, Cheryl," she commented, "but it was better than sleeping in the car!"

Joy led the kids inside their apartment and sighed in relief to finally be home. She felt blessed to find the power was on and the apartment was warm.

"Ok, you both need to take a shower and change into some clean clothes," she told them.

"First dibs on the bathroom," Cheryl shouted and took off running.

Joy sat down on the sofa and thought to herself about how good it felt. She closed her eyes for a moment and thought about what Cheryl had told her about her friend Carlese and her family living in an apartment without furniture. She could completely understand how it could happen. The struggle to pay rent and utilities, buy groceries, and keep her two children clothed was a never-ending one. Single parents were faced with difficult decisions every day. Choices had to be made, and priorities had to be set. A safe, warm, dry place to sleep took priority over luxuries and creature comforts. Keeping the lights and heat on was higher on the list than a dining room table or even a bed.

As she thought about it, her mind went back to school. Maslow's hierarchy of needs – that was it! The first level of needs was physiological. First, a person needed air, water, food, clothing, and shelter from the elements. That was what Carlese's family was addressing as best as they could with the financial resources that they had available. Furnishings for the apartment added comfort, but when push came to shove, addressing those primary needs came first. But there was a cost. Someone sleeping on the floor would mean a person wouldn't get a good night's rest and would wake up groggy and exhausted. Poor quality of sleep would negatively affect a child's performance in school and an adult's performance at work. It could lead to a child falling asleep in class or struggling to pay attention.

Joy wished that she had the means to go out and buy beds for Carlese's family, but she was barely covering her own with two growing children. She was jarred from the thought by Cheryl bouncing into her lap.

"Dry my hair for me, please!" she begged of Joy.

Joy grabbed the towel draped across her small shoulders and began drying her hair. By the time Joy had Cheryl's hair dry, she could hear the dull thump of Jeremy's feet coming down the hallway.

"Ok, y'all," Joy said, "it's been a long couple of days. I want both of you to get a good night's sleep."

"I'm alright," Jeremy piped up.

"Well," Joy began to reconsider. "There is no school tomorrow. I guess you could stay up a little while. But you better be in bed by midnight, mister."

"Score!" Jeremy exclaimed.

He plopped down on the sofa beside her and picked up the remote.

"Cheryl" Joy continued, "you, little miss, need to get in the bed."

"Yessum," Cheryl quickly responded.

She crawled up in her mother's lap and gave her a huge hug.

"Let's get you tucked in," Joy said, picking her up and starting toward the bedroom.

"Mama," Cheryl said looking up at Joy as she carried her down the hallway, "I want to figure out some way to get Carlese a bed."

"Me too, Princess," Joy said. "I've been thinking about that ever since you told me about it. I don't have anything figured out yet, but I'm thinking about it."

Joy laid Cheryl on her bed and flipped off the ceiling light. She could make out her daughter's face from the dim light of the nightlight across the room. Cheryl's eyes were closed. Joy sat down on the edge of the bed, and Cheryl started praying.

"Dear God," Cheryl said in a soft voice, "Thank you for getting us all home safe. Thank you for my warm bed and my mama and brother. Please bless Carlese with a bed, so she can sleep at night and make better grades in school. Amen."

Joy leaned over and kissed her on the forehead.

"Good night, Princess," Joy said softly. "I love you."

"I love you too, Mama!"

Joy stood and softly walked to the door. She quietly closed the door and returned to the living room where Jeremy sat fixated on the television.

"I'm going to bed," she called to Jeremy, who quickly glanced up at her.

"Don't forget," she reminded him, "in bed by midnight. If I wake up after midnight, and I hear that television, there will be problems."

"Yes ma'am," he replied, without looking up from his television-induced trance.

"Good night, son," she said. "I love you."

Jeremy did not respond. Joy turned back down the hallway to her room and retired for the night.

CHAPTER 30

J ust after 11 p.m., Samuel Mathews was sitting in the lounge area just across from the nurses' station sipping a cup of coffee and reading his Bible when a man approached him. Sam looked up at the approaching figure and tried to focus his eyes. He removed his wire-rimmed glasses and rubbed his tired eyes. He put his glasses back on and attempted to focus on the man that was now less than six feet away. For a moment, Sam thought he was dreaming. The man now standing before him was the living image of Santa Claus dressed in a faded shirt and camouflage pants, carrying a large sack on his shoulders. It was well after Christmas, and Sam felt foolish even entertaining the idea of Santa Claus. But the grey-haired gent with the long, grey, full beard and a large sack on his shoulders looked like he had stepped out of a Hallmark card – minus the traditional red suit, of course.

"Reverend Mathews?" the man asked, lifting one eyebrow.

Sam scrambled to his feet.

"Yes, sir," Sam replied.

The man set his large sack on the floor.

"Sir," the man said, "my name is Lewis Davis. This is going to sound like a bit of a strange story, but please bear with me. I am a homeless vet. I have lived on the streets of this city for more years than I want to acknowledge. Anyway, Miss Gladys is a friend of mine. We frequent the same building and cross each other's path practically daily. I was one of the people who found her in the snow the other night. I talked with my friend

Fred, another homeless man that I see a lot on the streets. We both sheltered at your church during the storm. He told me he thought you were sitting with Gladys. I had a bit of a time finding where she was in this hospital, but finally found y'all. I wanted to check on Miss Gladys and see if you or she needed anything."

Sam sat dumbfounded for a moment. A homeless man was checking to see if he needed anything. It seemed like some weird role reversal to him. He was a pastor. He should be coming to the aid of the homeless man. This man had walked several miles in frigid weather to check on Gladys and him. Sam was caught off-guard by the generosity of someone who had practically nothing but the clothes on his back. Finally, he spoke.

"That is very kind of you," Sam said. "You must be frozen to the core after walking all the way here from the church. How about a cup of coffee? They keep a fresh pot brewing right around the corner here."

"Alright," Lewis said, "that would be good."

Lewis nodded. Sam led him to the coffee maker and poured Lewis a cup.

Lewis looked up from his coffee and said, "Is there anything I can do for you? Do you have anyone to switch off with while you're sitting with her?"

Sam shook his head.

"No, honestly, I didn't make any real plan. I just knew the National Guard was sitting with her while she went through surgery, and eventually she'd be sitting up here alone," Sam explained. "I just couldn't stand the thought of that."

Lewis nodded his affirmation.

"Well, sir," Lewis responded, "with her breaking a hip, she is gonna be here and then in physical therapy for a while. You aren't gonna be able to do this alone. I figure we need a woman that can change shifts sitting with her. I think I know someone who would be willing to help."

Sam listened intently.

"I have her number in my cell," Lewis continued. "Her name is Karen. She is a homeless advocate that volunteers at the Atlanta Mission."

Lewis pulled a flip phone out of a coat pocket, opened it, and scrolled through the directory.

"Here she is," he said, pushing the dial button. Karen answered on the third ring.

"Miss Karen," he said, "this is Santa."

Sam smiled and shook his head.

"Do you remember Gladys, the lady who always has her hair up in a scarf and sits outside Chick-Fil-A at Colony Square most days?"

"Oh, yes," Karen answered, "I know her. I helped her get some shoes a couple weeks back."

"Well," Lewis continued, "she fell during the storm and suffered a broken hip. She's down here at Grady recovering from surgery. Pastor Mathews from Peachtree Street Church and I are up here sitting with her. I was wondering if you could help out rotating shifts with us sitting with her."

"Of course I will," Karen quickly replied. "Give the preacher my number. In fact, let me get a few things together, and I will head down that way."

"Thank you," Lewis responded. "How about you get a night's rest and plan on coming in the morning? We can cover the watch tonight. I just got here myself."

"OK," Karen said, "but don't hesitate to call me if you need me before then."

"Will do," Lewis said. "Good night."

"Good night, Santa," Karen said.

Lewis hung up the phone and looked at Reverend Mathews.

"She wants you to have her phone number," Lewis said.

"Oh, alright," Sam replied, and began digging into his inside jacket pocket. He retrieved an address book and a pen. Lewis read the number to him while Sam jotted it in the book.

"She is coming first thing in the morning to sit with Gladys, so you can go home and get some rest," Lewis reported.

"That's wonderful," Sam replied. "I didn't have any real plan. In fact, I rode here with the National Guard, so I don't even have transportation home."

Lewis nodded and smiled, "We will worry with details in the morning."

Sam nodded in agreement.

"So, Lewis," Sam said, "tell me your story."

Lewis looked up at him after taking a long sip of his coffee.

"I was your run-of-the-mill high school kid," Lewis started. "Nothing special. I played football but never got a scholarship to play college ball, so I joined the Army. They sent me overseas to some of the hottest and most humid jungles I ever imagined. I did three tours, made Sergeant, and a bullet to the leg sent me home. Once I got out of the VA hospital, I really couldn't get a good start at things. I worked construction jobs as a general laborer for 20 years but fell off a roof one day and broke my back. Ran up a hell of a bill in the hospital with surgery, physical therapy, and all. I didn't have any insurance, and the hospital put the bill collectors on me. What little I had, they got, and the State of Georgia ruled I wasn't disabled. I couldn't work construction with the issues with my back. I started working little odd jobs which were hard to come by and made very little money. I began sleeping in shelters. I got the hell beat out of me in a couple and robbed. So, I decided I wasn't sleeping in them anymore. For the last six or seven years, I've been sleeping in doorways and under bridges and such – wherever the city cops will leave me alone. I guess you'd say this isn't the retirement I imagined for myself, but here I am. This ol' rucksack holds everything I own."

Sam listened intently without commenting.

Lewis continued, "Miss Gladys there, I seen her a lot when I get meals at the mission and when we get one of the gift cards folks donate. On colder days, we both sit in the food court of Colony Square during the day to stay warm. Their security folks don't tend to harass us, and we can both generally come up with a couple of bucks for something to eat there. Fred usually hangs out in the soft chairs in the Starbucks there. I have seen him around for years. We three kinda check on each other, but we don't sit in a bunch together, as it draws too much attention. Attention when you're homeless results in you getting bounced out of a warm building. We sit tables apart and keep to ourselves to maintain a low profile."

Sam continued to listen. When he was confident Lewis was finished, he looked him straight in the eyes.

"Lewis," he said, "I really want to know the best way to make a difference in the lives of the homeless community in this city. I've always wondered what I could do. The Mission seems to do a good job, but it seems like the homeless community is so much larger than what they are equipped to address. If you were given the money to address the homeless situation in this city, what would you do differently?"

Lewis thought for a while, stroking his beard as he contemplated the question. After several minutes of complete silence, he answered.

"Well," he said, "I never have liked shelters, because you never had your own space. You were always in a room with 3 or more other folks. And I don't mean to come off as ungrateful, but there's got to be some way to retain your dignity. Showering with 20 other guys...you know, if somehow you could give each person their own space. Be it however small, their own space...where they could feel safe and get some rest without having to try to sleep light to protect your belongings and your own safety. And if I really wanted to just get crazy dreaming, I'd like to see nurses or doctors volunteer to address medical needs. Many of us are older, some are diabetic, some have asthma, you name it. Yeah, that would be pretty good if there was some way to do all that."

Sam listened and considered what Lewis was telling him.

"Instead of a huge building with bunks and large showers, maybe something like if someone renovated one of the old one- or two-story motels. Each person would have their own room and own bathroom. You'd have to figure something out for meals, but they'd have a permanent address, which is important for getting any kind of government assistance, and it would help to recruit medical volunteers. They would know where to find folks and could check on them regularly," Sam said.

Lewis nodded in agreement.

"Or maybe like if someone renovated a trailer park where each person had a trailer. They'd have a kitchen, bathroom, and everything," Lewis added.

Sam nodded as Lewis talked.

"In either scenario, the people establish a permanent address, which also helps with finding work for those who aren't disabled," Lewis continued. "There are a lot of homeless folks who can work and want to work, but it is hard to meet dress codes and such for a lot of jobs if you are living on the street."

Sam looked up and said, "Lewis, I want to figure out how we do something like this. If I have to retire from the church, launch an organization, and start fundraising, so be it. But something needs to be done. I'm half-expecting some backlash from the church for opening a shelter in the light of the church's financial situation. But it was the right thing to do. And if they decided I put them in a financial hardship and decide to dismiss me, I'll walk out knowing I did the right thing. But this was just a drop of water on the tongue of a thirsty man. Opening the church as a shelter during the storm helped for a couple of days, but what about the other 363 days? We return to status quo and act like there aren't people needing shelter just outside our doors?"

Lewis was staring at Sam.

"You don't actually think they would fire you for opening up the church as a shelter, do you?" Lewis asked in bewilderment.

"I honestly don't know," Sam quickly replied. "The finances have been so tight that we haven't been able to do more than just a Sunday morning service. The utility bill for heating the education wing and the sanctuary for the last two days will more than likely exceed what we normally spend in an entire month. The treasurer will probably have a stroke when the bill comes in. He'll call the head of the board, who will then call me. Who knows what will happen from there? But you know, I'm not troubled by all that. I'm trying to find a path to serve the community right outside our doors. That community and their needs have changed significantly in the last 20 years, but our church hasn't made any changes to address them.

Years ago, Martin Luther felt the Catholic Church had gone astray, and he nailed a list of grievances on the door of the church. It eventually spawned a reformation. Several days ago, a man froze to death on the steps of our church, and to me, it is almost like the community nailed a list of grievances on our door. I believe we have to do something. Our lack of funding doesn't absolve us of our responsibility to care for the hurting outside our doors."

Both men sat in silence, contemplating their thoughts. Eventually, Lewis broken the silence.

"Where would we find a trailer park or an old motor lodge in Atlanta these days?" he asked. "I don't think I've seen a trailer park anywhere in the city. And the last motor lodge I remember was torn down years ago to build a high rise."

"Right," Sam replied. "If we were to do something like this, we would have to find property away from downtown. The suburbs all still have trailer parks and older, two-story motels. But the homeless community would have to be willing to relocate away from the inner city."

"Well," Lewis said, "I would wager that there's a good many of us that would be willing to make the move if we knew it meant we would regain our dignity and have security."

CHAPTER 31

John woke as the sun rose over the city. He looked at the fuel gauge on his truck and could see he still had an eighth of a tank left. The heater was keeping the cab warm. He looked over to the passenger seat where the lady whose car behind him had run out of gas and her baby were sound asleep. He looked out the windshield and could see crews working in the distance to move a tractor-trailer that was jackknifed in the roadway. As he sat watching them work, he heard the familiar sound of ATVs. He looked around, trying to locate them. They were getting closer. After a few minutes, he saw headlights in the rearview mirror. ATVs maneuvering through the abandoned cars. He stepped out of the cab of his truck, and one of the ATVs came to a halt behind his truck.

"Good morning, sir," said a female voice from under the hood of a heavy parka. "National Guard. Anyone out of gas or needing a jump start?"

"Yeah," John quickly answered. He pointed to the lady's car behind him. "That car is out of gas and the lady and her baby are asleep in my truck."

"Alright," said the woman, "let's see if we can get her started. The gas station at the top of the ramp is open, so if we can get her started and up that ramp, she should be good to go."

"Sweet!" John exclaimed.

He walked back up to the passenger door on his truck and tapped on the glass with a knuckle. He gently opened the door.

"Ma'am," he said, "the National Guard is here, and they have fuel to get your car started. Could I get your keys and see if we can get it cranked?"

The woman groggily responded, "I left the keys in the ignition. I didn't think there was much chance of anyone stealing it with it out of gas."

John chuckled. "Good point," he said.

He closed the door and walked back to the car. The woman from the ATV had a funnel in the car's gas tank and was hoisting a jerry jug up to the spout. After a few minutes, she lowered the jug, removed the funnel, and fastened the gas cap.

"Alright, sir," she said, "let's see if it'll crank."

John crawled in the car and turned the key. He waited for several minutes for the fuel pump to direct fuel from the tank up to the engine. Then he turned the key to start. The engine began turning over. It coughed a couple of times. He tried again. The engine gave one more cough and started. He lightly revved the engine to ensure it had ample fuel pressure before crawling back out.

"I think she is good," John shouted back to the woman strapping the jug back onto the ATV.

"Good deal," said the woman. "On to the next!"

John walked back up to his truck. He looked up ahead to see a large loader had pulled the tractor-trailer off the edge of the interstate. Cars were slowly beginning to maneuver past. He knocked on the passenger door window again and opened the door.

"Ma'am," he said, "we got your car started." He pointed to the off ramp just ahead on the right.

"There's an open gas station just up that ramp, and it looks like they have it salted so you can drive up it," he said.

The woman climbed out of the truck cab while holding the baby in her arms. John got them settled back into the car, which was quickly getting warm. A couple cars to their right began moving. John held up his arms and motioned one behind the line to stop so the woman could pull over into the line. The car obliged, and the woman pulled behind the slowly moving line. He stood in the cold, watching her inch her way to the ramp and gradually proceed up the ramp and out of sight. He walked back to the cab of his truck.

"Wonder if that station has any diesel," he said out loud to himself.

He figured it would be a good idea to fill the truck up as the ride could take more fuel than normal at this creepy, crawly pace. He navigated his way over into the slow line and eventually up the ramp. When he reached the station, it was busy with cars fueling. He looked around, but the woman with the baby had apparently come and gone. He searched for a diesel pump, and to his pleasant surprise, he saw a green-handled nozzle on an end pump signifying diesel fuel. He pulled in line behind the pump and waited. After a few minutes, he reached the pump and filled the truck. From the station, he could see the slow-crawling line of cars on the interstate below. While the interstate was five lanes wide in each direction, he could only see two lanes that were moving.

"I'm not getting back into that mess," he thought.

After returning the nozzle to the pump and twisting the fuel cap on the truck's tank, John crawled back in the warm cab. He pointed the truck for Peachtree Street.

"Let's try some side streets and back roads," he said to himself. He punched the button on the steering wheel.

"Call Mary," he said.

"Dialing Mary using OnStar," the system responded.

Mary answered on the first ring.

"Hey, sunshine," he said. "I'm finally off the interstate. I got a tank of fuel and am gonna start up Peachtree."

"That's probably your best bet," Mary replied. "They're still trying to clear a lot of tractor-trailer jams on all of the interstates."

"Yeah," John answered, "give me a few hours, and I should be home."

"Love you, honey," she said.

"Love you, too, doll," he replied and pushed the button on the steering wheel to disconnect the call.

He cautiously began the drive north on Peachtree, avoiding abandoned cars that littered the roadway. He encountered light traffic along the route as more and more cars were being freed from the icy traffic jam that had gripped the entire city. Within an hour, he had made his way to Roswell Road. Within another hour, he had reached downtown Alpharetta. Main Street looked almost like a Norman Rockwell painting, with everything covered in snow. The streets of downtown were clear without any abandoned cars to mention. He proceeded north through town, and just outside of town, he hung a left. Around a curve and down a hill, and familiar horse farms came into his view. Everything around him was still and quiet and covered in a blanket of white. A few more miles and he turned left into his subdivision. Several blocks later, he steered the pickup into the driveway and up the hill to the house.

A snow man greeted him on the front lawn sporting a multicolored scarf, two charcoal briquette eyes, a carrot nose, what appeared to be Skittles candies forming his smile, and one of John's cowboy hats.

"Someone's been having some fun," he said out loud.

As he followed the walkway from the driveway to the front porch, he stopped and noticed a wide, packed path down the hill into the side yard. It only took a moment for him to recognize what he was seeing. Then he saw the round trashcan lid sitting at the bottom of the hill. The kids had discovered trashcan-lid sledding.

When he opened the front door, he was immediately greeted by Zeke, a 35-pound basset hound with long droopy eyes and a wagging tail.

"Hey buddy," John said, bending down to rub behind the dog's ears.

"DADDY!" came a yell from the kitchen and two sets of drumming feet before both children grabbed his legs. Mary followed them into the den.

"Welcome home, stranger," she said with a grin.

John laughed and embraced her, with two children still firmly grabbing both of his legs.

"I'm betting you're starved. There is Brunswick stew in the Crock-Pot, and the kids have been making cookies. Don't be alarmed, the kitchen has not been bombed – just two small children who are a little messy," she reported.

John sat down on the hallway bench and pulled off his cowboy boots. He stood and pulled off his rancher coat and hung it on the coat rack. He walked into the kitchen, made himself a large bowl of stew, and sat down at the breakfast table at the edge of the kitchen. Mary carried two cups of coffee over and sat down at the table across from him as he ate. Between bites of stew, John relayed the story of the last 24 hours stuck on the interstate and the lady and baby he assisted. Mary listened intently while sipping coffee and bouncing one of their daughters on her knee. John walked back to the Crock-Pot for a second bowl of stew and sat back down to eat it.

Mary told him of the stories the local news had been reporting during the day – stories of complete strangers helping stranded drivers and stories of homeless people forced to seek shelter. John listened and nodded while polishing off his second bowl of stew. Finally feeling full after the second bowl, he pushed himself back from the table a bit and began sipping his cup of coffee.

"You know," he began, "I've been thinking about something for the last couple of days. When Uncle Herschel died, he left us that piece of land down near the speedway. He made a little money on the mobile home park and kept the taxes paid renting camping spots for the races on the rest of it. NASCAR only comes to the track once a year these days since they revamped their schedule, and I don't think the mobile home park rental business is all that lucrative. But if we sell all that land, we are going to have one hell of a tax bill to pay. I'd really like to find a charity of some sort that could use some of that land for something useful and maybe donate a few acres to them."

Mary nodded in agreement. "Maybe Boy Scouts or a church would want land for camping or a retreat center," she said.

"Right," John replied, "and if we were to donate land, I would be inclined to donate the mobile home park, because it already has electric, water, and septic on it. I think I am going to do a little talking around and see what we can figure out. It's a good hour's drive down there, and I really don't want to have to continue to manage that whole deal on top of my job. I think there are only four, maybe five, trailers rented out still. We can give those renters non-renewal notices, so they can figure out where they are going to move while we figure out the rest."

"Sounds like a plan," Mary said in agreement. "I'm going to get these two in the bath and ready for bed. It's been a long, eventful day."

As Mary herded the children upstairs for baths, John cleaned up the dishes from dinner and loaded the dishwasher. Zeke sat quietly a few feet behind him watching his every move.

"Zeke, ol' boy," John said as he finished loading the dishwasher and started its wash cycle, "you about ready for a walk?"

Zeke's tail pounded the floor. He sprung up on all four feet and lumbered for the doorway, stopping at the coat rack where his leash hung, and began nudging the end of the leash with his nose. John laughed at the sight.

"I'm gonna take that as a yes," John said.

He pulled his boots back on, put on his coat, and grabbed the leash. Zeke jumped up on John's legs, making it easy to attach the leash to his collar. The second the latch clicked, Zeke jumped back down and quickly tugged John to the door. John opened the door, and Zeke led him out for their evening walk.

CHAPTER 32

Samuel Matthews set quietly behind the desk in his study, pecking on the keyboard of his laptop computer. He scrolled through the results of a Google search, clicked a link, and then clicked another. He sat for of a couple of hours reading article after article about the master-planned community being developed in Texas. As he read, Sam scribbled notes into a journal which was stationed beside the keyboard. After several hours, he had written four pages of notes. The more he read and wrote, the more his head was spinning with ideas. He knew he needed someone with business acumen to review what he was reading and discuss the viability of something similar being developed in the Metro Atlanta area. While having over half a decade of experience serving and pastoring, he knew he did not have the experience to even begin to plan something so complex and far-reaching.

Sam pulled out his old, flip-style cell phone and dialed Phil Portman. Phil answered on the second ring.

"Hello?" Phil answered.

"Phil, this is Samuel Matthews," said Sam.

"Good morning, Sam," Phil replied. "What's got you stirring at 7 a.m.?"

Sam looked up at the clock on the study wall. He had not even realized what time it was or even what day of the week it was, for that matter. He sat at the hospital for so long that he had lost track of it all. He glanced down at the computer screen and saw the date. He moved the mouse over it to see that it was a Wednesday. He quickly tried to regain his composure and continue his phone conversation.

After what seemed to Phil as an unusually long pause, Sam continued, "Phil, I have been doing some research on something someone mentioned to me at the hospital this week. I would like you to do some reading, and then let's get together and compare thoughts."

Phil responded without hesitation, "Sure, Sam. What have you found?"

"A planned community for the chronically homeless. Not a shelter, but a planned community with travel trailers, mobile homes, and tiny houses. A place where the chronically homeless can receive medical attention and attend addiction rehabilitation, and where each person has their own home," Sam explained.

"Whoa!" Phil exclaimed. "That is a radical departure from the local solutions. Does such a place currently exist somewhere?"

Sam smiled. "Yes, such a place exists just outside of Austin, Texas," he replied.

Phil's interest was piqued. He did not have any notions of cost or complexity. He was just filled with curiosity at the approach. He had seen shows on television from time to time about young people who were forgoing traditional housing to buy or build a tiny house that they could set in someone's backyard or could use for travelling. The idea of a homeless person living in one seemed like a genius solution compared to the old shelter approach.

From talking to the homeless that had sought shelter at Peachtree Church during the storm, Phil had learned of the pitfalls of the shelters. Anytime a large mass of people with disabilities or addictions are housed in one large facility for long periods of time, it seemed to breed conflict. Several individuals he had talked with told of wanting personal space and security. Some avoided the shelters because of physical abuse and theft. Others just wanted personal space which the shelters simply could not provide.

"Sam," he said, "give me the name of the place, and let me start reading."

Sam beamed, "Community First! Village."

"Thanks, Sam," he responded. "I am going to get studying up on this, and I will give you a call when I am ready to discuss."

"Sounds great," Sam said.

Sam hung up the phone and looked around the study. He had not been home in a couple of days, and a hot shower sounded like good medicine to him. He pushed himself back from the computer and slowly stood to his feet as his joints popped and creaked. He locked the study door behind him as he stepped into the hallway and shuffled his way to the door leading outside to where his old Ford Crown Victoria sat waiting.

The driver's door creaked when Sam opened it as if to remind him how tired the old car was. He gently slid behind the wheel and closed the door to another series of creaks. He put the key in the ignition switch and turned it. Nothing happened. He grabbed the shifter and rocked it between park and reverse a few times and tried again, but the old Crown Vic refused to wake from its slumber.

"Now isn't the time for this," Sam said out loud.

He pulled the key out of the ignition switch. He slid the key right back into the switch. He rocked the gearshift between park and reverse a couple dozen times and turned the key. The lights on the dash panel lit up, the starter steadily turned a few deliberate chugs, and the old car fired to life.

Sam pulled the shifter into drive, and the car made the familiar chug-chug-chug sound as it pulled out of the church parking lot toward his home. Shortly, Sam rounded the corner and into the apartment building parking. He sought out a parking spot where the old Crown Vic would be faced the main drive, in the event it would not start and would need a tow or a jumpstart. One could not be too cautious with these old cars, he reasoned.

Two tugs on the interior door handle convinced the door to unlatch, and it creaked as Sam pushed it open. As he crawled out of the car and stood up, Sam was almost sure his hips and knees made as much noise as the door on the car. He gave the door a solid shove to close it. When it latched, rust fell from the bottom of the door.

Sam quietly shuffled toward his apartment. He ascended the stairway to the door of his unit. He opened the door, flung his coat and scarf onto a wingback chair sitting just inside the doorway, and sat down to remove his shoes. His feet ached as he pulled off the shoes, so he paused and gently flexed his feet to try and relieve the pain.

After a moment, he rose to his feet and shuffled to his bedroom. He walked into the bathroom and turned on the hot water in the shower to give it time to heat up. He walked back into the bedroom, pulled a pair of flannel pajamas out of the dresser, and laid them on the edge of the bed. He disrobed and tossed his clothes into a waiting hamper just outside the bathroom door. He shuffled back into the bathroom, adjusted the water temperature, and eased himself into the shower.

Sam stood motionless under the warm water for several minutes allowing the warmth of the water to sooth his aching joints and feet. Winter seemed to be just a little more difficult to withstand every year, and a hot shower seemed to be the

only solution for him. After a few minutes of hot water therapy, he shampooed what remained of his gray hair and lathered
his body in soap. After rinsing all the shampoo out of his hair
and soap from his body, Sam again stood motionless under the
hot water.

Finally, he turned the water off, pulled a thick towel off a
hook on the wall and began to dry himself. Wincing, he attempted to dry his lower legs and feet before sitting on a
shower stool for momentary relief. He shuffled out of the
shower and across the bathroom, stopping briefly to catch a
glimpse of the tired figure in the mirror.

"Better give that old face a shave in the morning," he noted
to himself.

He shuffled back to the bedroom and pulled on the flannel
pajamas that he had laid out. He walked to the dresser across
the room and retrieved his daily medication. He had missed a
couple days' doses with the events of the week, so he wanted
to make sure to take them before he retired for the night. He
shuffled to the kitchen and poured himself a small glass of water from a pitcher in the refrigerator. He took the handful of
pills in three segments to prevent choking, and he finished off
the glass of water for good measure. He set the glass in the
sink, took a casual glance around the kitchen and living room,
and retired to his bedroom for a long overdue night of sleep.

CHAPTER 33

The next couple of days passed like a blur as Sam recovered from his prolonged research stint. By Saturday morning, he was well-rested and feeling normal again. The first thing on his mind when he awoke was the Sunday sermon, which needed to be prepared. He could not remember the last time he had gotten to Saturday without having already prepared a message. He shuffled into the kitchen and started a pot of coffee. He firmly believed nothing good had ever been accomplished without coffee. Once the coffee was ready, he poured himself a mug and sat down in one of the wingback chairs in the living room. He drew a long sip of coffee, before setting it on the table beside the chair, and retrieved a tablet and pen. Without much effort, he wrote across the top of the page: *"For God sent not his Son into the world to condemn the world, but that the world through him might be saved." (John 3:17).*

He sat and looked at those words on the page. For years, Sunday School teachers had taught children the verse just before it and even required they commit it to memory, but how many had read on to verse 17? Yes, John 3:16 proclaimed the good news that God has loved the world so much that he sent his Son to pay the price for their sin and died in their place as an eternal sacrifice for all, but the following verse iced the cake, as Sam liked to call it. For years, people struggled feeling condemned and unworthy of the love of a Savior, but God had removed all that condemnation.

Sam's pen began to fly across the page, pausing briefly for him to take a couple longs sips of coffee before continuing. At the end of the fifth page, Sam laid the pen down and read his draft while drinking the remaining coffee from the mug. Halfway through the reading, the mug went dry. Sam laid pages down on the table beside the chair and shuffled back to the coffee maker to replenish the mug. He drew a sip of the piping hot coffee and returned to his chair. He lifted the pages and resumed reading. When he had completed his review, he tucked the pages inside his weathered Bible, ready for Sunday.

Sam picked up the remote control for the television and pushed a button. The television came to life. He pushed another button a few times until the Atlanta Braves spring training baseball game came into view. He settled into the comfort and support of the chair and began watching the game.

About the third inning, Sam's cellphone rang. He flipped it open and answered the call.

"Hello?"

"Sam," the voice said, "it's Phil."

"Well, good morning to ya, Phil," Sam replied.

"Good afternoon, Sam," Phil responded, noting it was going on two in the afternoon, "Clear your calendar for the week and pack a suitcase. I have two airline tickets for you and me to fly to Austin on Monday and check out this homeless community you were talking about on Friday."

Sam was almost dumbfounded, "Really?"

Phil smiled. "Yes, really," he continued. "I did a lot of reading like you asked and was intrigued, so I gave them a call. They have a kind of bed and breakfast arrangement where we can stay on the grounds and see how things all work firsthand. I went ahead and booked us both a flight for Monday to go look at things. I'll pick you up at 6 a.m. on Monday, and we will head to the airport."

"Alright," Sam said, "I better start getting things ready."

"Sounds good, Sam," Phil replied. "See you in the morning."

Sam pushed a button on the phone to disconnect the call, closed the phone, returned it to his shirt pocket, and returned his attention to the baseball game. At the end of the inning, he shuffled into the kitchen, made himself a sandwich, and poured himself another mug of coffee before returning to his chair and the baseball game.

As he watched the game, Sam considered how much the city of Atlanta had changed over the years. He remembered going to Braves baseball games at Fulton County Stadium for years when he was in college. But the old stadium had been demolished for the Olympics and was replaced by a more modern facility dubbed "the Ted" for Ted Turner, who owned the Braves and TBS television network at the time. But this year, the Braves had moved to the north side of town into a newer, even more modern park. As he thought about the changes with the baseball stadium, he drew a parallel to Peachtree Street Church. When he became the pastor at the church, it was a thriving center of the community with hundreds of families attending each week. These days, they did not see 100 people attend at Easter or Christmas – the two biggest church days of the year. Times were changing all around the midtown and downtown communities, and he knew things were going to have to change at Peachtree Street Church.

CHAPTER 34

Sunday came and went for Sam as hundreds of Sundays had over his 40-plus years as the Senior Pastor at Peachtree Street Church. He dutifully delivered the well-prepared message to the group of 35 or 40 people who sparsely populated the pews in the old sanctuary. At the conclusion of the morning worship service, he stood in the lobby, shook hands, and smiled as the small group filed out of the sanctuary and out into the streets of midtown Atlanta.

Sam wondered to himself how long he would continue. He was past the age of retirement, and the diminishing congregation made him wonder if his work here was concluding. The board seemed dead set against selling the property despite numerous and lucrative offers. But he knew that if they wanted to continue, the church would at some point need to find a new pastor. Lately, that someday seemed to be quickly approaching for Sam. Every day that he ascended the stairs to the sanctuary from the street or the stairs to his study, his joints would remind him that their willingness was diminishing.

As Sam and a couple of remaining volunteers locked the doors and secured the building, Sam thought that soon he needed to initiate a difficult conversation with Phil regarding his retirement. The board would have to make the decisions on the trajectory of the church after his retirement. Sam knew that time was quickly at hand, and he was at peace with it.

Sam shuffled out to the old Crown Vic, managed to get it started, and pointed it to Mary Mac's for his traditional Sunday afternoon lunch.

CHAPTER 35

It was early Monday morning when Phil pulled into the parking lot of Sam's apartment and parked his car. A few spaces over, he noted the presence of the tired, old Ford LTD Crown Victoria that he recognized as Sam's. The faded paint, the one missing hubcap, and the crack at the base of the windshield all hinted at how tired the old car was. Phil was amazed that it still started and drove. As he walked to the door of Sam's apartment, Phil found himself drawing a comparison between the old Crown Vic and Sam. Both were weathered and tired, and both were still going after years of service.

Phil knocked on the door. He could hear what he thought was a shuffling sound. After a few minutes, he could hear several mechanisms being unlocked, and the door opened to Sam dressed in a pair of khakis, button down shirt, and a sports coat.

"Good morning, Phil," Sam said with a smile.

"Morning, Sam," Phil replied, "are you ready for this adventure?"

"As ready as I can be," Sam responded. "I'll warn you now that I may slow you down on the walking. I'm not the spring chicken I once was. In fact, I'm carrying my cane along with us. I try not to use it around the church much, unless I'm having a particularly painful day. I don't want the congregation worrying. But for getting through the airports and such, I figure it's in my best interest."

"Absolutely," Phil quickly replied, "and we can get some assistance from the airlines as well. No need to kill yourself getting through the airport. You need to save your strength for the destination."

Sam turned and pulled a rolling suitcase to the door. He retrieved his weathered Bible from the table beside his chair and looked up at Phil.

"Well, I think I have everything I need," he said.

"Let me get that bag for you," Phil said, reaching past Sam for the suitcase.

"Thank you," Sam responded.

He closed the door to the apartment behind them, pulled out a ring of keys, and secured three locks. The two proceeded to the parking lot – Phil rolling the suitcase and Sam following a bit slower, aided by his cane. When Phil reached his Mercedes, he opened the trunk and stowed Sam's suitcase beside his. He darted around to the passenger door and opened it as Sam was approaching. Sam slid into the car, laid his cane against the seat, and fastened his seat belt. Phil retreated to the driver side, hopped in, and started the car.

"If you want some relief for your back, this car has heated seats," Phil said.

"Oh, that would probably be a good idea," Sam said.

Phil reached over and pushed a button.

"I'm setting it on low," he explained. "If you want it warmer, just push this button again. It has three heat settings."

"Thank you," Sam replied.

Phil put the car in gear and began the route to the airport via the interstate. He had driven it many times, and now he drove it more from memory than anything. As they drove, Sam figured now was as good a time as any to start the difficult conversation that he had been putting off for a couple of years.

"Phil," he began, "I've given it a lot of thought, and I believe I'm going to retire from serving as the Senior Pastor at the end of the year."

While somewhat stunned about the timing of the conversation, Phil had known it was on the horizon. He glanced over at Sam.

"What was the final factor, the dwindling attendance or your mobility?" Phil asked.

Sam chuckled. "A combination of those factors and a few others, actually," he responded to the question.

"I can understand," Phil said. "The board has not put any plan together for contingency, so it's good you're providing 11 months for us to chart a course."

Sam smiled, "Precisely my line of thinking."

"Have you decided where you are going or what you are going to do yet?" Phil inquired.

"No," Sam replied, "I am going to be trying to figure that one out over the next several months as well."

"Well, I would say we all have a lot of decisions and planning to do over the course of this year," Phil noted. "So, regarding today's business, I really like this model they have implemented in Austin. Apparently, they initially tried to launch it a couple of times within the city limits, but they encountered resistance from neighbors at a couple potential sites and the obligatory zoning regulations. They settled on a site in the unincorporated area in the county just outside of Austin where they were not encumbered by all the zoning and other technicalities. They have a mixture of travel trailers, RVs, and tiny houses so that each resident has his or her own home that provides for their privacy and dignity. They have created a facility that serves as a sort of clinic where doctors, dentists, as well as social workers and lawyers can visit and provide pro bono services."

Sam nodded while he talked, listening intently to every detail. "You know, with the number of homeless veterans and homeless that are elderly, that sounds like an ideal environment for someone that is self-sufficient and does not need to be in a nursing home or such. The more I think about it, it even sounds like a place that could use a retired minister to live on property," he said.

Phil quickly glanced over at Sam. "I had not given that a thought, but you have a good point. If we had something like that in the Atlanta area, it might be a pretty good place for a retired minister who did not want to completely unplug from ministry," he noted.

Soon, Sam started noticing aircraft lights in the sky above them. A few minutes later, and they were arriving at the airport. Phil drove them to the covered parking closest to the terminal, opting to pay for the convenience of getting Sam as close to the main terminal as possible without dropping him at the door.

Phil pulled out his phone and snapped a shot of the parking sign near the car to make it easy to remember the aisle and section where they parked on their return. He opened the trunk and retrieved their two roller bags and his laptop bag. He latched his laptop bag to his roller bag and began rolling the two behind him.

"I can pull mine along, Phil," Sam said.

"It's not a problem, Sam. I can handle them both with ease," Phil replied, refusing to relinquish the bag.

"Alright," Sam conceded, "thank you."

"My pleasure, my friend," Phil replied. "I am going to get the airlines to get you a roller chair, so you don't wear yourself out walking through this airport. I want you rested and able to walk around when we get to Austin."

Sam started to protest, but Phil stopped him. "I know you can walk and don't need a wheelchair. But if you walk the length of this airport and aggravate your back and joints, you will be sitting in the middle of a large tract of land outside Austin and unable to get around. Why don't we go with a roller chair in the airport and save your energy for where it's important?"

Sam relented, "Alright."

Phil guided them to security and after several minutes of what Sam thought felt like a cattle drive weaving through mazes of lines, the two maneuvered through security and headed down a long escalator to the transportation tunnel. They boarded a tram and headed for their concourse. Four stops later, they exited the tram and walked across to another long escalator that took them up to the concourse where they would be catching their flight. Phil guided them to a customer service counter and requested a roller chair for Sam. After a few minutes, a skycap appeared with a chair. Sam eased himself into the chair and sat quietly as they proceeded to their gate at the other end of the concourse. Once at the gate, Sam thanked the skycap and moved to one of the seats at the gate. Phil palmed the skycap a twenty-dollar bill and thanked him for his service.

"Sam," Phil called out, "I'm going to walk over to Starbucks for a coffee. Can I get you something?"

"I never turn down coffee," Sam replied with a grin.

"Anything in it?"

"No," Sam answered, "just black coffee."

Phil returned shortly with two large cups and handed one to Sam. "I got my usual Flat White. I got you a Blonde Roast. Hope it's to your liking," he said.

"Thanks," Sam replied, "I'm sure it's fine."

While the two sipped their coffees, Phil pulled out his laptop and quietly began working on something. Sam, a natural student of human nature, watched the people moving around the airport with great interest. The Atlanta airport was a gateway for international flights entering the United States, so there were people of all nationalities. He saw hair of every color in the big box of Crayola crayons and clothing of every style from current times to 50 years ago.

After another 30-45 minutes, the airline gate agent made a call for early boarding for passengers needing assistance or a little extra time for boarding. Sam knew this was his call. With the aid of his cane, he cautiously rose to his feet. Phil stowed the laptop back in his bag, retrieved their boarding passes, and followed him to the gate attendant. He handed her Sam's boarding pass and then his own. He followed Sam aboard with the two bags in tow.

When they arrived at their seats, Sam was surprised to see Phil had purchased them both first class seats. He was grateful for Phil's generosity, knowing the seats would be more spacious and comfortable. Sam slid into his assigned seat, and Phil stowed their bags in the overhead. He slid into the seat beside Sam.

"This is some pretty expensive seating," Sam quietly noted to Phil.

Phil smiled, "Perks, my friend, from all of my international travel. I have been saving up flyer miles and have never used them. This seemed like a good use," he said.

Sam nodded. "Well, thank you. It's very generous of you," he replied.

Once the flight was airborne, the flight attendants served breakfast to the first-class cabin. Once Phil finished eating, He retrieved his laptop and began working again. Sam admired the man's work ethic and wondered if he ever rested or relaxed.

He did not inquire as to what he was working on, but instead pulled out his Bible and began to read.

When the flight landed in Austin, another skycap was waiting to greet them when they stepped off the plane into the jetway. Sam slid into the chair and laid his Bible and cane across his lap. Phil followed them with the two bags in tow. They crossed the airport, making their way to the rental car pickup area. Phil had a large SUV waiting for them when they arrived. Again, he palmed the skycap a twenty-dollar bill while Sam was not looking and thanked him for his service. He stowed their bags in the back of the vehicle while Sam climbed into the passenger side.

Phil climbed in under the steering wheel and started the vehicle.

"Oh look," Sam exclaimed, "heated seats!"

He pushed the button on his side and settled in for their drive. Phil smiled and pushed the button on his side as well. He pulled the vehicle into gear and navigated for the exit. He pulled his smartphone from his pocket and made a couple of selections and then laid the phone on the console between them. Sam looked down to see an animated road map. A voice began providing them directions to their destination. Sam chuckled at the thought. His flip phone did not provide that functionality.

Soon they were on a Texas highway. Sam was amazed at the stark difference in the landscape here in Texas compared to Georgia. Lush green was replaced by the shades of red and tans, and there was an absence of the abundant trees to which he was accustomed. Phil maneuvered the twisting roads without a word while Sam gazed out the windows, focusing on older buildings and the rolling hills in the distance.

Following the guidance of the voice on his cell phone, Phil made a turn onto a smaller country road. Sam looked up in time to see a solitary road sign. "Hog Eye Road" the sign read. Sam smiled as he thought to himself, it doesn't get more country than Hog Eye Road. He continued to take in the countryside around them – an old, weathered barn leaning to one side surrounded by a well-worn fence constructed of mesquite fence posts and barbed wire. Further down, the road began to bend, and Sam could see a village begin to appear. As they descend a hill and passed through open gates, Sam could see little houses scattered across the property. Some were metal structures with modern design, others were traditional wood frames with screened porches, while even others were travel trailers and RVs.

Phil pulled the vehicle to a stop and put it in park. They both sat motionless for a few minutes, simply soaking in their surroundings. They both looked up and saw a figure slowly approaching them – a grey-haired, bearded man with a toothy grin wearing a baseball cap. Phil rolled down the window on the driver's side and greeted him.

"Good morning," Phil called out.

The man walked to the window, stretched out his arm, and responded, "Good morning, welcome to Community First! Village. My name is Dominic."

"I'm Phil," Phil responded, shaking the man's hand, "and this is Reverend Samuel Matthews."

"Just call me Sam," Sam quickly interjected.

"Would y'all like the 50-cent tour?" Dominic asked.

"You bet!" Sam exclaimed.

Phil shut off the engine of the SUV and both men climbed out – Sam shuffling with his cane. Dominic led them to the Bed and Breakfast composed of tall teepees and shiny Airstream travel trailers.

"You boys will be sleeping in one of our Airstreams while you are here. We didn't think Sam's joints would withstand sleeping in a teepee for a couple of nights," he said, as Phil and Sam quietly surveyed their surroundings.

He then led them to the amphitheater and fire pit.

"A lot of community is created here," he continued. "We hold a summer film festival and invite families to visit with us. On cooler nights, we light up a fire in the fire pit, roast some weenies, make some s'mores, and play guitars. It's a really good place for community gathering and fellowship, and it's a great place for neighbors to get to know each other."

After a few minutes, he led the two men to the Health Center building where mental care, health care, hospice, and respite care services are provided to residents of the community. The men were speechless in amazement of the level of care and services that were available. They saw the market and the hospitality center before wandering through the community farm complete with goats, chickens, beehives, an aquaponic system for raising catfish, fresh vegetable garden, fruit trees and nut trees.

Then, they toured the blacksmith shop and the carpentry shop where classes are provided and items are created for sale. Their tour ended in the center of the village in a garden containing a huge chess set and playground surrounded by beautiful flowers.

Sam broke the silence.

"It is breathtaking," he said. "I could never imagine this in all of my wildest dreams. I probably wouldn't believe it existed without seeing it with my own two eyes. I have spent most of my life wondering what it would have been like to live in the

Garden of Eden. Now, I feel like I have actually experienced it myself firsthand."

Phil chimed in. "You know," he started, "ever since the storm, things have really changed in my mind and life concerning the plight of the homeless. After spending two and a half days interacting with those in our community struggling with a place to call home, I have kept saying to myself 'there has to be a better way.' But I could not come up with a workable solution. I knew the shelters were not the ultimate solution for a variety of factors with the biggest being the inability to restore an individual's dignity. But y'all have done it here. Individuals have their own home. They have privacy they haven't had in years. They have personal space where they can sleep in peace without worrying about having their shoes stolen. They do not have to worry about where their next meal is coming from, because they can walk right out their front door and collect eggs or pick fruit or vegetables. They have ready access to health care. They can even learn a new skill or craft. But most importantly, they can feel a sense of community and belonging."

Dominic smiled as he listened to their observations. "You clearly see the vision, gentlemen. I believe that we are able to provide those who want it restored dignity, genuine community - where everyone knows your name and you feel like you belong, and the power and freedom of choice that they have not had for years."

Sam and Phil accepted an invitation to join other visitors and community residents for lunch at the Community Center. They sat down at the wooden tables, elbow-to-elbow with complete strangers, and enjoyed a completely organic meal prepared from food produced on the grounds. As they ate and visited with those at their tables, they were encouraged by the

stories of the community residents. Many of their stories started much like the stories they heard during the two and a half
days they provided shelter in the storm in Atlanta. But these
stories changed. They did not end with the individuals walking
out warm and with a full belly back into the cold Atlanta
streets. These stories ended with individuals being awarded an
RV or a tiny house, a sense of dignity, and a sense of community. They woke each morning knowing they were surrounded
by people who cared and genuinely wanted good things for
their lives.

Sam and Phil spent the remainder of the day visiting with
members of the community: feeding animals, cooking dinner,
carrying split firewood to the fire pit, and simply enjoying the
community that existed. When they arrived back at the Airstream travel trailer that was their room at the Bed and Breakfast, Phil struggled to shut his mind down to be able to get to
sleep. He finally gave up. He quietly crawled out of bed,
walked to the other end of the Airstream, and sat down at the
sofa. He retrieved his laptop and began typing away.

Unaware of how long he had been typing, Phil glanced
down at the corner of the laptop screen and noticed it was 2
a.m. He closed the laptop, quietly walked back to the bedroom
area, and crawled back into the bed. Within minutes he was
sound asleep.

CHAPTER 36

John kissed his family goodbye and tossed his suitcase in the passenger side of his pickup. He crawled in and fired the truck to life. He took a long swig of coffee from his travel mug before dropping it in the cup holder in the console. He looked around and backed the truck out of the driveway and headed for the airport. He had made the journey down Georgia 400 and I-75 to the airport. It almost seemed automatic to him, but this trip seemed different. He glanced out the side windows as he passed 14th Street and the area just south of it where he had spent the night with a total stranger and her baby in the cab of his truck during the winter storm.

In just over an hour, he pulled into the parking deck and found a parking spot. He shut off the truck, pulled out his cellphone, and noted his parking details in an app on the phone for future reference. He walked around the truck to the passenger side and took out his suitcase, set it on the ground next to the truck, and extended the handle. He threw his laptop bag over his shoulder, closed the truck door, and pressed a button on the key fob to lock the truck. It responded with two quick chirps of the horn. He set off for the terminal at a fast-paced walk with his roller bag in tow. Across the parking deck, down a ramp to the ground level, he made quick work to cross the roadway between the parking deck and the main terminal, anxious to get out of the cold wind. When he stepped through the automatic doors into the terminal, he slowed his pace a bit and continued toward the queue line for security. While the crowd in front of him steadily snaked its way through the ribbon maze, he emptied his pockets into his laptop bag and retrieved his driver's license and boarding pass.

After about 15 minutes of the slow-snaking queue line, he reached the TSA podium and presented the agent his driver's license and boarding pass. The agent prudently reviewed his license and boarding pass before making a mark on the boarding pass with a highlighter and returning it and his license to him. John looked up at the eight lines in front of him that all appeared congested, so he elected to try his luck by going to his right around to two other lines. Down a narrow corridor, he followed several other travelers and was pleased to find a small group in front of him proceeding at a decent pace. He grabbed a tray and placed his shoes and belt in it along with a bag containing toothpaste and other liquids and gels. He grabbed a second tray, pulled his laptop out of his laptop bag and placed it in a tray by itself. He placed the two trays, his suitcase, and laptop bag on the conveyor feeding an x-ray machine and then stepped toward a body scanner. He stopped and looked at a TSA agent who motioned for him to step into the scanner. He placed his feet in the outlines on the floor and held his hands up as if someone had said: "Stick 'em up". He stood motionless for several seconds until the agent told him to step through. He stepped out of the scanner onto a rubber mat where he waited and watched a red light in front of him. When the light turned green, he stepped forward to a conveyor belt and retrieved his laptop bag, suitcase, and the two trays he had prepared. He repacked the laptop into his laptop bag, stowed the bag of liquids and gels back in his suitcase, stepped into his shoes, threaded his belt back through his slacks, and put his other belongings back in his pockets. He stacked the two trays on top of a stack at the end of the conveyor and proceeded to the long escalators down to the transportation level.

Once at the bottom of the escalator, he began walking through the level bypassing the airport train system, electing for a bit of exercise on his way to the concourse for his flight. After another 15 minutes of walking, he arrived at the escalator up to the concourse and stepped on it, relaxing for a brief moment. When the escalator delivered him to the concourse, he stepped off and headed down the concourse toward his gate. Halfway there, he stopped at a Starbucks and purchased what he referred to as a "cup of inspiration". He began sipping his coffee as he headed to the gate. When he arrived at the gate, he checked the display above the gate agent's podium for the flight's estimated arrival and departure times, which appeared unaltered, indicating no delays. He then scanned the available seating and found an open seat near the podium, which he figured would help in boarding. He sat his laptop bag on top of his suitcase, sat down in the seat he had chosen, and began enjoying his coffee. He checked his phone and responded to a few emails.

He had grown tired of all the travel his job required, but at least this would be a short trip. He would meet with the leaders from a developer starting a new master planned community outside of Round Rock, Texas, just north of Austin. The area had seen a great deal of growth over the years, and a master planned community offered families neighborhood shopping and restaurants as well as schools, doctors, and dentists offices all within walking distance of their homes. Their meeting would last most of the day, so he would spend the night and be on a flight home tomorrow – things could be worse, he figured.

Half an hour had passed when John heard a noise and looked up to see a gate agent opening the door to the boarding ramp. Soon, a wave of humanity began pouring from into the gate area. Several men in suits came off at a brisk pace and headed for the escalators. Next came a college kid in a sweatshirt, with a guitar bag slung over his shoulder. Another hundred or more people followed in step. Once the plane had emptied, the gate agent made an announcement that the crew was cleaning the plane, and they would begin boarding shortly. John checked his watch, and to his surprise, it appeared the flight might depart on time. A rarity, he figured, for the airline and for the busy Atlanta airport. He tossed his empty coffee cup in a nearby trashcan which initiated the sound of an electric motor for a moment. John figured it must be an automatic compactor.

Several minutes later, boarding began. John's frequent travel and first-class ticket got him on-board quickly. He stowed his roller bag in the overhead and his laptop under the seat. The flight attendant brought him coffee and a hot cloth and asked if he would like anything else to drink. John declined. After several minutes, the steady line of passengers dwindled down, and the flight attendant began the flight safety speech demonstrating how to buckle a seat belt. John wondered if there was anyone on the face of the earth that had ever boarded an airplane and did not have the rudimentary knowledge of how to fasten a seat belt. Heck, his youngest buckled and unbuckled the harness all the time in the car seat. Did they really need to demonstrate this every flight? The seat belt demonstration was closely followed by the five exits of the plane, the lighting on the floor, and the demonstration of oxygen masks falling from the overhead with the reminder to put on your own mask before trying to help someone else.

John rolled his eyes and thought, "Of course, because if you pass out due to lack of oxygen, you won't be able to help someone else."

This thrilling demonstration was followed by an explanation of how your seat cushion could be used as a floatation device. John wondered if anyone who had ever been in an emergency landing in water had to forgo using their seat cushion as a flotation device because it had been soiled on the landing.

Finally, the flight attendant's presentation concluded. One flight attendant walked the length of the plane ensuring all the overhead compartments were closed and latched. Two others walked the aisles to ensure everyone had figured out how to buckle their seat belt and that they had their seat in the upright position, their tray table stowed, and any items neatly tucked under the seat in front of them. One final check to ensure the door was securely latched, and the flight attendants took their jump seats.

A few minutes later, the captain came on the public address system and thanked everyone for choosing this airline, gave a synopsis of how long the flight would take and where they were in line to taxi out to the runway. The ground crew pushed the plane back from the gate, and the flight crew took over. A few short engine revs and several stops, and the aircraft was in line behind 10 or so more waiting for their turn on one of Atlanta's runways. After several more minutes, the pilot reached the end of the taxi strip and turned the plane for the runway, stopping at a line on the asphalt while the aircraft in front of them accelerated and took flight. Finally, it was their turn. The pilot rolled the aircraft onto the end of the runway and centered it on the dotted line. The aircraft sat motionless for a few minutes before a sudden rev of the jet engines, and they were underway. John considered that this must be what if felt like to launch a NHRA drag car off the line at the Atlanta Dragway. The nose of the aircraft lifted, and the plane was in flight. John could hear hydraulics folding up the landing gear and wing flaps changing position.

After several more minutes, John heard a doorbell chime twice. The flight attendants unbuckled their seat belts and began working in the galley. Thankfully, breakfast was served to the first-class passengers, because John was more than ready to eat. The flight attendant refilled his coffee mug before leaving John to enjoy his breakfast.

CHAPTER 37

Sam woke up several times during the night. As he got older, this was becoming the norm more than the exception. He made a couple of trips to the bathroom in the Airstream over the course of the night. When he woke up at 5 a.m., he decided there was not much point in trying to get back to sleep again. He quietly arose, made the bed, changed out of his pajamas into the day's clothes, folded the pajamas, and neatly put them back into his suitcase. He stepped into the bathroom, plugged in his electric razor, and gave himself his daily shave. He washed his face, brushed his teeth, and combed what was left of his gray hair. He returned the toiletries to his suitcase, sat down in the swivel chair by the door, and slowly put on his socks and shoes. This had become the hardest part of getting ready in the morning over the last couple of years. If he spent too long with a sock or tying a shoe, he would get breathless.

Once completely ready, he grabbed his cane from beside the door and used it to help himself get up from the swivel chair. He opened the door, carefully maneuvered down the two foldout steps, and closed the trailer door. He began walking with no particular direction in mind, admiring the beauty of the different design of tiny houses scattered across the community. After a couple of minutes of walking, he came upon a sight he had not noticed yesterday. Nestled between several of the houses was a small chapel with a red door and a breathtaking, stained-glass image that Sam quickly recognized. It was the repentant criminal that was crucified next to Jesus. Sam could remember Jesus' words to the man, "Today, you shall be with me in Paradise."

Sam walked around the little chapel paying painfully close attention to every detail. Once he had completely circled the building, he walked to the red door and reached his hand out for the knob. He was surprised to find it unlocked. For so many years they had been so careful to ensure all the doors were locked at Peachtree Street Church that it seemed odd but refreshing to him. He stepped inside the chapel and stood motionless, mindfully eyeing every square inch of its interior. After a while, his hips and knees started aching from standing so long, so he found a place to sit. He sat in wonderment of everything he had seen over the last 24 hours at this incredible place. He bowed his head in silence and began to pray.

Back at the Airstream, Phil had awakened and realized Sam was nowhere to be found. He found it odd, but he was not alarmed. He elected to start his day with a shower in the trailer's small bathroom, and then he conducted his morning routine – shaving with a safety razor, brushing his teeth, combing his hair, and sprinkling a dash of cologne for good measure. He walked into the Airstream's galley kitchen where he eyed a coffee maker. In the cabinet just above it, he found filters, packs of coffee, and mugs. He prepped the coffee maker and turned it on to brew. He walked over to the foldout dining table and fired up his laptop while he waited for the coffee.

After several minutes of typing, the travel trailer was filled with the aroma of freshly made coffee. He poured himself a mug, sat back down in front of the laptop, and continued his work.

CHAPTER 38

John awoke from a nap to two chimes that sounded like a doorbell. He opened his eyes and looked around to see that the flight attendants were busy collecting mugs and dishes from the first-class passengers. The Captain's voice came over the public address system and told the passengers that the flight would be beginning its descent into the Austin area. He relayed the current weather conditions and estimated they would be touching down in 30 minutes. He concluded with the customary seatbelt light going on, no moving around the cabin, and other details that John had heard too many times previously.

A few minutes later, the lead flight attendant began her announcement for passengers to move their seats in the upright position stow their tray tables. John had heard it so many times, he halfway expected to hear them say, "With every head bowed and every eye closed, we're gonna sing the last verse of Amazing Grace six more times," like he had heard a hundred times in the Baptist church where he grew up. He reached across the empty seat beside him, opened the window shade, and stared out at the vast rolling landscape beneath them and the occasional wisp of a cloud between. His mind wandered across hundreds of topics, but today's meeting was not one of them. He was confident that he was prepared to handle the discussions. Because he had previously planned all the details, he didn't have any concerns about what was coming. No, the dominant recurring thought this morning was how to deal with Uncle Herschel's land. Atlanta Motor Speedway had been reduced to one NASCAR event a year, and they had made acres of the speedway property open to campers. The days of Uncle

Herschel renting out part of the land to fans camping a few miles down the road were over. The mobile home park tenants were almost completely gone. With his work schedule, his time with his family was precious, and he would much rather spend time with his wife and children when he was home than worry with mowing that piece of land.

Looking out the window, John could tell they were now on their final approach. He set back up in his seat, planted his feet directly on the floor, and crossed his arms. This was something he had done so many times, he did not even think about it anymore. He heard the landing gear drop into position, and he heard the hydraulics setting the wing flaps. Within minutes he felt the rear wheels touchdown, and he immediately heard the pilot reverse the engine thrust as he quickly slowed the plane. The front gear touched down, and he heard the braking.

"Welcome to Austin, the live music capital of the world!" the captain said in his final address on the public address system. He chattered away about what gate they would be arriving at and how they knew the passengers had a myriad of choices in air travel and they appreciated them selecting this airline. John wondered if there was any sincerity in that whole speech or if it was as meaningless reciting it as it was repeatedly hearing it.

When the door opened, he stepped into the aisle, grabbed his laptop bag, tossed it over his shoulder, and retrieved his suitcase from the overhead. He extended the handle and rolled it along behind him as he walked off the plane and up the jetway to the terminal. Once inside the terminal, he turned and headed for the ground transportation. He walked by numerous shops selling books and magazines and "Keep Austin Weird" shirts, hats, and mugs before reaching the ground transportation area. As he walked out of the secured area of the terminal into the ground transportation area, he spotted a middle-aged man in a black suit holding a small whiteboard with his last name on it. He walked directly to the man.

"Hi," he said, "I'm John."

"Good morning, sir," the man replied, "My name is Randall. I will be driving you to the company's headquarters. Allow me to get your bags."

"Thanks," John replied, handing over the roller bag. "I'm good with the laptop bag."

Randall led him out of the terminal to a waiting black SUV. He opened the rear door for John and headed to the rear of the vehicle where he loaded his suitcase. Randall walked briskly around to the driver's door and crawled in under the steering wheel.

"You picked a good day to visit Austin," Randall said, as he started the SUV and pulled it into gear. "No rain on the radar and mild temperatures."

"Awesome," John replied.

Randall turned on some jazz music on the stereo, pulled the SUV onto the Interstate, and headed for Round Rock. John pulled out his phone and sent a quick text to his wife: "On the ground in Austin, heading for Round Rock. Hope you have a wonderful day. I love you."

He scanned a few emails on his phone and slid it back into his pocket. Lying in the seat beside him was a copy of USA Today, so he picked it up and began reading.

194 | ALLEN MADDING

CHAPTER 39

After a couple of hours at the keyboard of the laptop, Phil looked down at the corner of the screen and noticed it was almost 11 a.m. He stretched, stood up, set the coffee mug in the sink, turned off the coffee maker, and decided to find Sam. He slid on a pair of tassel loafers and stepped out of the Airstream. Closing the door behind him, he pondered momentarily which direction to head. He finally decided on a direction and set off walking. He checked the hospitality center, the community market, the garden, the dog park, the amphitheater, but to no avail. After almost an hour of wandering, he saw a sight that drew his attention – a small chapel. He did not recall seeing it the day before, but then again, they had seen a great deal in one day. He was suddenly certain he knew where Sam was. He increased his pace toward the chapel. When he reached the red front door, he quietly opened it and stepped inside. There he found Sam seated with his head bowed, silent, and motionless. He quietly put his hand on Sam's shoulder. Sam opened his eyes and glanced upward.

"Well," he said, "good morning, Phil."

"Good morning," Phil replied. "Been here all morning?"

Sam chuckled. "Yes, I have," he said. "For the life of me. I couldn't tell you for how long."

Phil smiled, "If I were forced to guess," he said, "I'd say about five hours."

Sam furrowed his brows, "Seriously?"

"Seriously," Phil replied, "I've been up a little over three hours, and you were long gone when I awoke."

Sam nodded. "Well yeah," he said somewhat sheepishly. "My internal alarm doesn't seem to let me sleep past 6 anymore it seems. I've quit fretting it or fighting against it. I have resigned to just get up and get on with my day."

"Are you hungry?" Phil asked.

"Now that you mention it," Sam replied, "I am."

Phil smiled, "Well, you are in luck," he said. "The community center has some sandwiches and fruit they were setting out when I was by there a few minutes ago."

Sam reached for his cane. "I guess we better get a move on then," he said with a grin.

The two men walked across the grounds back to the community center.

"I see why you insisted on the roller chair in the airport. This place is huge. There is a lot of walking around here," Sam commented.

"They have a couple of golf carts if you get needing one," Phil said, "but I thought if I could convince you to save your energy at the airport that you would probably enjoy strolling around this community."

"I really have," Sam replied, "I have been thinking all night that this is the kind of place I could retire, enjoy, and feel useful. We need to find a way to do something like this in Atlanta."

Phil smiled. "How did I know you were thinking that?"

"Probably because you are thinking the same thing," Sam responded.

"Guilty," Phil exclaimed. "I just keep thinking that we have so many homeless veterans and elderly in Atlanta that would enjoy a place like this, and it is such an improvement over the shelter model. Nothing against the shelters, but they are a temporary solution. Transitional at best. This is a sustainable model – a permanent solution to address several underlying issues instead of just addressing shelter."

Sam nodded in agreement and said, "But the magnitude of a project this scale and the money it must cost to complete it is staggering."

Phil shook his head. "I completely agree with you," he said. "It's not a project one church or four or five people can complete. It would take a community of corporate sponsors, churches, civic groups, doctors, dentists, lawyers, and other volunteers all working together. We would have to clearly define the vision and begin pitching it to other churches, civic groups, and businesses and ask them to partner with us. But think about it, Sam. We have the corporate headquarters of Home Depot in Atlanta as well as the corporate headquarters for hundreds of other companies. And some of us are fortunate enough to rub elbows with some of those CEOs at lunch in Mary Macs, in Lions Club meetings, and on the golf courses. You might be surprised at some of the contacts some of the board members at the church have."

Sam stopped walking, looked up at Phil and said, "What you are saying is, you think it could be done."

Phil looked Sam straight in the eyes. "There is not a doubt in my mind. I have already made a list of folks whom I have contact with that I want to talk to when we get back," Phil said. "And I've been working on some ideas on what we need and what a sponsorship for each building or service might look like. We're just going to have to find some land outside of the city. Somewhere that is not strangled in zoning and subdivisions that would fight something like this. Dominic told me that they tried to launch on two or three other tracts of land

and constantly encountered resistance before landing on this property."

Sam resumed walking toward the community center.

"I would say we have a good deal of work ahead of us," he said as he walked, "and in a little over 10 months, I can be there – wherever there is – fulltime."

The two reached the community center and walked into the shared kitchen where they found a couple trays of freshly picked fruit and a tray of sandwiches. They both filled a plate and grabbed a bottle of water before walking out to one of the wooden tables where they sat down to eat.

"You know," Phil said between bites, "we are going to need someone with experience at developing a master plan for something of this scale. Because you cannot build it all at once, so you need a master plan to map out where everything will be once it is completed. Then you can build it in phases."

Sam silently nodded as he listened and ate.

CHAPTER 40

R andall pulled the SUV into the circular driveway and up to the tall, glass front doors of the tallest building in the office park and put the vehicle in park. John let himself out before Randall could get the door for him, so he continued around the vehicle, opened the rear door, and retrieved John's bag for him.

"Thank you, sir," John said.

"Don't mention it, sir," Randall replied.

John gave him a twenty-dollar bill as Randall handed him the bag. He turned and headed in the doors, across the marble-lined lobby, and to the elevators. He paused for a moment at the directory and confirmed the floor before punching the elevator call button. Within a couple of minutes, the elevator door opened, and he pushed the button for the 12th floor.

"Going up," John said to no one. "Penthouse suite."

He watched the numbers change on the digital display above the button panel as the elevator passed the other 11 floors. When the display showed 12, he said "Yahtzee!"

When the elevator doors opened and he stepped off, he was immediately greeted by one of the district managers for the firm.

"Hello, John," the man said, "How was your flight?"

"Pleasantly uneventful," John said with a chuckle.

The man grinned. "Well, that is always good," he said.

He led John to a conference room surrounded by glass windows. Six people were gathered around the table when he walked in the room. They all stopped mid-conversation to greet him. He headed for an empty chair and sat down at the table. At the head of the table was the Senior Vice President of the development company, Dennis Smith.

"Alright, looks like everyone is here. Let's take a final look at the revised master plan," he said as he clicked the mouse on his laptop and a multicolored map appeared on a screen at the end of the room.

"So," John started, "let's begin at the front entrance and work our way through the grounds. As you enter from the highway, you turn onto a brick paved drive that circles a large fountain. Once you pass the fountain, you arrive at the community main square."

John continued his presentation detailing the entire planned community for the next 25 minutes.

A discussion followed with everyone at the table asking questions, and John answering them and detailing items on the map. One by one, he answered every question to the satisfaction of the requestor. Dennis sat at the head of the table admiring John's command of the room. Everyone had input on the original design and every tweak John had made to the design over the last six months. His attention to everyone's concerns and his attention to detail was noticed and appreciated. When the last question was answered, a young woman opened the door of the conference room and wheeled in a cart with boxed lunches. John had not even noticed the time, but he welcomed the break. A hush fell over the room as everyone concentrated on eating. John recalled as a child one summer revival preacher had joked that there was nothing more silent and reverent than a group of people with food in front of them.

After lunch, John became a silent observer as the team discussed budget, construction bidding, zoning, permitting and all the fine details involved in the development. These discussions went on for several hours. Once concluded, Dennis asked for a motion to approve the master plan. A motion was made and seconded, and a unanimous vote approved the plan. Dennis tasked two of the team members to prepare a presentation for the zoning board and to draft the documents for building permits. He turned to John.

"John," he said, "we greatly appreciate your work creating this master plan. You have done a spectacular job of designing a beautiful live/work community that I believe will be a great success. The teams will be in touch if they need any support for their preparation for zoning and permitting."

John stood and shook his hand. "Dennis, it is always a pleasure to work with your firm. If I can assist in any way moving forward, feel free to contact me."

Dennis walked him to the receptionist area just outside the conference room and asked the girl at the counter to call John's car service. The two shook hands again and Dennis returned to the conference room. John retrieved his suitcase from the receptionist and headed to the lobby where he found a comfortable sofa to wait for the car service. Within a few minutes, a black town car pulled up in the circular driveway and to the glass doors. John stood up, grabbed his suitcase, and rolled it behind him as he walked out the glass doors.

"John," said the driver as he opened the rear car door, "my name is Miguel. I understand you are staying at the Hyatt. Is that correct?"

"Yes, sir," John said.

"Excellent," Miguel replied.

John slid into the back seat as Miguel stored his suitcase in the trunk. Miguel crawled into the driver's seat and turned to John.

"Would you like me to drive you to a local restaurant for dinner?"

"That would be nice, but I hate to be an inconvenience," John replied.

"No inconvenience at all, sir," Miguel said. "I am at your service. What are you hungry for?"

John thought for a moment and responded with a knowing grin, "Barbeque."

Miguel flashed a wide smile, "I know just the place for you!"

Within a few minutes, Miguel pulled up in front of a large adobe building with an old covered wagon out front and an array of cacti surrounding the building. When he opened the door for John, he could instantly smell the aroma of meat cooking over mesquite wood.

"Oh, that smells divine," John said as he stepped out of the car.

"The food tastes even better than it smells," Miguel noted. "Take your time and enjoy your dinner. I will be waiting just past that sign," he said, pointing to a section of the parking lot.

"Thank you, Miguel," John said and headed to the front door of the restaurant.

He was quickly seated at a corner table and a waitress took his drink order. Within a matter of minutes, she returned with a Lone Star beer and a bucket of parched peanuts. John ordered a beef brisket dinner and sipped his beer. He retrieved his phone and texted his wife: "Meeting went well. The plan was unanimously approved, and they are headed to zoning and permitting. I'm sitting in a barbeque joint enjoying a Lone Star and waiting for brisket. I love you."

Moments later, his phone buzzed. He looked down at a text message in reply: "John! How could you! Having brisket with-

202 | ALLEN MADDING

out me? I am wounded to the core. I love you, too. Eat some for me."

He laughed at the response and emptied the beer. Before he had the bottle back on the table, the waitress arrived with another. Just a few minutes later, she returned with a huge platter of succulent meat, baked beans mixed with bacon and ground beef, corn on the cob, and coleslaw.

"Now THAT is what I'm talking about," John said as she sat the platter down in front of him. John savored every bite of the meal until there was nothing remaining on the plate, taking the last piece of Texas toast and mopping the platter clean.

When the waitress returned and saw the empty platter, she giggled and said, "I guess you didn't like it."

John held up the end of the platter, "I cleaned it so well, you don't even need to send it to the dishwasher. You can just put this platter back in the cabinet," he joked.

"How about a bowl of hot blackberry cobbler for dessert?"

John blew out his cheeks, "I couldn't eat another bite, unfortunately," he said, somewhat disappointed at turning down cobbler.

She smiled and handed him the check. He stuck a credit card in the book holding the check and finished off the remaining Lone Star while she closed his check. When she returned, he totaled out the check, put the receipt in his wallet, stood up and headed for the door. Once outside, he spotted the town car right where Miguel said he would be. As he approached the car, Miguel popped out and opened the rear door for him.

"Well," he said, "how did I do on the recommendation?"

John patted him on the shoulder. "That," he said, "was amazing."

"I'm glad you liked it," Miguel replied with a smile.

Miguel drove him to the hotel and stopped in front of the door to the lobby. John tipped him, and Miguel handed him a business card.

"When you come downstairs for breakfast in the morning, call me," he said. "And when you have eaten, I will be here ready to take you to the airport."

"Sounds like a plan," John said.

Miguel retrieved his bag for him and rolled it to the lobby door.

"Have a good night's rest," Miguel said.

"Thanks, Miguel," John replied, "You, too."

John walked into the hotel lobby as Miguel drove off into the night.

CHAPTER 41

P hil awoke to the alarm on his phone. He shut it off and sat up, looking at the other bed, noticing that it was vacant and made as if a maid service had visited. He turned his head toward the front of the Airstream to see Sam fully dressed, sitting in the swivel chair, drinking coffee, and reading his Bible. Phil shook his head. He got out of bed and headed for the shower. He completed his morning ritual and dressed for the day. He returned to the bedroom area and finished repacking his suitcase. Following Sam's lead, he made the bed. Then he walked to the front of the trailer and poured himself a cup of coffee in a paper cup.

"Are you ready to head to the airport?" Phil asked Sam.

Sam looked up over his glasses. "I don't know if I ever want to leave here," Sam quickly replied.

"Understood," Phil responded. He opened the trailer door and put Sam's suitcase just outside the door, then retrieved his own and carried it out. He loaded both suitcases into the back of the SUV before heading back into the Airstream for his laptop and his cup of coffee. Sam pushed himself up out of the chair with the aid of the cane and carefully descended the two folding steps from the trailer to the ground.

They climbed into the SUV, and Phil cranked the motor. They both took one look around as Phil pulled the shifter in drive and headed out to Hog Eye Road. They snaked along a couple of roads until they reached Farm to Market Road and eventually ended up on Texas Highway 71, just outside the front gate to the airport. Phil followed the signs to the rental car return and stopped in a line of returned cars where a young man in a vest waved him over. While the young man scanned the tag on the windshield and checked the fuel and mileage, Phil retrieved their suitcases from the back and tossed his laptop bag over his shoulder. The young man printed Phil's receipt from a handheld device and handed it to him. Phil thanked him and walked around to the passenger side where Sam was slowly exiting the vehicle.

"You look exhausted," Phil noted.

"Well," Sam began, "it has been a big week."

Once inside the terminal, Phil requested a roller chair for Sam. A skycap quickly appeared and helped Sam get seated. They then headed for the security line. Security moved Sam through quickly, while Phil went through the normal, slower process. Once cleared, Phil stopped to put on his belt and shoes and repack his laptop.

"Alright, Sam," he said, "let's get to the coffee."

Sam grinned. They rolled up to a kiosk where Phil bought them both a large cup of coffee, and they followed the skycap pushing Sam to the gate. The skycap wheeled the roller chair to a row of seats at the gate directly in front of the gate agent podium. Sam used his cane to help push himself up to a standing position. He thanked the skycap and shook his hand. Phil walked behind him and as Sam sat down in one of the padded chairs at the gate, Phil palmed the skycap a twenty-dollar bill. He then returned to where Sam was seated, handed him his coffee, and sat down in the seat next to him. Phil's phone vibrated, so he pulled it out of his pocket and pushed a button. He shook his head as he read the screen of his phone.

"Well, Sam, this flight has been cancelled, and they have moved us to another flight scheduled to depart 20 minutes later than our original," he said.

"Well, 20 minutes isn't too bad I guess," Sam said staying positive.

"We are going to have to walk to another gate," Phil added. "Fortunately, it is just three gates down."

Phil stood and pulled his laptop bag over his shoulder. Sam stood up, using the cane for leverage.

"I'll pull my bag," Sam said. "You have your hands full with a coffee and a suitcase."

Phil nodded and tugged his bag over onto its wheels. Sam shoved the cane under his arm so he could carry coffee in one hand and pull his bag with the other. They gradually walked to the new gate assignment and found two seats near the gate agent podium just like they had selected at the prior gate. They quietly finished their coffees and divided their attention between people watching and the news on the overhead televisions.

Within an hour, the gate area became flush with passengers. Sam looked around and wondered how they would all fit on the plane. He was a bit anxious, having heard stories of airlines bumping passengers off flights and the thought of sitting in an airport for hours on end. A gate agent walked up to the podium and began typing on a keyboard to a computer. After a few minutes, she began calling passengers to the podium and handing them boarding passes. Sam and Phil were the last two names she called. They both received their new boarding passes and sat down together reviewing them.

"Well," Phil noted, "looks like we aren't sitting together, but the good news is that we are still in the first-class section."

When boarding began, Sam boarded early to allow him the extra time he needed to walk the jetway at his regular pace. A flight attendant stowed his bag in the overhead bin above his seat, and Sam slid into the window seat on his row. After several more minutes, the remaining first-class passengers began boarding. A tall, dark-haired, bearded man stopped at the seat beside him and hoisted his bag into the overhead bin. He pulled a laptop bag off his shoulder and pushed it under the seat. He sat down in the seat next to Sam.

"Good morning," he said.

"Good morning," Sam replied.

The man stuck out his hand. "I'm John," he said. "What's your name?"

Sam shook his hand, "I'm Sam."

"Nice to meet you, Sam," the man replied. "Are you from Atlanta?"

"As a matter of fact, I am," Sam answered. "Born and raised."

"Me, too," John replied, "What brings you to Austin?"

Sam reached into his sports coat pocket and pulled out a pamphlet. "Well, I pastor a church in downtown Atlanta, and we have been discovering the overwhelming homelessness around our area. We heard about this village just outside of Austin, so we came to look at what they were doing and see if we could learn a little something," Sam explained.

John took the pamphlet and began browsing it. John was stunned and silent for several minutes as he read about a master planned community tailored to the needs of the homeless population in the Austin area. He could not believe his eyes. Finally, after a few minutes, he was able to overcome the rush of emotions he felt bursting inside him.

"Sam," he said, "you are not going to believe this, but I design master planned communities for a living. In fact, I came to Austin to deliver the final design to a developer here for a master planned live/work community on the north side just outside of Round Rock."

Sam snatched his head to look John in the eyes. "You're kidding me," he said.

"Actually," John continued, "I'm as serious as a heart attack. And if that doesn't shock you, this next bit of information I am about to share just might."

"Try me," Sam responded.

"Well," John continued, "my uncle passed away several months ago and left me a large tract of land down near the Atlanta Motor Speedway, and a section of it contains a mobile home park. It's over an hour's drive from our house, and I have been struggling to try and manage it."

"Wow," Sam replied and reached down and pinched his own thigh. He squirmed from his own pinch. "I guess I'm not dreaming, because that certainly hurt."

John laughed.

"My wife and I have been talking about trying to find a church or group to donate the mobile home tract. If you started something like this village," he said, referring to the pamphlet, "you could have probably 10 people living on the property within a matter of days before even drafting a master plan."

Sam's eyes grew wide as he said, "You said you were entertaining the idea of donating the tract with the mobile home park?"

John laughed again. "Yeah, this is quite the opportune meeting," he replied.

"Yes. Yes, it is," Sam replied. "A divine appointment, I believe."

Through the remainder of the boarding process, take off and flight, the two continued to talk. Sam relayed the story of Peachtree Church's current operation status, the events during the winter storm, and his impending retirement. The more John listened, the more he was encouraged to support the idea of designing and creating a community outside of Atlanta that those struggling with homelessness could call home. When the flight landed in Atlanta, Sam knew he needed to connect John and Phil. He looked around the first-class cabin to locate him. Finally, he saw him four rows ahead of him on the other side of the aircraft.

"John, I want to introduce you to the president of the board of our church who came out here with me to see the village outside of Austin. Any chance you would have a few minutes when we get off for a quick introduction?"

"I'll do you one better than that," John replied. "Why don't we sit down and have lunch at one of the restaurants together here in the airport?"

Sam was surprised by the offer. "Well, I don't want to be an imposition. I am sure you have things to do and places to be," he said.

John smiled. "I am going to need to eat lunch anyway. Why not make it productive?"

When the plane landed, it took several minutes for the pilot to taxi across the myriad of taxiways at the huge Atlanta airport and finally pull up to the assigned gate. Sam hardly heard the flight attendant or the captain's announcements. Once the aircraft door was open, Phil quickly appeared in the aisle next to Sam's row to help with his suitcase.

"Phil," Sam said, "I want to introduce you to John. He designs master planned communities."

Phil was stunned for a moment as he thought to himself, "What are the chances?" He quickly gathered his composure and shook John's hand.

"Pleasure to meet you," Phil greeted him.

As the three began their walk up the jetway, Sam gave Phil his second surprise of the day. "John has invited us to lunch to discuss the possibilities of launching a master planned community for the homeless outside of Atlanta."

Phil quickly glanced at John. "Seriously?" Phil asked, in a bit of shock.

John chuckled. "As serious as a heart attack, sir. I even have a piece of land I can donate to get it started," he said with a wide grin.

Phil smiled, "Well then, lunch is on me."

"Oh no, I can write it off as a business expense. You're not stealing my tax write-offs," he joked.

John led the three to a restaurant on the concourse that had sit-down service on the second level, providing a quieter place to talk. A young waiter took their orders and John began the conversation. "Sam has told me a bit about your experiences over the last couple of weeks and what you just observed in Austin, and it sounds like you would like to do something similar in Atlanta."

Phil nodded in agreement. "Yes, sir," he said. "Over the last few days, I have been working on the paperwork we need to launch an independent nonprofit separate from Peachtree Street Church. I believe this will allow us to acquire grants, corporate sponsorship, as well as support from other churches regardless of denomination. I have made a list of business leaders in the area that I have relationships with that could possibly serve on the board. And I have been drafting the vision and mission statements, so we have something to begin massaging once we have a formal board."

It was Sam's turn to be shocked at this point. "Is that what you have been working on during this whole trip?"

"As a matter of fact, it is," Phil said with a smile, "I figure we need something established before you retire."

Sam smiled. "I guess we do," he said.

After the waiter delivered the food, Sam said a prayer, and the men began eating.

John continued, "Well, as it happens, I have several acres near the Atlanta Motor Speedway in an unincorporated area that I inherited from my late uncle. It has become more than I can keep up with and frankly, it's wearing me out. There is a mobile home park on the land that we are beginning the process of closing down. The mobile home park has five trailers on it that we own that are in pretty good shape. Each one is a two bedroom, so theoretically, you could put ten people on the property on day one."

Phil looked at Sam. "I think I need to pinch myself."

Sam chuckled. "Don't," he said. "I already did, and it hurts like the dickens."

Phil laughed.

John handed his business card to both men. "Here is my card," he said, "I like this idea so much I'm going to make you an offer. One – my family will donate the mobile home park to your organization once you have inspected it and determine it is up to your requirements. Two – I will provide the organization first right of refusal on the remainder of the land. Three – I will design the master plan for developing the entire property to the organization's requirements pro bono. And, four – at some point, I would like to be considered for the board of directors. You do not have to respond to this four-part offer immediately. Let's set up a time to ride out and look at the property, and you can see what you think. I will send you a copy of my portfolio, so you can see what kind of work I have done in the past for other clients. Y'all can consider all of the offer, and we can get back together in a few weeks to see how you would like to proceed."

When he concluded his statement, he noticed both men had stopped eating. Phil looked at Sam and Sam looked back at Phil. Almost simultaneously as if choreographed, the two men looked back at John.

"Are you sure you want to engage this far this early?" Phil asked. "That is an awfully big leap of faith for partnering with two guys you just met on a plane"

John chuckled, "Guys, I'll be honest with you. This sounds like the best use of that land I have ever imagined. And with the enormity of the homeless population in Atlanta, I cannot think of a better cause to get behind."

The men continued to chat until they had all finished their lunch. The waiter returned with the check, and John quickly grabbed it and placed his American Express card in the book and closed it.

"I was serious when I said I was expensing this as a business luncheon with a potential client," he said and handed it to the waiter.

"Well, thank you," Sam said. "Thank you for lunch. And thank you for this generous offer."

"Yes, thank you," Phil said. "Check your calendar once you get back into your office and let us know a good time to tour the property."

"Sounds like a plan," John replied.

The waiter returned with the check, John completed it, signed a copy, and tucked the other copy in his laptop bag.

"Well, if you gentlemen will excuse me," he said, "I am sure my wife and kids would like to see me before dinner."

"Absolutely," Sam replied.

They stood up, shook John's hand and thanked him again. The three started for the escalator to the transportation level. Sam and Phil fell behind John's quick pace, and he was quickly out of sight. The two men boarded the airport tram. Sam found a seat in one end of the tram and sat down. Phil stood in front of him, holding onto an aluminum pole. After several stops, they reached the stop for the main terminal, exited the tram, and stepped onto the tallest escalator that Sam had ever been on. After a few minutes, they ascended into the bustling main terminal near the baggage claim. Phil led Sam to the exit directly across from the parking deck. Sam was beginning to tire from the walk, and his pace showed it.

Once outside the terminal, they stopped at the curb for a break in traffic to cross the airport road to the parking deck. When they stopped, Phil noticed a heavy sigh from Sam.

"You OK there, Sam?" Phil asked.

"Yeah, it's been a long week," Sam replied.

Phil spotted a break in the seemingly endless line of traffic, and they started to cross. He led them up a ramp where he stopped in front of a vending machine and paid for his parking. He then led them to an elevator that took them to the floor where Phil's Mercedes was parked. A little more walking, and they reached Phil's car. Phil opened the passenger side door for Sam and helped him get seated before stowing their luggage in the trunk. Phil opened the driver's door and slid into the driver's seat.

"If you like," Phil said, "that seat reclines with the button there on the door rest."

Sam looked at the armrest on the door and located a button. He reclined the seat a bit and settled in for the drive back into Atlanta. Phil wound his way out of the parking deck to one of the many exit gates. He stopped in front of a kiosk screen at one of the booths and inserted the ticket he had received at the vending machine where he had paid for parking. The kiosk opened the gate and printed out a parking receipt. Phil took the receipt, rolled up his window, and drove out of the gate onto the busy airport road. A couple of lane changes and Phil had the car pointed north on I-85. He turned to check on Sam and noticed that he was asleep.

CHAPTER 42

Sam woke up several times in the early hours of Friday morning, but not because he was in pain – no more than normal anyhow – nor was he awakened by a fitful bladder or things that rattle garbage cans and window shutters. He was waking up thinking about the homeless men, women, and children he had encountered during the winter storm and those he had met outside of Austin who now had homes. He marveled at the difference in the quality of life and the glimmer of hope and light that he saw restored in those eyes. Finally, he could not bear tossing and turning over anymore, so he got up, heated a kettle of water on the stove, and brewed himself a cup of hot tea. He sat down in his chair in the living room area and picked up the book he had bought while in Austin. He sat motionless and silent, reading and sipping his tea, stopping only for a moment to wipe a tear from his eyes and then resuming to turn pages. When he finished the book, he looked up at the clock on the wall and realized he had been reading for two and a half hours. He stretched his tired joints and carried his mug back to the kitchen and sat it on the counter. He turned back to the bedroom and began his morning routine.

When he walked back out of the bedroom, his cell phone was ringing. He unplugged it from the charger, flipped it open, and answered it.

"Hello?"

"Good morning, Sam," said the voice. "It's Phil. Are you about ready to ride down and take a look at John's property?"

"Absolutely," Sam replied, "I couldn't sleep from the antici-
pation. Hurry over here and let's get moving."

Phil chuckled, "I don't recall you ever being in much of a
hurry, Sam."

"Well, now you've seen it," Sam replied with a laugh.

"I hope it is alright with you," Phil continued, "I have invited a couple guests to join us."

"Oh?" said Sam.

"Yeah," Phil replied, "I talked to a couple guys in my circles
who I thought might be interested in corporate sponsorship
and asked them if they would like to join us for the first look."

Sam smiled, "That sounds great."

"OK," Phil said, "we will see you in a few minutes."

Sam wondered who Phil might have with him while he
waited for his arrival. He knew Phil moved in some influential
circles, so it made it hard for him to narrow it down to one or
two community leaders. He walked over to the window and
opened the blinds so he could look out on the parking lot.
Shortly he saw the lights of the Mercedes turn in to the parking
lot. He grabbed his cane and scurried for the door. He walked
out of the door to the apartment, locked the door behind him,
and scurried down the steps the best he could. As Phil was
stepping out of the car, he saw Sam approaching.

"Slow down there, tiger!" he exclaimed. "We don't need you
taking a tumble."

"Thanks for the concern," Sam responded. "I'm alright."

The passenger door of the Mercedes opened and out
stepped a man in a suit. The rear door of the Mercedes opened
and out stepped another man that Sam swore he recognized
but could not quite place him. The first man approached him
with an outstretched hand.

"Reverend Matthews," he said, "it is nice to meet you. I'm Roger Phillips."

Sam shook his hand. "Nice to meet you, Roger. You can call me Sam."

"Roger heads up community involvement with a large building supply corporation headquartered here in Atlanta," Phil noted.

The second man approached Sam and greeted him with an outstretched hand as well.

"Reverend Matthews, I'm Bill Hammond," he said, "I'm Vice President for a national fast food franchise group headquartered here in town."

Sam shook his hand. "Nice to meet you as well, Bill."

Roger looked at Sam. "Sam, why don't you ride up front here? I'll ride in the back with Bill."

Phil escorted Sam over to the passenger side and helped him into the car. They all buckled in and Phil started the car, put it in gear, and started out of the parking lot. He paused momentarily at the exit onto the street and pushed some selection on the screen in the middle of the dash.

"I've got the address entered here, so we can use navigation to get us there," he explained.

"So, fellas, I understand that you looked at a large master planned community in Texas for the homeless," said Roger. "What kind of housing did they utilize?"

Phil quickly began explaining, "They had a variety of housing elements in the village: travel trailers, recreation vehicles, and tiny homes. I don't know how much you gentlemen have been exposed to the tiny home movement, but there is quite a variety of homes under 500 square feet that are becoming very popular these days. Some of the ones we saw had large, wraparound porches while others were two story loft arrange-

218 | ALLEN MADDING

ments. The builders were quite creative in maximizing every inch of space and leveraging outdoor space as well."

Roger nodded his head. "Yes. We have seen a lot of development across the country in the tiny home segment from construction on 8x12 trailer frames, railroad caboose renovations, and storage container-based homes. It seems to be a booming trend in the starter home segment," he noted.

Sam chimed in, "They are economical solutions that really fit the need for providing a home to someone who has been without. It is certainly a step up from sleeping in a doorway, under a bridge, or even in a tent. Tiny homes provide a restoration of privacy and self-sufficiency. Several of the people we talked to were ecstatic to be provided a 12-foot travel trailer with a clean bathroom, a dry mattress, and a working stove and refrigerator. We tend to take a lot of things for granted until you sit and talk with someone that has been struggling with survival while homeless."

"If you had available utilities and basic infrastructure, a tiny house could be built for $10,000 to $15,000," Roger said. "Theoretically, a $100,000 grant or corporate sponsorship could provide 10 homes."

"Those are the numbers I have been working on," Phil commented. "I figure we could completely furnish an 8' x 12' home for just under $15,000."

Bill had been listening attentively to the conversation. "You show any corporation in the Atlanta metro area that you can provide a proper home to someone for $15,000, and I think you will be pleasantly surprised how many would be willing to sponsor a couple of homes," he said. "And you know, we both have friends that work for other corporations in the area. If we get involved, we are going to tell a couple of friends and they get their companies involved. The next think you know, you have a considerable level of corporate support."

"That is my hope," Phil responded. "It may seem a like a bit of conflict of interest at first, but the gentleman who is going to show us this land designs master planned communities. He has offered to donate a tract of this land that has a working mobile home park on it as well as his services to design a master planned community on the remaining land."

"That is a pretty significant donation," Roger said. "The design work alone can run in the six figures. Then you figure in the value of the land donation on top of that - it certainly isn't an offer to take lightly."

"Has he mentioned his asking price on the remaining land?" Bill asked.

"No, he hasn't at this juncture," Phil responded. "Just that we would have the right of first refusal on it."

"Where are you on organizational development?" Bill asked.

"I have drafted the vision, purpose, and articles of incorporation. And I have started drafting the application for 501(c)3 nonprofit status for the IRS," Phil replied.

"Excellent," Bill said. "It is kind of exciting to be given the opportunity to become involved at the ground level."

Phil had purposely avoided the interstate option and chosen to take Highway 41 instead. He had seen all the interstate congestion he could possibly want for a while. They passed the main entrance to the Atlanta Motor Speedway and after a couple more miles, he turned onto a two-lane road. At first, the road led them between subdivisions, but after a while they gave way to single homes on a few acres of land. Then they saw livestock and barns on bigger expanses of land. As the road curved around, they could see the outline of the grandstands for the race track off in the distance, while both sides of the road were dotted with pine trees and pastures. Finally, they arrived at the entrance to a mobile home park. It was neatly mowed and seemed well-kept. There were several empty lots and five homes sitting on adjacent lots. All the homes were freshly-painted and neat in appearance.

Phil pulled up next to a pickup truck and parked the car. He shut the car off, and they all got out and looked around them. The nearest trailer had an office sign next to it. The door to that trailer swung open, and John stepped out to greet them.

"Good morning, gentlemen," he said with a smile.

He walked across a small deck and down the steps to where they were standing.

Phil introduced him to Bill and Roger.

John began, "This mobile home park consists of 25 acres and has 60 pads on it that can support single or doublewide trailers. These 5 homes in front of you belong with the property and are two-bedroom units. You would be free to place mobile homes, RVs or even tiny homes on the remaining 55 lots. There is county water at each pad and the park has its own private septic system. The park has underground utilities, so you will notice a panel and meter base at each pad. As I mentioned before, if you choose to accept the mobile home park as a donation, you could house 10 people right off the bat while you conduct fundraising to build out the other 55. When you fill this up, our family has an adjoining 200 acres that we would be willing to provide you first right of refusal."

Sam looked at the other three men standing beside him. "I cannot see any reason why we wouldn't accept the offer," he said.

Phil smiled. "Can we take a look inside the trailers?"

"Sure," John answered. "Three still have renters living in them, but they have been provided notice that we are closing business. They are in the process of relocating but are happy to let you see the inside of their units. Why don't we start here with the office unit? The manager has lived here and managed the property from the living room. He has already vacated, so it's clean and empty."

The men walked through the mobile home and were pleasantly surprised by how clean it was. Every room looked spotless as if it were a brand-new home. They toured the other four units and returned to the deck of the office unit.

"What kind of zoning regulations do you have to contend with here?" Phil inquired.

"The county has the basic building permit process, but it isn't anything like inside the city. As you probably noticed on the way in, this is still a rural agricultural area. This tract is surrounded by my family's land, so you will not have issues with neighbors complaining. There has been a mobile home park here for 30 years," John replied.

Roger looked at Phil. "I am pretty sure I could get you a grant to build ten homes here once you have your 501(c)3," he said.

Phil and Sam smiled at each other.

Bill chimed in, "I will personally donate enough to build two and get our company to fund another ten."

Sam looked at Phil. "I guess we need to get busy."

John stood to one side of the deck watching the conversation take place. "Am I to take it that this meets your inspection?"

Phil stepped toward him. "Yes, sir. It certainly does." He shook John's hand. "Thank you for this generous offer."

John smiled. "My family is happy to support this cause. I will contact my attorney's office and have them draft the closing documents. Call me when you have your articles of incorporation filed, and we will schedule the closing."

Every one of the men shook John's hand and thanked him. They walked around the park for several minutes before returning to Phil's car.

CHAPTER 43

Lewis' cell phone rang. It caught him by surprise, as he did not get many calls. He looked down at the caller ID display before flipping it open to answer it. The number did not seem familiar to him, but he decided to answer the call anyhow.

"Hello," he said with his forehead wrinkled, wondering who was calling.

"Lewis," the voice on the other end said, "this is Reverend Samuel Matthews. We met at the hospital waiting room when Miss Gladys was having surgery after the storm."

"Oh yeah," Lewis replied. "How are you doing, Reverend?"

"I am doing pretty good, Lewis," Sam said. "I was wondering if you would be interested in a project we have started."

"What sort of project would that be?"

"Well," Sam continued, "I want to offer you your own home. A group of us have acquired some land several miles outside of town. We have a couple furnished mobile homes that we are giving to a few deserving souls. And you came to the top of my mind. We are trying to create a community that looks out for one another. After seeing how you came looking to see about Miss Gladys, I thought this would be a perfect opportunity for you."

Lewis was stunned. He did not know what to say or how to react. Was this real? Could this really be happening?

"What's the catch?" Lewis asked intently.

"What do you mean?" Sam asked in response.

"What do I have to do?"

"You don't have to do anything Lewis," Sam explained. "This is a no-strings arrangement. If you want to accept it, you will become the owner of a fully furnished two-bedroom mobile home. If you decide that you would like to share your home, you are welcome to offer the second bedroom to anyone of your choosing. You do not have to decide this minute. But if you are interested, I would be more than happy to drive you out to see the home, and let you see what you think."

"Well, I don't have anything on my calendar for the next..." Lewis stopped himself mid-sentence. "I have no plans. I guess I could go see it with you whenever you like."

"Alright then," Sam said, "when could you meet me in front of the Chick-Fil-a at Colony Square?"

"In about 15 minutes," Lewis replied.

"OK. I'll meet you there. We can grab a couple of lunches and drive out to see the home," Sam suggested.

"Alright. I'm headed that way," Lewis said and closed his phone. He started walking the six or so blocks toward Chick-Fil-A. When Lewis rounded the corner, he saw an old ex-cop car sitting in the circular driveway right in front of a "No Parking" sign.

"Reverend Matthews," Lewis said as he approached the driver's window.

"Hello Lewis," Sam replied.

"Reverend, these folks are bad about booting cars around here, so you better stay with your car. I'll go inside and see what I have left on my gift card," Lewis suggested.

"No, sir," Sam sternly responded. "I'll stay with the car, but you take this $20 bill. Lunch is on me."

Lewis started to protest, but Sam already had his hand up. "I won't hear it, Lewis," he said.

"Alright, alright. But can I get you something?" Lewis relented.

"Sure, just a sandwich and a sweet tea, since they dropped the coleslaw I loved so much from their menu. I sure don't want a kale salad," Sam replied.

Lewis laughed, "Alright. You sit tight."

"Why don't you put that big backpack in the back seat. I'll keep an eye on it for you," Sam suggested.

Lewis smiled, "You know, I didn't even think about that. I'm so used to having to guard it and keep it with me all the time," he explained. "Pretty sure I can trust you with it," he added.

Lewis opened the rear car door and laid the backpack on the backseat. He then disappeared down the stairs toward the front doors. After several minutes, he popped up carrying a paper bag and two drinks. He walked over to Sam's window and handed him a drink. He then walked around to the other side and crawled in the car and closed the door.

"Thank you for lunch," Lewis said. "It's kinda like Christmas – a free lunch and an offer of a free house."

Sam smiled, "You are more than welcome, my friend."

Lewis handed a foil wrapped sandwich to Sam.

Sam said, "Mind if I bless it?"

Lewis looked directly at Sam and replied, "Not at all."

Sam prayed out loud, "Lord, please bless this food and my brother Lewis. Bless our time together and help us bless those we meet. In Jesus name we pray, Amen."

Lewis emphatically said, "AMEN!"

Sam cranked the old tired Crown Vic and took a bite of his sandwich. "Let's go see your new home, Lewis," he said. While Sam drove, both men ate their sandwiches and savored the southern delight that is Chick-Fil-A sweet tea. After several minutes, Lewis polished off his sandwich and tossed the empty foil wrapper back in the paper bag.

"So, Miss Gladys has been completing physical therapy in an extended stay wing of the hospital. When I saw her yesterday, they said they could release her. The social worker lady has been trying to get her to check into a shelter when she gets out," Lewis said.

"What's Gladys think about that idea?" Sam asked.

"Not a whole lot," Lewis replied, "She's not a big fan of the shelters."

Several miles later, they rounded the corner of the two-lane road and came up to the community. A metal archway stretched over the entrance that read "The Home Place". Sam stopped the car, and Lewis mindfully looked around.

"It's a pretty far ways outside of the city," he observed, "but this is quiet and peaceful."

Sam eased the car down the driveway toward the first trailer and pulled to a stop in front of the deck.

"What is that over there?" Lewis asked pointing off to the left of the driveway.

"Those are chicken coops," Sam explained. "There are laying hens in there that produce eggs. If you like, you can walk over there and get you a couple of eggs and make yourself breakfast, or you can boil a couple for lunch."

Lewis nodded his head. "I do love a couple of eggs in the morning on the occasion I can get some," he said.

Sam smiled. "Here you can get some anytime you want."

Lewis squinted his eyes looking a little further down the driveway path. "Is that a garden over there?"

Sam shook his head and replied, "Yes, it is. There is sweet corn, green beans, tomatoes, squash, cucumbers...all sorts of vegetables growing there, free for the picking."

Lewis paused in amazement. "Who keeps all this up? Who feeds the chickens and weeds the garden and such?"

Sam smiled. "Well, there is a fellow living in this first trailer here that was homeless. We met him during the storm. He stayed in our church for shelter that night. He loved to stay busy and work. We offered him this trailer, and he wanted to help manage things. He is the manager and a pretty good handyman."

The door to the trailer opened and out stepped Fred.

"Howdy, Sam. Who ya have there with you this fine day?"

"Fred, this is Lewis," Sam said, introducing him. "Lewis, meet Fred."

"Hello, Fred," Lewis said. "I think I have seen you around before."

Fred nodded, "I believe you are right. I think we have seen each other on the streets of downtown. Thinking about joining us?"

"Thinking about it," Lewis admitted. "Kind of far to the free clinic or anything, isn't it?"

"It is," Fred said, "but we have a Physician's Assistant that comes out twice a month to check on us, and he gets free samples of any medication that you have to have – takes good care of us."

Lewis raised his eyebrows. "Well, alright," he said.

Fred stepped off the deck down to where Lewis and Sam were standing. "Lewis, let me show you the home that is available, if you decide you want it," he said. "Walk this way."

He led Lewis over to the second trailer and unlocked the front door with a key on a ring hanging from his belt. Lewis stepped inside and could not believe his eyes. There was a comfortable-looking recliner, a sofa, and a small television. He walked on in a little further and saw a wooden table and two chairs and a kitchen with a stove, refrigerator, microwave oven, a toaster, and even a coffee maker. His head was jerking from side to side trying to take it all in at one time.

"Walk on back past the kitchen," Fred suggested.

Lewis stepped into a hallway to see a washer and dryer. A few more steps and he could see a nice size bathroom with handles on the wall of the shower/tub combo and another beside the toilet. He walked on down the hallway and stepped into a large bedroom with a bed that was made up with sheets and a comforter and two fluffy looking pillows. Lewis turned around and looked at Fred and Sam standing in the hallway.

"It all looks new," he noted.

"Because it is," Fred explained.

He looked at Sam.

"This is for me?" He asked, almost bewildered.

"If you want it," Sam responded, "it is yours for the asking."

"Heck, there is another bedroom on the other side of the living room, isn't there?" Lewis asked.

"There is," Fred answered, "with another full bathroom."

Lewis smiled and shook his head in disbelief.

"Preacher, you said I could pick a roommate if I wanted, right?" Lewis asked.

"That's right," Sam answered him.

"Would it be OK if we got the social worker lady to let Miss Gladys have that front bedroom? I don't want to upset church folks thinking we're shacking up or anything."

Sam smiled. "I think that would be fine, Lewis. She is going to need someone to help her get fully back up to speed. And I'm pretty sure we could get the local social services to help her right here."

Lewis nodded, "Well, if Miss Gladys can have the front bedroom, then I'll take it."

Sam reached out to shake Lewis' hand, but saw tears rolling down his cheeks. He wrapped his arms around the big man and gave him a hug.

"Welcome home, Lewis," he said.

Fred walked up behind them and patted Lewis on the shoulder. "Welcome home, Lewis," he said.

Lewis wiped the tears from his cheeks and looked at Sam. "What do I have to do to move in?"

Sam chuckled. "Get your backpack out of my car and carry it into that back bedroom," he said.

Lewis looked up at him in disbelief.

"Really? I don't have to sign something or anything like that?"

"No," Sam answered him, "it is yours. It's a free gift."

Lewis walked over to Sam and gave him a huge bear hug while tears rolled down his cheeks.

"This is the most wonderful thing I have ever been given," he exclaimed.

Fred quietly walked out of Lewis' trailer and stopped at the edge of the deck that ran the length of the front of the trailer. He looked off in the distance and shook his head. A tear rolled down his cheek and fell off his jaw. Fred never tried to wipe the tear away. He just kept shaking his head.

He looked up toward the sky and said, "This is good stuff right here, God. This is good stuff."

A few minutes the door to the trailer opened and Sam and Lewis stepped out onto the deck.

"There you are," Lewis said. "I wondered where you got off to."

Fred looked up at Lewis and shook his head.

"Just enjoying the air. It smells so sweet and clear here – so different than downtown," Fred replied.

Sam stepped near the two and said, "Guys, I would like to pray a blessing over Lewis' new house, if that is alright with y'all."

Lewis nodded his head. "Sure," he said.

Sam bowed his head and began praying. "Gracious Lord and Savior, thank you for all of the blessings you pour out on us each and every day. Thank you for these two men. Please bless Lewis and his new house. Let it be a blessing to him. May he be blessed coming and going, and may he bless everyone that he meets every day. We pray this in Jesus name, Amen."

"Amen!" Lewis and Fred said in unison.

"Were going to be getting more neighbors soon," Fred told Lewis. "We have three more trailers that I am finishing up the final touches on. Once those three are filled, we have 60 more spots that have all the utilities already ran. We just need a tiny house, a mobile home, or a RV of some sort for those spots. There is a fella coming out tomorrow that will be putting up a large metal carport kind of structure that will be in the open area near my trailer. We have a large Barbeque grill and 10 wooden picnic tables that will go under it for a community area."

Lewis smiled. "You know I do love some good barbeque!"

He walked back to Sam's car and opened the back door and retrieved his backpack. He tossed it up on his shoulders and started back to his new home. He stopped at the door and turned to Sam and Fred.

"You know," he said, "this is going to be the first time I've ever unpacked."

Fred nodded his head. "Go slow," he recommended. "It is a lot to adjust to in one afternoon. Take it at your own pace. I was almost overwhelmed with it all when I first came out here. If you get bored during the day, you are more than welcome to hang out and talk to me while I work around here. But pace yourself; tonight will be the first time in a long time that you slept on a mattress with clean sheets and a brand-new pillow. I'm hoping it's the best night of sleep you have ever had."

Lewis nodded as he listened to the advice.

"If you guys will excuse me, I think I am going to take a shower," Lewis said.

Fred nodded. "There are clean towels and washcloths under the sink in the two bathrooms. And if you open the top drawer on the chest of drawers in the bedroom, you will find new underwear and socks."

Lewis turned to Sam and Fred. "Thank you again. Thank you very much," he said.

He opened the door and walked into his new home. Closing the door behind him.

Sam looked at Fred with a smile. "You did pretty well for your first new resident," he said.

Fred grinned. "Thanks," he said, "I just kept thinking about what it was like when you and Phil brought me out here that day. It kind of helped me understand what he was feeling and thinking."

"Well," Sam started, "I think I am going to head back into town and try to catch up with Miss Gladys and her social worker and see if we can't get arrangements made to bring her out here if she is interested."

Fred shook his head. "I was really surprised that Lewis suggested that idea," he said.

"I wasn't," Sam replied, "Not for a minute. The second he said it, I thought 'That is the Lewis that I know.'"

"Have a good afternoon and drive safe," Fred said.

"You have a great afternoon and evening, Fred. Call me if you need me," Sam said.

Sam shuffled back to the tired old Crown Vic, cranked the motor, and drove toward the large archway entrance.

Fred stood motionless watching Sam drive off and out of sight. After a few minutes, he headed to trailer number three to assemble some furniture.

CHAPTER 44

Gladys was just polishing off the breakfast tray when the nurse knocked on her door.

"It's open," she responded, while finishing off the last fork full of grits and eggs.

The nurse walked to her bedside.

"Well, are you ready for a road trip this morning?" the nurse asked, with a smile.

"Honey, nothing personal, but I am just ready to be out of this hospital," Gladys quickly answered.

"No offense taken, Miss Gladys. I completely understand. Are you sure you feel up to a long car ride?"

"Oh yeah," Gladys responded without a single thought, "I'm a tough old bird."

"OK," the nurse replied. "I have some discharge papers for you to sign. Miss Karen is out at the nurses' station. She will be in to see you in a minute. Let's get these papers signed, and I will get you a wheelchair."

Gladys began signing the papers and continued the conversation as she signed. "I don't need a wheelchair. Y'all have had me up and down the hall with the walker and my funny-looking cane."

The nurse smiled.

"Sorry, Miss Gladys. Hospital policy due to insurance requirements. Anyone leaving the hospital goes to the front door in a wheelchair, even if they had a mole removed from their nose," she explained.

Gladys shook her head.

"Alright. I guess I won't win this fight, huh?" Gladys sighed.

The nurse looked over all the paperwork, tore out a couple duplicate pages, and slid them in a binder.

"These are your copies. We recommend your see your surgeon for follow up. His office address and phone number are in this binder," she explained. "You weaned yourself off prescription pain relievers. If you have any pain, I recommend taking an Aleve once every 24 hours as needed. Continue to walk and do the exercises the physical therapy staff taught you."

"OK," Gladys said, trying to patiently weather the sea of follow-up information.

"I'm going to go get you a wheelchair now," the nurse said, and headed for the door.

As she stepped into the hallway, Gladys heard another voice.

"Miss Gladys?"

"Yes?"

Miss Karen walked in the room with a large smile on her face. "Well, look at you. Aren't you looking good today!"

Gladys laughed. "Kind of early in the morning to already be hitting the liquor isn't it, Miss Karen?"

Karen shook her head, "Gladys!" she laughed. "I came over in the mini-van, because I thought you might have a better time getting into it."

"Oh, OK," Gladys replied.

"Reverend Mathews and I have been talking and it sounds like they have a nice home arranged for you. He wanted me to make sure you would be comfortable sharing the house with Lewis," Karen said.

Gladys nodded her head.

"Lewis is as harmless as a butterfly and has a heart of pure gold. He is kind of the male version of you Miss Karen," Gladys said.

"OK," Karen said, "I consider that a pretty good referral. Reverend Mathews is going to meet us at the home. Nothing is written in stone. If you don't like it and choose not to move in there, I can make arrangements for you in one of our shelters in town."

"Thank you, Miss Karen," Gladys responded. "I have always appreciated how you have looked out for me and the rest of the homeless community. Even though I haven't set foot in it yet, from what Reverend Matthews has told me, I can't see myself not accepting the offer."

Karen smiled as she said, "Alright. But just remember if anything changes, we can look at options for you. If you decide to move in there, they have arranged transportation so you can make your follow up appointments with the doctor. They also have a local social worker that checks in with the community there on a regular basis."

Gladys nodded her head. "Wonderful! I wondered how I would make that work."

The nurse appeared at the door to the room pushing a wheelchair.

"Are we ready to get rolling?"

"No pun intended, I hope," Gladys said.

"I thought that was clever," the nurse replied.

"Don't quit your day job," Gladys quipped.

Gladys sluggishly twisted herself sideways until her feet were hanging off the edge of the bed. She pushed herself closer to the edge until her feet touched the floor and lifted herself to standing.

"Couldn't have done that a week ago," she said proudly.

The nurse guided her into the wheelchair while Miss Karen collected her pack sitting by the edge of the bed.

"Miss Karen," said the nurse, "there is a large hospital bag just inside the wardrobe door there next to the bathroom, too."

Karen walked over and opened the wardrobe door and picked up a large hospital bag.

"There's a couple of items the nursing staff bought as farewell gifts and a few toiletry items as well," the nurse noted.

The nurse began rolling Gladys down the hallway and toward the elevator while Karen followed behind carrying the bags. When they reached the elevator, the nurse pushed the down button and they waited. After several minutes, a down arrow above the elevator illuminated and a chime sounded. The doors to the elevator opened, and the nurse wheeled Gladys inside and turned her around to face the door. Karen stepped inside and stood beside her.

When they reached the ground floor, the elevator doors opened, and the nurse rolled Gladys a short distance to the exit doors. Karen went around them to the parking lot to get the van. She returned shortly and pulled to a stop right in front of where they were waiting. She walked around to the passenger side and opened the sliding door. Karen and the nurse helped Gladys getting into the van and getting seated. Karen loaded her walker and two bags in the back of the van while Gladys kept the three-legged cane by her side. Karen pushed a button on the key fob and the sliding door closed. She walked back around and climbed under the steering wheel.

She turned to Gladys. "Are you all buckled in and comfortable?"

"Oh yes," Gladys replied, "this seat is pretty comfortable."

"I tilted it a little to try and make you as comfortable as possible," Karen noted, "There are buttons on the door beside you that will let you adjust it however you like."

"Thank you, Miss Karen," Gladys said. "You are too kind."

Karen pressed some selections on the touch screen in the center of the dash, and a navigation system began providing directions. Karen pulled the van into gear and pulled out of the driveway and onto the street. She followed the directions up onto the interstate and began travelling south.

After a few miles, Gladys struggled to keep her eyes open. Within a few minutes, she was asleep. Karen glanced in the rear-view mirror. She smiled when she noticed that Gladys was napping during the ride.

When Gladys awoke, they were traveling down a small, two-lane country road.

"Are we close?"

"As a matter of fact, we are," Karen answered her.

They rounded a corner, and they could see the large metal arch over the entrance. Karen gradually drove down the driveway and pulled the van up to a large shelter. Smoke wafted from a grill cooking in the far end. She parked the van and pushed a button, and the door by Gladys slid open. Karen retrieved the walker from the back of the van and carried it to the opened door.

"Miss Gladys, I think they have lunch ready for us!"

Gladys' eyes sparkled and danced. "I don't know what they are cooking, but it sure smells good to me!"

Karen helped Gladys out of the van. Gladys took the walker and began making her way to the shelter. She could see wooden picnic tables with balloons tied to the corners. She looked around and then looked at Karen.

"Miss Karen, is it somebody's birthday?" Gladys asked.

Before Karen could manage an answer, they heard a noise to their right. They turned to see Sam.

"Welcome to The Home Place, Miss Gladys," Sam said.

"Well, thank you," Gladys said with a huge toothy smile. "Is it somebody's birthday?"

Sam chuckled. "No, dear," he replied, "this is a welcoming party for you."

Gladys looked around her. "There must be a dozen people here," she thought. "Who are all these folks?"

Sam led her to a table that had a large cushioned chair at the end of it.

"We thought you would be a little more comfortable here than on one of the wooden benches," he said.

"Oh mercy! Thank you."

Sam helped her get seated and set the walker to one side of her.

"I want to introduce you to some people, Miss Gladys," Sam said.

He pointed to two men working at the grill. "I think you will recognize Lewis over there cooking. I'm not sure if you know him, but the other gentleman there is Fred. Fred lives here and serves as the Community Manager. Anything you need, you tell Fred, and he will take care of it."

He motioned to a group standing off to one side of him.

"These folks here are members of the board of directors for The Home Place. They are responsible for making this dream a reality," Sam explained.

He introduced each board member to Gladys, and they each stepped to her and shook her hand.

"This gentleman's name is John. His family donated the land for The Home Place, and he designed the master plan for the development of the community," Sam said.

John took his ball cap off and held it in his hand as he shook Miss Gladys's hand.

"It is a pleasure to meet you, Miss Gladys," John said. "I have heard a lot of great things about you from Sam and Lewis. I hope you enjoy the community."

Next Sam introduced Bill and Roger.

"Miss Gladys," he said, "these two gentlemen represent two corporations headquartered in Atlanta that are sponsoring the construction of 15 tiny houses that are being added to the community. Four are currently under construction, and we plan to have the rest completed by the end of the year."

"Wow!" Gladys exclaimed, "There are a lot of homeless in Atlanta that would love having a house here."

"We hope so," said Phil, who was now standing beside Sam. "We started with five mobile homes and by the end of this month, those will all be fully occupied. We are getting busy beginning the next phase. After lunch, I would like to show you around the property. Do you think you could stand a ride in a golf cart?"

"Oh, I imagine I could," Gladys replied. "I'm kind of anxious to see the rest of the beautiful place."

Lewis walked over to where they were with a plate in his hand.

"Miss Gladys. It sure is good to see you out and about," he said, almost tearing up.

"It's so good to see you, Lewis," Gladys responded.

"Well, I have a plate for you here. There's ribs, baked beans, tater salad, and coleslaw," he said, setting the plate down on the table in front of her.

One of the board members brought her a solo cup filled with sweet iced tea and plastic utensils and napkins.

"There is banana pudding for dessert," the lady said with a smile.

Gladys beamed with excitement. Everyone else lined up near the grill and began making up their plates. Sam and Karen came over and sat on either side of Gladys. Once everyone was served, Lewis and Fred brought over their plates and set down with them. Sam stood up.

"Thank you, everyone, for coming to this celebration. Let us pray," he said. "Father God, we thank you for the blessings of this day. Especially for this wonderful smelling food and the blessing of sweet iced tea. Thank you for Miss Gladys' continued healing and restoration. Thank you for everyone here and their dedication to providing homes to those who are homeless and a community where everyone feels welcome. In your Son's holy name, Amen."

"AMEN," the group said in almost perfect unison.

When everyone finished their meals, Lewis and Fred began delivering small bowls filled with banana pudding. Gladys was amazed. She thought the food in the hospital had been pretty good - a huge improvement over some of the things she had eaten living on the streets of Atlanta. But this meal far surpassed anything she had eaten in years.

"Lewis," she shouted, "You never told me you could cook ribs that good. Man, you ought to be running a restaurant!"

Fred fiercely nodded his head in agreement. "I've been telling him that for weeks now," he said.

When Gladys finished her lunch, Phil walked over to her.

"Miss Gladys are you ready for the fifty-cent tour?" He asked jokingly.

"It depends," she replied. "Can I put it on my account? On account I don't have any money!" She laughed heartily at her own joke.

"That's a deal," Phil said.

Phil and Karen helped her up from the chair. She grabbed her walker and began shuffling alongside Phil as they walked over to a waiting golf cart. He helped her get seated and the put her walker in the back of the cart. They started driving down the driveway.

"This is Fred's home and the community office," Phil said, pointing to the first trailer. "Right in front of it are the community mailboxes. Each one has a number corresponding to the house number."

They rode a little further.

"This is Lewis' home," he said pointing to the second trailer with a large deck running the full length of the front of the trailer. "And yours if you decide to accept it," he added.

"We will come back and walk through it in a minute," Phil said as he drove on slowly.

"This is the third house which will have two sisters moving in later this week. The fourth house has an Army Veteran and his best friend that will be moving in next week. The fifth house here has three candidates who have applied for it. The board will be selecting this afternoon on who will be moving in there," Phil continued.

Just past the last trailer, Phil stopped the golf cart for a moment. Gladys looked up at a structure with four walls. The roof had not been built yet. Windows and doors had been framed out in the walls but were presently empty openings.

"This is going to be the community chapel," Phil announced. "It will only seat about 18-20 people. It's not necessarily designed to house Sunday morning services for the entire community. It is designed for a quiet place of reflection, meditation, and prayer."

Gladys smiled. "I bet Reverend Matthews is in love with this already."

Phil smiled and in a hushed voice asked, "Can you keep a secret?"

"Why yes," Gladys replied.

Phil whispered, "Sam doesn't know it yet. He thinks it's the next house. We have some amazing, stained-glass windows from an old, country church that was torn down that will go in these window frames."

Gladys smiled. "He will absolutely love it!"

Phil pulled a little further down the drive, and Gladys could see signs in front of each lot. The signs displayed the name of the house that would be built there and had a listing of the sponsors responsible for funding the construction.

"These are the 15 tiny houses you spoke about earlier," Gladys remarked.

"Yes, ma'am," Phil said with a large smile.

"Are you ready to tour the home that Lewis is offering to you?" Phil asked.

"Absolutely!" Gladys answered quickly.

Phil turned the golf cart around in the driveway and started back to the second trailer. As they got closer, Gladys could see a couple of people playing horseshoes just to one side of the shelter where they had eaten lunch.

Phil stopped the golf cart at the edge of the deck. He stepped out of the golf cart and retrieved Gladys' walker. As he helped her to her feet, she stood up, grabbed the walker, and looked toward the trailer. Instantly, she noticed three wooden steps leading to the front door. Before she could comment on the issues climbing steps with the walker, she noticed to her left there was also a ramp leading up onto the deck. As she made her way toward the ramp, she heard a couple of voices.

She turned to one side to see Sam and Lewis approaching from the shelter.

With a little assistance from Phil, Gladys made her way up the ramp with ease. Lewis hurried up the steps and across the deck to open the front door for her. Gladys crossed the deck and stepped into the living room and stopped dead still.

She carefully looked around in wonderment. It was spotless. New furniture, a fully furnished kitchen, and clean as a whistle. Lewis walked in behind her and fed her the details of the floor plan, and to her surprise, he told her about the washer and dryer just down the hallway.

"Are you ready to see your room?" Lewis asked.

"Yes, please," Gladys said softly.

Lewis pointed to a door at the end of the living room. Gladys shuffled her way to the door, opened it, and stepped into the bedroom. She stopped just inside the doorway looking at a queen size bed, dresser, chest of drawers, two night stands on either side of the bed, and in the corner, a wing-backed chair. Lewis stepped in behind her.

"Over there," he said, pointing to a door, "is a full-size bathroom with a shower that is handicap equipped. The door next to it is a walk-in closet."

Gladys stood stationary, just gazing around the room. Sam and Phil walked into the trailer and through the bedroom door before pausing to read Gladys' expression.

"Well, Miss Gladys," Phil said, "what do you think?"

Gladys turned toward him with tears rolling down both cheeks.

"I think this is the most wonderful gift I have ever received. I have wished and prayed for a dry place to sleep for years. I never dreamed of something this nice," she said, wiping at her cheeks and jaw line.

Lewis looked at her. "I would be honored if you would live here as my housemate," he said. "I will take care of the entire house including cooking and laundry until you feel like cooking and get tired of mine."

Gladys smiled and threw an arm in the air toward Lewis. He reached over and hugged her neck. The two smiled and cried. Karen walked in the trailer with Gladys' bags and set them down in the living room.

"Gladys," she said, "can I help you unpack and move in?"

"Oh, heavens yes," Gladys replied.

Lewis stepped toward the bedroom door. "I will let you ladies tend to this. I better get back over and get things cleaned up from lunch."

As Gladys settled into her home, she couldn't help but feel overwhelming gratitude for that terrible snowstorm. If it weren't for the storm and the Reverend's temporary shelter setup, she wouldn't be sleeping in her own bed tonight. For the first time in years, she unpacked her bag and hung her clothes in her very own closet.

Woke

"Housing will never solve homelessness, but community will. It's not a transactional thing. It's a relational thing."

ALAN GRAHAM,
Founder and CEO,
Community First! Village
and Mobile Loaves and Fishes

Dedicated *to my good friend, Bill Barton, who relentlessly campaigned for a third book and final story. I am grateful for your constant encouragement and your friendship. The Bible talks of iron sharpening iron, and you are a living example. I am a better man for the time you have poured into my life, quietly calling me out when I am wrong and always willing to provide wisdom when consulted.*

CHAPTER 45

The cell phone alarm went off at 8 a.m. Jim Harris rolled over and silenced it as he slowly slid his way out of the foot of the bed. Now standing in the center of his tiny home, he reached to the counter and turned on the coffee maker. He turned and pushed the door next to his bed and stepped into the small bathroom. He brushed his teeth and took a long look in the mirror. He washed his face and combed his unruly beard. He stepped back out of the bathroom and returned his attention to the coffeemaker. He placed a cup under the dispenser, put a pod in the machine, and pushed a button. As the machine made a groaning noise, he gently pulled on a pair of faded blue jeans and a sweatshirt. He opened a couple window blinds to let the morning light stream into his home and retrieved his cup of coffee. He took a long sip before pulling on a set of floppy-topped boots.

Jim stepped out the door of his tiny home onto the three-foot porch, closing the door behind him. He gazed around the property. He stepped off the porch and walked toward the community building. He strolled across the concrete driveway past the MARTA bus stop as a golf cart whizzed by him. A twenty-something girl with curly blonde hair, blue eyes, and a huge smile was at the wheel.

"Morning, Jim!" she shouted with a smile as she passed.

"Morning, Cathy."

He stepped into the archway of the community building and into the front office. A young intern behind the counter greeted him as he entered.

"Good morning, Jim! I have a group of six volunteers for you this morning. What do you have for them?"

Jim looked up. "We need to do some weeding in the garden."

"Sounds good," she replied. "I'll give the introduction speech and then turn them over to you."

Jim stepped out of the office and walked back out into the sunshine.

After a few minutes, a group of people began arriving. They headed into the front office and eventually emerged with volunteer name tags. Shortly after, the intern appeared and provided the volunteers with an introductory speech. She discussed how The Home Place had come about and its overall goal to establish community and dignity to those who had become homeless by the loss of family and community. She introduced Jim, and he spoke up.

"We have a vegetable garden that I maintain here on the property. Every Saturday, we host a farmer's market where our residents can come and get fresh vegetables for free. Today, we are going to be doing some weeding in the garden. If y'all will follow me, we'll head out that way."

As he led them to the community garden, they walked a meandering path that weaved between varying styles of tiny homes. As they walked, he pointed out different features of the homes.

"If you'll notice the panels on the roofs, all of the homes have solar power. Also, do you see the big silver drum beside the home with the PVC pipe running up to the gutter? That's a rainwater catchment system. We use that water to flush toilets and water flowers."

As they rounded a bend in the walkway, chicken houses came into view.

"We have enough laying hens here that everyone receives a dozen farm fresh eggs each week for free. It's my goal that nobody living here ever goes hungry. We all experienced that on the street. Never again, if I have anything to do with it."

They arrived at a large garden with raised beds full of every vegetable imaginable. He walked to a large shipping container sitting near the garden, opened the door, and handed out gloves and gardening tools.

"Please take extreme care not to step in a bed and not to damage any of the plants. If you have trouble distinguishing between a plant and a weed, ask me before you pull."

The volunteers spread out across the garden and pulled the weeds that had pushed through the weed-proof mat. As they worked, one of the volunteers asked Jim to share his story.

"Well, I was working construction. I had a bad accident on a job site and broke my back. They put me on some pretty strong pain medication, and I went home in a plastic brace with a prescription for more meds. I took the meds and was drinking some to deal with the pain. After they released me from therapy and everything, I went back to work and was still taking pills for the pain. When the prescription ran out, I started buying some from a guy a few blocks from where we lived. In the meantime, I got behind on the rent, and we got evicted. My wife went to live with her parents. But they told me I wasn't welcome because I was an addict, and they weren't having that in their house.

"So, I started sleeping in my truck. I missed a couple days at work, and the foreman started in on me. He said I had liquor on my breath and fired me. Not long after that my truck got towed and impounded by the city, and I couldn't afford to get it out. So, I started sleeping under the overpasses and anywhere someone wouldn't run me off.

"I had been on the streets about two years when the big snowstorm hit, and I stumbled into a church that was opened as a storm shelter. It was different than the ones I'd been in before. Instead of handing you a bowl of soup and blanket and walking off, some of their folks sat down and talked to me while I ate. Like I was a real person – not a street person you walk by and ignore.

"One of them figured out where my camp was and started coming by once a week with groceries, toiletries, and socks. Heck, he even came out and spent the night out there under a bridge a couple of times with us. When this village started, he came by and invited me to come check it out to see if I wanted to live here.

"I was skeptical at first, but come to find out, this dude had moved out here and was offering me a tiny house right next door to him. At that time, there were like 5 people living here, and they were still developing the infrastructure and building some of the main buildings. I guess you could say I got in on the ground floor."

As they worked in the garden, the volunteers continued to pepper him with questions.

"It seems kinda remote," one of them observed. "What do you do if you need to see a doctor?"

Jim smiled. "We have a clinic that is staffed six days a week by doctors and nurses from Atlanta. We also have a rehab center, which has been a big help to me. With their help, I've been clean for 6 months now. We have a lot of residents who struggle with mental and emotional issues, and we have a center with staff for that as well."

"Do you have to pay rent?" another asked.

"Sure do," Jim replied, "But there are a bunch of opportunities to earn an income here. For instance, if you sign on to clean the bath house, it takes about two hours a day and pays $650 a month. We have a carpentry shop where folks build furniture, and they get 40% of the sales. You might have noticed when you came in, just inside the gate is our post office, which also has job opportunities."

A few minutes before noon, Jim raised his hand in the air.

"OK, folks. Let's put up the tools and gloves. Thank you for your hard work in our garden. The hundred and fifty residents living here will appreciate and enjoy the vegetables this garden produces from your efforts today. After we put away the supplies, you're invited to join us at the pavilion area. Lunch for the entire community is being provided from a church in Jonesboro. Volunteers have been manning the grills, and there's plenty of food to go around."

He walked to the storage container and began storing the gardening tools and tossing the gloves in a large box by the door. Once all the tools and gloves were collected, Jim closed the heavy door and bolted it shut. He led the group to the closest bath house and restroom facility.

"You can wash up for lunch here and use the restrooms, and then I will lead y'all over to the pavilion."

As the volunteers entered the bathrooms, they were impressed by how clean and accommodating the facilities were – complete with handmade soaps created onsite. A couple noted that the building was powered by an array of solar panels on the roof, solar heat being used to heat the water for the showers and sinks, and rain catchment systems utilized for flushing toilets.

Jim met them outside the doors of the restrooms and led them over to the pavilion. At noon, a dinner bell rang.

"We're right on time," Jim noted as they approached the large crowd gathering at the perimeter of the pavilion. A silver haired man with wire-rimmed glasses stood up on a picnic table bench and raised his hands.

"Welcome, everyone! For those visiting, I am Sam Matthews, Chaplain and Director of The Home Place. We would like to thank First Church of Jonesboro for providing the community lunch today. Let us pray. Heavenly Father, we thank you for a beautiful day, good food, the fellowship of friends, and the love of a community where we can all belong. Amen."

A line formed at the end of a row of tables, and the entire community started fixing their plates and sitting at the numerous picnic tables under the pavilion's expansive roof. A group of people stepped onto the stage at the front of the pavilion and began playing music. Sam smiled and turned to the group of volunteers behind him in the line.

"Not every day you get lunch and a live band," he said with a smile.

The group soon reached the serving line and were served their choice of ribs, hamburgers, hot dogs, beans, and chips.

"Is lunch served to the whole community every day like this?" one of the volunteers asked.

"No," Jim answered. "We usually have a community lunch once or twice a week. One of the families here holds what they call a "Prayer and Pancake Breakfast" on Tuesdays. We have a community dinner every Wednesday evening, and these community lunches happen a little more randomly when a volunteer group offers to host."

Jim led the group to a row of available picnic tables, and they sat down to eat. While they were eating, Reverend Matthews walked up.

"I wanted to thank y'all for volunteering today. Did Jim work y'all hard?"

The group chuckled in response.

"Not too bad," one of the volunteers spoke up.

"Yeah, he's a pretty good guy to work with," Sam said. "And he's not a bad gardener."

Jim smiled. "Thank you, Sam," he replied.

Sam patted Jim on the shoulder and walked to another row of tables to talk with another group of people. Jim wiped the corners of his mouth with a napkin.

"You know, after I moved out here was the first time in years that I could actually rest. You probably don't realize it, but when you're sleeping on the streets, you never really rest. You know that you're sleeping somewhere that someone doesn't want you to be. Business owners don't want you sleeping in the doorway of their closed businesses. People don't want you sleeping on the park benches. The Georgia DOT doesn't want you sleeping under their bridges. There's always someone coming to run you off. The police come by and poke you with a nightstick and tell you to move on. You have to worry about someone stealing your pack or your shoes. It's hard to rest worrying about all that all the time, and you're never really able to get comfortable sleeping on the ground or a sidewalk. The first night I moved in my tiny home and laid down on a mattress with sheets and a pillow, it was the best rest I had in years. It's amazing how good you feel after a peaceful night's sleep!"

Once the volunteers finished their lunch, Jim escorted them to the guest parking area.

"Thank y'all for volunteering at The Home Place. We simply couldn't function without the support of volunteers like y'all. Tell your friends about us and encourage them to check us out and consider volunteering with us. Y'all have a great afternoon and drive safe."

The volunteers all shook his hand and said goodbye. Jim turned and headed toward his home.

CHAPTER 46

John took a long sip of coffee from a stainless-steel travel mug. He checked the time on the clock on his truck's radio. Traffic had once again delayed him. It was quarter after 9 when he drove under the archway over the driveway entering The Home Place. He drove to the main parking lot and shut the truck off. He retrieved his tool pouch, a thermos, and a soft sided cooler from the rear passenger floor and walked to a waiting golf cart nearby. He pulled a key ring out of his pocket, unlocked a padlock and removed a chain that secured the golf cart to a steel post. He tossed the lock, chain, and his tool pouch into the back of the cart. He crawled under the steering wheel, turned the key in the switch and started down a stone pathway. He drove past several tiny homes, rounded a corner, and stopped at the edge of a lot where four tiny houses were under construction. Metal roofing had been completed on all four houses, and siding had been started on one.

John scooted out of the golf cart, retrieved his tool belt, and strapped it around his waist. He walked over to a small job trailer sitting between a couple of the houses. He unlocked the trailer and pinned the doors open. He set out a pair of sawhorses, strung out an extension cord to an outlet on a temporary utility service pole, and plugged up a circular saw. He pulled a few siding boards from a stack just inside the framed walls of the house and placed them on the sawhorses. He pulled a tape measure from his tool pouch and took a measurement for the siding. He returned to the sawhorses and started cutting boards. He carefully stacked the cut boards near the side of the house.

After a few minutes, he heard someone call his name. He turned to see Lewis Davis leading a group of volunteers his way.

"Good morning, Santa!" John called out.

"Good morning, John boy!" Lewis replied. "I got you a siding crew here to help out."

"Good morning, everyone," John greeted the volunteers. "We've got four houses that need siding. I bet you can knock it all out before lunch," John said with a grin.

John demonstrated how to use an air nail gun and how to use the homemade jig to determine the overlapping of the siding. They quickly caught on and began nailing on siding. John returned to the sawhorses to continue cutting. Two teams attacked the work on two of the houses. John was busy keeping up with demand for siding. Within a little more than an hour, they had completed the siding on the first two houses and turned their attention to the remaining two houses. Within an hour, all four tiny houses were completely sided.

"Good job, y'all!" John shouted.

Lewis smiled. "You know it amazes me how quickly these tiny homes come together."

John grinned. "Yeah, it goes a lot faster when you're building a house that is 250 square feet."

John helped the volunteers store their tools in the job trailer, and Lewis led them to the pavilion for lunch. John continued working. He cut out the window openings in the newly hung siding and hung the windows in the first house. The house had double windows on each side and a single window offset on one end where a bedroom would be. Windows had already been installed in the eves at each end of the house to provide indirect light without compromising privacy.

Once he had completed the windows on the first house, he walked over to the golf cart and retrieved a thermos of coffee to refresh his insulated mug. He opened a small, soft-sided cooler and retrieved a sandwich and an apple. He quietly ate his simple lunch while gazing across the landscape of the developing village. He struggled to believe it had been two years since they had launched The Home Place, and it already had over 200 residents. Many were former homeless who were seizing the opportunity to heal from the devastating loss of family and receive a sense of belonging, while some were middle class suburbanites who had chosen to retire into the community to encourage and support their new neighbors.

John finished his lunch and turned his attention to the second house. He had one window left to install when he felt his phone vibrating. He stopped and took the call.

"Hey Cowboy!" said his wife, Mary. "What ya doing?"

John smiled. "Installing windows in a couple tiny homes," he explained.

"Should we expect you for dinner tonight?" she asked.

"Absolutely!" John replied. "I plan to be wrapped up here a little before 5."

"Perfect," Mary responded. "Just in time for Atlanta traffic." she said playfully.

"Don't remind me," John said with a chuckle. "How's your day going?"

"Going good," she answered. "I met with a shop owner down on Main Street in Alpharetta who is going to start carrying some of the art and jewelry the artist group in The Home Place have been creating. She seemed really excited to work with them."

"That's awesome," John responded. "Well, I better get back to work so I can get this knocked out before dark. I love you."

"I love you too, cowboy!" Mary replied. "Drive careful on the way home. Nobody else will."

John ended the call, snapped the phone in its holster on his belt, and returned to installing windows. He completed the second house and moved to the third. When he finished sawing the openings in the siding for the windows, Lewis returned.

"Hey John," Lewis called.

"Why hello, Lewis!" John responded.

"Thought you might could use an extra hand over here for a bit," Lewis said.

"I never turn down free help," John said.

They installed windows in the house while they chatted.

"How have things been going with you, Lewis?" John asked.

"I don't have any complaints," Lewis said as he lifted a window into the opening in the side of the house. "I've been struggling to control my diabetes, but the medical center here has been helping me out."

John nodded as he sunk screws into the window securing it into the opening. "Sam mentioned that you had been hospitalized a couple weeks back."

"Yeah," Lewis replied. "Apparently my old prescription and diet weren't doing the trick anymore."

"Feeling better now?" John asked.

"Yeah. I've had three really good days so far this week. I'm hoping they got it figured out. My diet has really changed, but I'm getting used to it."

"I'm glad to hear it, buddy!" John said.

"Well you know, two years ago it probably would have killed me," Lewis continued. "When I was on the street there wasn't any real hope for getting any long-term medical care for something like diabetes. You'd go into the ER, and they'd do the bare minimum it took to shuffle you back out the door because they knew you couldn't pay the bill. Since I moved in here, they've helped me get my Social Security check and my Medicare. And the Medical Center staff here seem to really care about the residents and aren't so focused on the dollars and cents."

Soon the two completed installing windows in the four new tiny houses. John gathered up the tools and stored them in the job trailer. Lewis stood proud, admiring their work.

"This is good stuff, John," he noted. "Four more lives are gonna be positively impacted by these houses. Somebody is gonna finally be able to get a good night's rest for the first time in a long time without worrying the cops are gonna poke 'em in the ribs with a baton and tell them to get moving or worrying that someone is gonna steal their pack while they're asleep."

John smiled. "That's my hope, Lewis."

Lewis patted him on the back. "You're a good man, John. First you designed this community, and now you are out here donating your time building homes."

John looked at the ground and back up to meet Lewis' stare. "Just glad I can be a part of something that is making such a positive impact on the lives of people."

Lewis gave him a bear hug. John wiped the corner of his eyes and locked up the job trailer.

"Well, Lewis, I better get headed to the house. Can I give you a lift?"

"Sure," Lewis replied. "I'll ride up to the main parking lot with you. I need to check my mailbox."

CHAPTER 47

It was 3 a.m. when Sam Matthews woke. The room was filled with red light. He turned onto his side and moved the curtain to look out the corner of the window above the bed. An ambulance and fire truck were parked across the cul-de-sac directly in front of the tiny house belonging to Bobby Carpenter. Sam snatched his glasses and cell phone off the table, slipped on some shoes, and grabbed a jacket. He headed directly to Bobby's. As he stepped onto the small front porch of Bobby's home, he could see Bobby lying on the floor and paramedics working on him.

One paramedic drew a hypodermic needle and a vile of meditation that Sam assumed was Narcan, a medication used to counteract an overdose of Opioids.

"2mg Narcan administered," the paramedic announced.

The second paramedic gave Bobby a hard sternum rub with a knuckle.

"Wake up, buddy!" the medic called to Bobby.

While the paramedic felt for a pulse and listened for breath sounds with a stethoscope, the first paramedic drew a second dose of Narcan.

"No noticeable improvement in respirations," the paramedic reported.

"Alright," the first paramedic replied. "Administering second dose 2mg Narcan."

Again, the other paramedic gave Bobby a hard sternum rub with a knuckle.

"Wake up!" he called to Bobby.

Bobby flinched. He fluttered his eyes and began coughing.

"Easy, buddy," said the paramedic. "Relax. You've over-dosed, but you're going to be alright."

Bobby turned his head from side to side and tried to focus his eyes. He looked at the doorway and met Sam's eyes. He quickly diverted his eyes back to the paramedics in shame.

Sam knew that Bobby was struggling with addiction when he moved into the village. He also knew there was no hope of him overcoming the addiction while living on the streets of Atlanta. His only hope of ever beating the addiction was in a community that supported him and could walk with him through the rehabilitation process. While he didn't judge Bob-by for his addiction, it broke the old preacher's heart to see him in this situation.

Had he overdosed on the street, the chances of him getting emergency treatment were slim. But because he was here at The Home Place, he had neighbors who regularly checked on him and fortunately one found him and called 911.

"OK, bud," said the paramedic. "We're gonna carry you to the ER and have you checked out."

Bobby started to argue.

Sam held up his hand.

"Bobby," Sam said, "Let's just take a ride to the hospital and make sure you're alright. I'll bring you home once they've checked you over."

Bobby dropped his argument mid-sentence.

"Alright, Sam," he said quietly.

The paramedics lifted Bobby onto a stretcher and carried him out of the house. Gladys closed the door to Bobby's house and locked it.

Sam walked over to her and gave her a hug.

"Good job, Gladys. You're a great friend and wonderful neighbor."

Gladys wiped her eyes.

"Damn fool! I keep telling him the poison isn't the cure for his demons."

"I know, Gladys. I know," Sam replied. "We just got to keep praying and loving him through it. I need to go get dressed and head to the hospital.

While the paramedics loaded Bobby into the ambulance, Sam walked back to his house. He changed out of his pajamas and into slacks and a shirt. The ambulance was gone by the time he walked out of his tiny home, locked the door, and walked to his old faded white Ford Crown Vic sitting at the edge of the cul-de-sac. The door on the old Ford creaked as it opened hinting at its age. He crawled into the car and cranked it to life.

Sam quietly drove to the nearby hospital and parked in the small emergency room parking lot. He retrieved a clergy name tag from the glove box and clipped it on his shirt pocket. He stepped out of the car and walked across the parking lot and into the entrance of the emergency room. The lobby was empty with only a kiosk to greet him. He walked to a triage room and popped his head into the doorway.

"Good morning," Sam said to a nurse typing on a computer.

The nurse looked up. "Hi. How may I help?" he responded.

Sam told the nurse he had come with a patient brought in by the ambulance and provided Bobby's name. The nurse typed his name into the computer and pulled up his information.

"Alright," he said. "Right this way, please."

He quickly led Sam to an exam room where Bobby was connected to an EKG and surrounded by medical staff.

"Sorry to get you out of bed, Sam," Bobby said upon seeing Sam walk into the room.

Sam smiled. "Not to worry, Bobby," he replied. "I needed to get up anyway."

One of the nurses had started an IV on Bobby.

"We're gonna keep an eye on you for a bit and let you finish that IV," the physician's assistant reported. "Then, we'll probably cut you lose."

After the room cleared of medical staff, Bobby laid silent with Sam sitting in a chair just to the side of the head of the bed. After several minutes, Sam broke the silence.

"Bobby, it's time we find you a path out of this cycle before someone doesn't find you or we're too late getting you help," Sam said softly.

Bobby closed his eyes and dropped his head. "I've really tried, Sam," he said, "but Methadone isn't the answer."

Sam nodded.

"I understand," Sam responded. "When we get back to The Home Place, I want you to go over to the clinic and meet with the addiction recovery team. They will help you develop a recovery plan. It will be more than just a prescription. There is no magic bullet, so they don't suggest a band-aid fix. They will develop a recovery plan that is custom designed for you."

Bobby rolled his head to the side and looked Sam in the eyes.

"I'll give 'em a try," Bobby said skeptically.

After an hour of small talk, a nurse walked back in the room.

"How ya feeling, Bobby?"

"I'm alright. Gettin' kinda hungry," he answered.

The nurse pushed a button on a monitor near the head of the bed, and a blood pressure cuff slowly inflated. There was a ticking sound, and the cuff gradually deflated. A dinging sound soon followed, and the cuff deflated completely.

"Your vitals look good. Looks like you finished the IV, so let me get it disconnected."

She clamped off the IV line, disconnected the tubing from the catheter, removed it from his arm, and taped a folded piece of gauze over the puncture site. The physician's assistant soon appeared at the door.

"Ready to leave us?" she asked.

"Believe so," Bobby replied.

She reviewed discharge paperwork with Bobby and provided him some literature on addiction recovery. The nurse helped him sit up and to his feet. Sam walked with him out to the old Ford Crown Vic waiting in the parking lot.

"How about a little Waffle House?" Sam proposed.

Bobby smiled for the first time in hours.

"I could go for a little smothered and covered," he answered.

After a few minutes, Sam wheeled the old Ford into a parking spot in front of the Waffle House. Bobby and Sam crossed the parking lot and walked into the brightly lit restaurant. They were greeted by the smell of bacon grease and coffee. They slid into the corner booth, with Sam sitting with his back to the wall. A waitress with a scorpion tattoo on her neck quickly greeted them.

"Morning boys!" she started. "Whatcha havin'?"

"Black coffee, All-American, eggs over easy, bacon, and plain hash browns," Sam answered without glancing at the menu.

"What about you, Honey?" the waitress asked.

"I'll have the All-Star," Bobby answered. "Scrambled, sausage, hash browns smothered and covered, pecan waffle, and coffee."

"Alright boys. I'll get that started for you," she said while scribbling on a pad. She ripped the sheet off the order pad and clipped it above the grill. "One bacon, one sausage, scrambled and over easy, plain hash and one smothered and covered!" she shouted in no particular direction as she grabbed two mugs and started pouring the coffee.

She came back to the booth and slid coffee in front of both men. She pulled a handful of creamer packets from her apron and dropped them in a small bowl, which she set in front of Bobby.

Bobby grabbed three creamers and quickly poured them in his coffee before beginning to pour what Sam estimated to be a quarter cup of sugar in the mug.

"You like a little coffee with your milk and sugar?" Sam asked.

Bobby laughed. "You're hard-core, Preacher, drinking it black. I don't know how you do it."

Sam chuckled. "Years of experience, my boy. Years of experience."

"I don't know the demons you're fighting, son," Sam continued, "But you have worth, and you are valued in our community. We're all here for you and support you."

Bobby looked up from stirring his coffee. "Thanks, Preacher. That's the only reason I agreed to move into The Home Place, because y'all are the only folks who ever even acknowledged I existed in all the years I lived on the street. I figure if you come out with a sleeping bag and sleep under a bridge with me, living in a tiny home on that parcel, out there with y'all couldn't be too bad. It's been an adjustment hearing my name so much and every morning when I get up, the neighbors speaking to me. That kinda stuff didn't happen on the street. But you know, after living on the street for 10 years, I got into a lot of stuff to make myself numb so I couldn't feel the hurt and shame. And once you've been on some of this stuff, it grabs you and don't let go."

Sam nodded as he sipped his coffee.

"No one expects you to overcome 10 years in weeks or months. We're just glad you're alive to see another sunrise," Sam said watching the sun peek through the corner windows.

Once they finished eating, Sam got a coffee to go and paid the bill. They walked back to the old Ford. The driver's door gave a loud squeak as Sam opened it.

"Ya know, Preacher," Bobby started. "I used to work in a car shop. Ever think of having like an oil change, tire shop kinda place at The Home Place as another opportunity for folks to work?"

Sam smiled. "As a matter of fact, we have. When we visited Community First! in Texas, they had one and it seemed like a real good idea. We just need someone to head it up."

Bobby looked across the car at him with serious stare.

"I ain't no business manager, mind you, but I could darn sure take care of some cars," Bobby stated.

"Well, tell ya what," Sam replied. "As soon as we get a manager, you'll be the first guy he puts to work."

Bobby nodded. "Alright. Thinking this old car might need to be the first in for service."

Sam drove them back to The Home Place and parked. Bobby gave him a bear hug before walking back to his home.

"Thanks for being there for me, Preacher," he said. "Two years ago, I woulda just died lying on a sidewalk somewhere."

Sam wiped a tear from the corner of his eye. "Anytime, Bobby. We are here for you. I love you, buddy."

Bobby quickly turned and walked toward his home. Sam could seem him wiping his eyes on his shirt sleeve.

Sam walked into his tiny home. He had been trying to ignore the pain in his chest for the last hour, but it had intensified. And now his arm was beginning to ache. He retrieved a small pill box from his pocket and popped a nitroglycerin tablet under his tongue. He got undressed and flopped into bed, lying on his back, staring at the ceiling boards. After a few minutes, his head started pounding. He knew this meant the nitroglycerin was working. A few more minutes and the chest pain began to ease as he drifted to sleep.

Sam awoke a few hours later. The chest pain had subsided. He brushed his teeth, shaved, and dressed for the day in a button-down dress shirt and a pair of khakis. He filled his travel mug with coffee and stepped out onto the small front porch. He descended the three steps down to the ground and made his way to the offices. When he walked into the front office, several volunteers were signing in to serve for the day, and the receptionist was busy attending to them. Sam smiled and greeted the crowd, thanking them for coming out. He proceeded down the hallway and around the corner to his office. Before he could sit down behind his desk, an intern stepped into the doorway and called his attention.

"Good morning, Sam," she said cheerfully. "The crew from WSB-TV called and are about 10 minutes out for your interview."

"Splendid!" Sam replied.

He thumbed through some mail lying on the desk and sat down to check his email on the computer on the corner of the desk. Another intern stepped into his doorway.

"Hi, Sam," he said. "I'm going to be joining you this evening along with Fred and Lewis."

"That's great," Sam said looking up at him over the top of his glasses. "Have you ever slept on the street with the homeless before?"

"No, sir," replied the intern. "I've volunteered at the Atlanta Mission on occasion, but I haven't ever slept on the street."

"If you've worked in the shelters, you might run into a face you recognize tonight," Sam noted. "I always carry a cooler full of water, snacks, extra blankets, and of course socks to handout. Do you have a sleeping bag or something?"

"Yes, sir," the intern answered. "I have a sleeping bag and a small pillow I use when I'm hiking. I think I'm good."

"Awesome," Sam responded. "We'll meet at my car around 5. I imagine the boys will want to stop at The Varsity for a couple hot dogs before we go to the camp we'll be visiting."

"Sounds good," the young intern responded before disappearing down the hallway.

A couple minutes later and the first intern reappeared at Sam's doorway.

"OK, Sam," she said. "The TV crew is set up in the conference room and are ready for you."

"Thank you," Sam replied.

He pushed himself from behind the desk and slowly to his feet. He walked down the hallway stopping at a coffee maker to refill his travel mug. He continued down the hallway and stepped into the conference room where a camera was sitting on a tripod with two bright lights behind it. A reporter stood at one side talking to a man Sam assumed was the cameraman.

"Welcome to The Home Place," Sam announced.

"Thank you," the reporter replied. "I'm Susan, and this is Bill," she said, motioning toward the cameraman. "Are you good with standing, or would you prefer to sit at the table?" she asked.

"Standing is good with me," Sam answered with a smile.

They stepped in front of a large map on the wall of the conference room that illustrated the master plan community.

The cameraman made some adjustments and called out to them.

"OK," he said. "We're rolling."

"Hello, Atlanta!" she started. "I'm Susan Miller with WSB-TV. "Today's Community Action Series is looking at The Home Place, a large master planned community for the chronically homeless in Atlanta, situated near the Atlanta Motor Speedway just outside Hampton, Georgia. I have with us today Reverend Samuel Matthews, former pastor of Peachtree Street Church and founder of The Home Place. Reverend Matthews, tell us what your organization has going on here. It's very different than any shelter we have ever visited."

"Thank you, Susan," Sam responded. "We aren't a shelter at all, because shelters are temporary transitional housing for homeless. The Home Place is a community designed for the chronically homeless to come live and be restored. We believe that the primary cause of homelessness is a catastrophic loss of family. While there are a lot of other contributing factors that come into play, the catastrophic loss of family is the root cause. Feeding someone a meal, giving them a warm, dry place to sleep, and providing them with dry socks is all well and good, but it doesn't address the underlying cause – the catastrophic loss of family. You see, when you or I have a major crisis in our lives, we rely on our family to surround us and aid us through the crisis. With that support network, we can recover from the crisis and be restored. But if we experience a major life crisis and at the same time experience the loss of family, we are in an overwhelming tragedy. We have no one to turn to for support and assistance and are left to our own devices. This results in alcohol and drug use to try and escape the situation, loss of jobs and homes, and the overall deterioration of the quality of life."

Sam paused for a moment to let his response set in before he continued.

"Now, if we encounter someone who has experienced a major life crisis coupled with the catastrophic loss of family and we provide them a chicken sandwich and a cup of coffee and say, 'Go well with God," we haven't solved anything. We have just provided a Band-Aid. Here at The Home Place, we want to address the underlying issue. We do that by first providing a community where people are valued, cared for, and have a name. On the street, one of the first things that someone experiences is invisibility. The people that encounter them look away or down at the sidewalk. They won't make eye contact with a homeless person, let alone speak to them. Over an extended period of time, this chips away at their self-worth."

Sam continued, "As you walk through our community, you'll notice that homes are arranged facing each other. Every tiny house we build has a front porch that faces a couple other homes. So, when you wake up in the morning and step out on your porch, you are immediately facing your neighbor. This provides an opportunity for interaction, something the homeless person has missed for years. And once a person has developed self-worth and regained dignity, then and only then can we begin to address issues like addiction and mental health."

Susan nodded. "So, how does a homeless person become a resident here?" she asked.

"First we have to establish that the individual is what we refer to as chronically homeless," Sam responded. "That is, they have been living on the streets of the Atlanta metro area for a period of one year or more. Many of these folks we already know, because we've been out where their camps are, and we've developed relationships with them. Typically, a homeless man or woman is hesitant to move into a shelter because of past experiences and trust issues. A couple of times a month, groups from our organization go out and spend the night under bridges or in parks where the homeless camp. We get to know them, and they get to know us. They develop trust with us, and we work from there."

Susan smiled. "Do the residents pay rent here?" she asked.

"Absolutely," Sam quickly responded. "There are five different-size models across the grounds, and each has a different rent level. While some residents have social security benefits which they can use to pay rent, we also provide job opportunities within the community so our residents can earn a respectable income to pay rent and purchase items. One of the first things we do when a new resident joins our community is assist them with accessing many of the benefits that they've been unable to obtain on the street. Without an address, the government doesn't work well with providing social security or other benefits. When they move in here, they have an address and as you probably saw coming in, a community post office right out front."

The cameraman pointed to his watch and made a winding motion toward Susan.

"Thank you, Reverend Matthews, for inviting us out to see the community your group has built here," she replied. "And thank you for the work you're doing in our community. I'm Susan Miller for WSB-TV."

"That's a wrap!" the cameraman exclaimed.

"Thank you for coming out to see us," Sam said.

"It is our pleasure," Susan responded. "The young lady that greeted us has a golf cart waiting outside, so I believe we are going to take a tour and film some footage of the community."

"Sounds great," Sam replied. He noticed the young intern was standing silently in the corner of the room.

"All yours, Mary!" he said.

The cameraman began disassembling his gear, and Sam shook his and Susan's hands before walking out of the conference room.

Sam walked down the hallway and out of the office and made his way to the pavilion. He could already smell food. When he got closer, he could see that the volunteers for the day had lunch ready and community members were beginning to gather. Just entering the other side of the pavilion, Jim Harris was leading a group of volunteers in for lunch. Sam approached the serving line and checked in with the volunteers there. When he was confident they were ready to begin serving, he banged his travel mug on one of the picnic tables and stepped up on the seat.

"Good afternoon everyone!" Sam greeted the crowd. "We would like to thank this group of volunteers that have brought out a delicious meal, and we would like to thank this other group of volunteers who have been busy building our five newest homes. Without volunteers like y'all, we wouldn't be able to make this dream a reality. Let's pray.

"Father God, thank you for another gorgeous day in Georgia. Thank you for volunteers who commit their time to serving their community. And thank you for this wonderful meal we are about to enjoy. Bless it and bless those who partake of it. Amen."

Sam stepped down from the picnic table as the line of people filed through the serving line, where they were served plates of food. He walked over to one of the coffee urns and refilled his travel mug. One of the volunteers approached him, holding a plate full of food.

"I got you a plate, Sam," she said. "Pick out a seat, and I'll bring it to you."

"Oh!" Sam said, surprised by the generosity. "Thank you."

He shuffled across to a row of picnic tables and sat down next to a group of volunteers. The group rattled questions at him while he ate and answered. When he finished eating, he answered a few more questions before excusing himself. He walked to the edge of the pavilion where Cathy was standing chatting with one of the interns.

"Cathy," he said. "If anyone starts looking for me, I'm going to go lie down for a little bit. I was up all night at the hospital and I wanna take a short nap before we need to head out for our street camp out."

"Sure thing, Sam," Cathy said. "Do you want me to stop by and wake you later?"

"If you don't mind," Sam replied. "Make sure I'm up no later than 4."

"I got ya," Cathy replied.

Sam made his way back over to his tiny house. Once inside, he changed into a pair of pajamas and collapsed into bed. Within a few minutes, he was sound asleep and snoring.

CHAPTER 48

S am awoke to knocking on his door. He arose from his bed and stepped to the door. He opened the door to see Cathy.

"This is your 4 p.m. wakeup call!" she said cheerfully.

"Thanks, Cathy," Sam responded.

"No problem, Sam," she said. "Can I get you anything?"

"No, no. I'm good. I just need to get ready for our street camp-out," he answered.

"Alrighty then," Cathy replied. "I'll see you later."

She stepped down from his small front porch and headed across the way. Sam closed the door and walked back across his tiny home. He changed into a pair of soft jeans and a sweatshirt. After a quick trip through the bathroom, he made his way back to the offices.

Sam walked down the hallway to a storage room, retrieved a rolling cooler, and filled it with bottled water, a 12-pack of Coca-Cola, a 12-pack of Gatorade, and filled it with ice. He filled an empty cardboard box with random snacks off the shelves – beef jerky, peanut butter crackers, pop tarts, and snack mix.

An intern walked into the break room pulling a four-wheel dolly.

"Hi Sam," he said. "I've got a dozen blankets and a large bag of socks. Is this the rest of the stuff that needs to be loaded into your car?"

"Yes," Sam replied, happy to have the assistance.

"Alright," the intern replied. "I'll get it loaded for you."

The intern loaded the items onto the dolly and headed down the hallway. Sam returned to his office, locked his desk, and turned off the lights. He shuffled down the hall to the receptionist area in the front lobby.

"Alright," he called out to Cathy, who was sitting at the receptionist counter. "I'm headed into town for our camping trip. Thinking we'll probably end up under 85 near Buford Highway."

"Y'all be careful out there," Cathy responded.

Sam shuffled out to the tired Crown Vic. Fred, Lewis, and the male intern were congregated near the car chatting when he approached.

"Fred, Lewis, I take it y'all have met Brad?" Sam asked.

"Yeah," Fred replied. "We've been kinda telling him what to expect tonight. Sounds like he's seen a good bit, so there shouldn't be any great surprises."

"Good, good," Sam responded. "Who's up for The Varsity?"

Brad perked up.

"Oh yeah. I could do damage to some chili dogs."

Fred chuckled.

"I bet you can, young buck. I bet you can."

The men piled into the old Crown Vic. All the doors squeaked complaining of age and wear. The once light-blue seats were cracked and now more dark-gray than blue. Sam turned the key and the car cranked to life.

Sam wheeled the tired, old Crown Vic into the parking lot at The Varsity on North Avenue in downtown Atlanta. The guys filed out of the car and walked across the parking lot into the massive restaurant. They made their way through the sea of humanity and stepped into one of the lines at the counter. Sam stood at the back of the group as everyone ordered. He knew that hot dogs, French fries, or greasy onion rings were foods he should be avoiding, but he figured once a month would be al-right.

When it was his turn to order, he ordered a chili dog, two slaw dogs, onion rings, and a frosted orange (an orange-flavored milkshake). Twenty years ago, he would have ordered three chili dogs, but he had recently developed reflux. Over time, he learned if he buffered the chili dog with a slaw dog, he wouldn't experience the discomfort of heartburn.

Once the group all had their trays of food, they made their way to one of the TV rooms and settled in to eat. Sam dumped the onion rings onto a stack of napkins and did his best to mop up as much grease that was still on them before eating. As he ate, Sam wondered how many times he had grabbed a couple hot dogs at The Varsity over the years when he had served at Peachtree Church.

When the team finished their dinner, they dumped their trays in a trash can near the door. Sam returned to the counter and told the man at the register he had a catering order to pick up and gave him the order information. A few minutes later, the man reappeared with a cart with several trays of food. The guys carried the food back to the old Crown Vic and loaded them in the trunk. Sam started the car, turned, and looked at his passengers.

"Guys, we've been going out and sleeping under the bridges with our neighbors for a couple years now. Each trip is a unique and special opportunity to learn about them and love them. It's never an easy experience. The ground is hard to sleep on, and a lot of the areas smell of dirty, smelly, unbathed bodies and human excrement. There's always some mental illness tossed in the mix. But we're called to love our neighbors and the self-sacrifice we make tonight shows this community that we're invested and that we care."

The car was silent for a few moments as everyone contemplated Sam's words. Lewis looked up.

"Can I pray?"

Sam smiled.

"Of course you can."

Lewis nodded and bowed his head.

"God, we thank you for having warm food in our bellies and a safe place to sleep at night these days. We thank you for the opportunity to go back to the streets where we once spent the night every night. We thank you for the opportunity to bless the folks that are right where we were, struggling with many of the burdens we struggled with. Let our love shine like a candle in the night and help us to get out of your way to do what you want done. Amen."

A grin slipped across the face of everyone in the car.

"Amen," they said, nearly in unison.

Sam drove a short distance across the city streets and pulled to the curb under an overpass. A passing motorist on their way to or from work might have never noticed this was a homeless encampment. But for the men in the car, it was all too familiar, and the two shopping carts sitting next to the curb served as a reminder. The men crawled out of the car, which creaked when the doors opened. They began unloading the contents of the trunk into the shopping carts. They spread the aluminum trays of hot dogs, chili dogs, onion rings, and French fries across the hood of the Crown Vic and laid out paper plates. Sam gradually climbed the embankment under the bridge to where the homeless community sat.

"Good evening, friends. I have a load of hot dogs down at my car for anyone who would like a hot meal."

Several bodies stirred from inside tents and several raised up from where they had been lying. A few heads popped around a cement pillar under the bridge.

"Reverend Sam!" one man called out.

Sam smiled.

"In the flesh!"

Sam carefully descended the embankment back toward the car, with twelve people following behind him. They arrived at the car, and the guys served dinner to them. Sam stood at the edge of the crowd and watched the serving line.

"There are drinks on the trunk. Coffee, hot chocolate, and there is a cooler with Cokes, Gatorade, and water right behind the car."

Many people sat down on the edge of the curb to eat.

One man with matted dreadlocks whom Sam had not seen before looked up at him from his plate.

"You're taking a big chance feeding us, ya know."

Sam nodded.

"The thing is, they had a local city ordinance making it illegal to feed the homeless. The city police hated to enforce it so they kinda did it halfheartedly. But we raised a big enough fuss that a local law firm challenged it. It got struck down about 6 months ago by the Federal Circuit Court. It didn't much matter to us. Fine us. We'll pay it and be right out here next week."

The man smiled.

"You're alright, Preacher man. You're alright."

Sam smiled.

"Thanks. You can call me Sam. What's your name?"

The man's eyes opened wide.

"Nobody's asked me my name in two years. I'm Jacob."

Sam stuck out his hand. Jacob wiped his palm on his dirty pants and shook Sam's hand.

"Nice to meet you, Jacob."

Jacob quickly devoured four hot dogs and a pile of fries. He mopped his face with a napkin and looked up at Sam.

"Thanks for dinner, Sam."

Sam smiled.

"You're welcome, Jacob. I'm going to be spending the night. Do you have room up there for another sleeping bag?"

Jacob stood motionless for a moment.

"You're planning on sleeping under the bridge with us?"

Sam nodded.

"I have been a couple nights a month for the last couple years."

Jacob looked Sam in the eyes.

"Well, you'd be welcome to sleep in my tent."

Sam shook his head in disagreement.

"I wouldn't think of moving you out of your space. I just need a little bit of ground to unroll my sleeping bag."

Jacob cautiously scanned Sam from head to toe.

"How old are you, Sam, if you don't mind me asking?"

Without blinking, Sam replied, "I just crossed 70, but I'm spry as a young chicken."

Jacob grinned.

"And your 70-year-old back is content with sleeping on the ground?"

Sam chuckled.

"I wouldn't call it content, but I don't pay much attention to complaining."

Jacob took a long sip of hot chocolate.

"If you won't use my tent, you're welcome to sleep outside my door where I can watch out for you at least."

"Mighty obliged," Sam replied.

Sam recognized several faces and walked over to speak to them.

"Ronnie, Howard, Lester, how y'all doing?"

Three men raised their heads and looked in Sam's direction.

One jumped to his feet, tossing his plate to the curb. He scurried over to Sam and gave him a bear hug.

"Are y'all really fixin' me a house out there at your farm?"

Sam smiled.

"Yes we are, Ronnie! From what they tell me, it sounds like you're gonna be moving in next Friday."

Ronnie shuffled his feet as if he was dancing a jig.

"That's awesome, Sam! I haven't had a place of my own in three or four years."

Sam patted him on the back.

"The welcome wagon will be out to pick you up Friday morning, so be prepared!"

Brad started collecting trash into a black, 55-gallon garbage bag, while Fred and Lewis hawked the remaining food.

"OK, who's ready for seconds?" Fred shouted. "We still have a couple chili dogs and some onion rings over here."

Howard popped up off the curb and scrambled to the hood of the car.

"Hey Fred, let me help you out," he said laughing.

Fred grabbed two chili dogs with a set of tongs and placed them on Howard's plate.

"How ya been doing lately, Howard?"

Howard cut his eyes to the ground.

"I've been making do. You know the drill. You were on these streets. Constantly shuffling to try to keep business owners and cops from hasslin' ya. Somebody stole my backpack two weeks ago while I was sleeping in a shelter when it was the coldest. I always try to stay out of shelters."

Fred nodded all too knowingly.

"When you get full, go over there to those shopping carts. There are some backpacks, blankets, and socks. We should be able to get you fixed back up."

Howard looked Fred in the face.

"Thanks, man. I appreciate it."

Fred nodded.

"Have you considered coming out to the farm? It's a lot different than the shelters. You'd have your own place with a lock on the door. And neighbors who look out for you. Heck, you could even be my neighbor."

Howard shook his head.

"Nah, I had so many problems at the shelters, I never really considered it."

Fred nodded.

"Understood. Maybe you ought to think about checking it out sometime. Sam or Cathy would be happy to pick you up, carry you out there, and give you the ten-cent tour. You'd probably snag a pretty good lunch out of the deal."

Howard shifted his eyes for a moment and looked back up at Fred.

"Well, I guess if you went there and stayed, it must be a fair deal. Maybe I should check it out."

Fred smiled.

"At least take the tour. If you don't like it, it won't cost you anything but your time."

Howard nodded.

"I got a lot of time."

Sam stepped up and put his hand on Howard's shoulder.

"I couldn't help but overhear this conversation. You have my cell number. Call me Monday morning. Tell me where you're at. I'll pick you up. We'll grab some breakfast at Waffle

House, then I'll bring you out to the farm to hang out and look around, and you can eat lunch with the community. When you're ready to leave, I'll bring you back. Or if you're really adventurous, you can stay in one of our guest cabins for the night and see what it's like to live in a tiny house."

Howard grinned.

"Alright, I'll do that."

Sam looked him in the eye.

"If I haven't heard from you by 7:30 Monday morning, I'll be calling you."

Howard chuckled.

"Deal."

Lewis called out to the crowd who was finishing their dinner.

"Alright. In the two shopping carts over here, we have backpacks, blankets, and socks. If your backpack needs to be replaced, grab a new one, move your belongings into it and just drop your old one by the shopping cart. On the trunk of the car is some snacks to put in your packs for the next several days. We'll bring the cooler up to the campsite after we clean up here."

Fred and Brad finished cleaning up the trash from dinner while Sam and Lewis helped pass out blankets, socks, and snacks. Once the goods were distributed, they tossed three large trash bags in the trunk of the old Crown Vic. Lewis and Brad grabbed the cooler and headed up the hill for the camp. Sam and Fred grabbed the sleeping bags and pillows out of the car and followed the crowd back up the hill.

CHAPTER 49

Under the overpass, one of the members of the home-less camp had built a fire in a metal barrel. Most of the community sat around the barrel while a couple bedded down – one in a worn and dirty tent and another in a sleeping bag on the bare ground.

Lewis climbed the embankment carrying a plastic tote. As he approached the group gathered around the warming fire, one of them called out to him.

"Whatcha got there?"

Lewis grinned.

"I got a little surprise for y'all."

He set the tote on the ground and pulled out a piece of ex-panded metal that was just long enough to lay across the top of the barrel. The group silently watched his every move with great expectation. He reached back in the tote and revealed a smoke-stained coffee pot. Without a word, he pulled the top off the coffee pot and shook some coffee grounds from a foil bag into the top of the percolator basket. He set the basket aside for a moment and filled the coffee pot with bottled wa-ter. He placed the basket back in the coffee pot, secured the top and set it on the expanded metal atop the burn barrel.

"That's a pretty slick idea. You planned ahead. You musta been a Boy Scout," a voice called out from group.

Lewis grinned again.

"You ain't seen nothin' yet."

Lewis reached into the tote again and pulled out a couple foil pans.

"What the heck is that?" a man in the group asked.

Lewis smiled a toothy smile.

"Jiffy Pop popcorn. You just hold it by this wire handle and shake it over the fire, and directly you got yourself some popcorn. Who wants one? I have several."

The group suddenly stirred. A couple of men approached Lewis and were rewarded with a pan.

Lewis grabbed another handful and approached the men that were standing back taking it all in.

"Y'all like popcorn?"

He extended the pans toward them, and they quickly accepted. Shortly, half a dozen men were shaking Jiffy Pop popcorn pans over the burn barrel, carefully avoiding the coffee pot resting on the edge.

Lewis was still smiling.

"Man, all the nights I slept under this very overpass, I never even dreamed I would be cooking popcorn here. Coffee, yes. I used to make some in an old soup can. But popcorn? Nah, never dreamed of it."

Over the flicker of the flames, Lewis could see a couple snaggletooth grins as he spoke. Soon, the pans of popcorn swelled, looking like a large turban. The group pulled their pans off the fire and carefully tore the aluminum foil tops open, and steam arose from the contents. Lewis turned his attention to the coffee pot, which was percolating nicely with a repeating thump. He retrieved a sleeve of Styrofoam cups from the tote and held them up.

"Who's ready for coffee?"

Within a few minutes everyone in the group had a cup. Lewis directed them to a gallon bag with individual packets of sugar and creamer and wooden stir sticks. When the pot was empty, he quickly prepared another and set it back on the fire.

Howard made himself a cup of coffee and noticed the last person to pour a cup was Sam.

"'The last shall be first' or something like that?"

Sam chuckled.

"Something like that."

Jacob walked up to where they were standing.

"Preacher Sam, I'm gonna lay down and read a bit. You sure you won't take me up on my offer to use my tent?"

Sam shook his head.

"No, no. I'll be fine. I've slept several nights here on the ground with my sleeping bag."

Jacob realized he wasn't going to change his mind.

"Alright then, I'll read until I can't keep my eyes open. Holler if you need anything."

Sam smiled.

"Thank you, Jacob. I appreciate it."

After finishing his coffee, Sam made his way to where his bed roll laid just outside Jacob's tent. He pulled off his shoes and crawled into the sleeping bag.

Lewis and Brad put the unused items back in the tote, leaving the coffee pot and cups out for overnight refreshments. Brad carried the tote back to the car while Lewis trekked down the embankment with him for company.

"A little different than the shelters?"

Brad smiled.

"Kinda like a cross between camping in the woods and a night stay in a shelter all in one."

Lewis nodded in agreement.

As Brad was putting the tote into the trunk of the car, he noticed a woman pacing back and forth about 50 feet away. He looked at her curiously as she paced. Lewis noticed his inquisitive stare.

"That's Kendra."

Brad looked at Lewis.

"You know her?"

Lewis nodded in affirmation.

"Yup. She's lived on the streets for years. If you ask her what she's doing, she says she's waiting for a train."

Brad's furrowed his brow.

"The closest train station is 5 or 6 miles away."

Lewis nodded.

"Yeah and the closest MARTA bus stop is 5 blocks. But she does this every night just after dark. By 11 or so, she'll be gone."

Brad shook his head in disbelief.

"Alrighty then."

The two men climbed the embankment back up to the community. Brad sat down on the ground by the burn barrel, while Lewis made his way to his sleeping bag and settled in for the night.

CHAPTER 50

A round 2 a.m., Sam woke up to the sound of rain. He opened his eyes to recognize that it wasn't rain at all, but one of the group urinating on the concrete support holding up the overpass just a few feet from where he was lying. His back was aching, so he rolled to one side and tried to go back to sleep. After another hour, he was awake aching again. He slowly managed to get to a seated position and put on his shoes. He shifted to a standing position and ambled over to the warming fire. As he approached the fire, he felt that familiar ache in his chest. He looked around, saw a concrete block stood on end, and sat down. He lowered his head, resting it in his hands, with his elbow on one knee. He concentrated on slow, deep breaths while waiting for the pain to ease. After a few minutes, he raised his head and looked down the embankment toward his car. He rose to his feet and started the descent to the street. Once he reached the car, he opened the passenger door and the glove box and retrieved a Ziploc bag containing his nitroglycerin. He popped the pill under his tongue and sat down on the front seat of the car. He leaned back and closed his eyes as he waited for relief. After a few minutes, he felt the intense headache that assured him the medication was working. After a few more minutes, the chest pain began to ease, and he fell asleep sitting up in the car.

Sam awoke around 4:30 a.m. to the sound of a voice calling his name. He opened his eyes to see Jacob standing next to the car, peering thru the window at him.

"Preacher Sam, you OK?"

Sam nodded in affirmation and opened the car door.

"Yeah, I'm alright, Jacob. I came down to take my prescription and fell asleep in the seat."

Jacob stared intently at Sam.

"I got up to pee, and your sleeping bag was empty. I figured I better find you. On the streets, we have to kinda stick together in the dark. There's a lot of meanness on the streets."

Sam nodded again.

"I appreciate it, Jacob. I'm thinking I am going to go back up to camp."

That sounded like a good idea to Jacob. He offered Sam his hand and helped him out of the car and to his feet.

"I found an old pallet we can break some wood off to build the fire back up."

They gradually walked up the embankment. Jacob slid the expanded metal back to one side of the top of the barrel and dropped broken pieces of wood from the discarded pallet into the fire. Once he had a good amount of wood in the barrel and the fire was warming back up, he slid the expanded metal back across the top of the barrel.

Sam made his way back to his sleeping bag and kicked off his shoes. He knelt down and crawled back into bed. Jacob followed behind and flopped back into his sleeping bag in the tent.

"If you need anything, Preacher Sam, you just call my name."

"Thank you, Jacob," Sam quietly replied.

Sometime around 7 a.m., Sam woke up to the sound of voices. He opened his eyes and realized that most of the community was up and stirring about. Brad approached, knelt next to him, and held out a Styrofoam cup of coffee.

"Morning, Sam. I brought you a little gift."

Sam gladly accepted the warm cup of coffee.

"Thanks, Brad."

Brad nodded.

"Guess they're all about to start their morning routine."

Sam took a long sip of coffee before responding.

"Yeah, some will be going down to the nearby shelter for the daily free breakfast. Some will probably head to a nearby coffee shop, get a cup of coffee, and sit in the warm, comfortable chairs as long as they can before someone runs them off."

Brad understood the routine, having served in area shelters.

"I've passed out what was left in the cooler, so I'm going to carry it down to the car. I'll be back up in a few."

Sam and the team rolled up their sleeping bags, collected trash, packed up their belongings, and carried them down to the car. Some of the community descended the hill and stopped at the car. Some thanked them for coming and some gave hugs, while others quietly began walking down the street.

As the guys packed into the car, Sam quietly asked Brad to drive.

"If you don't mind, how about taking us to Waffle House for a little breakfast on the way back to The Home Place?"

Brad grinned.

"We can make that happen."

CHAPTER 51

S am woke on Monday morning without the need of an alarm. Once showered and dressed, he made his way to his office. As he stepped into the reception area, he could smell coffee. He headed straight over to refill the mug he had started at home. He proceeded down the hall and to his office and sat down behind his desk. He looked at the time on his phone, 7:30 a.m.

"Someone didn't call, and I made a promise."

Sam dialed Howard's number. He answered on the second ring.

"You weren't kidding were you, Sam?" Howard said answering the phone.

Sam laughed. "Not at all, Howard. I believe offering a man who is living on the street a decent place to live and a community that supports him is a priority. I don't ever want to miss the opportunity to offer someone a better situation. Have you had breakfast yet?"

Howard cleared his throat. "Yeah, I just finished a plate at the mission and was fixin' to walk down to one of the benches in Grant Park."

"Alright," Sam responded. "Still up for taking a tour today?"

Howard paused for a moment. "Sure, I wouldn't mind a little change of scenery. Not like anyone's gonna miss me if I'm not out here."

Sam smiled.

"OK. I'm gonna get one of the staff and a van, and we will head your direction. Morning traffic in Atlanta is never easy, so I won't even pretend to guess when we'll get there, but I'll call you when we reach Grant Park."

"Deal," Howard replied.

Sam closed his phone and walked back to the reception area.

"I need a driver and a van for a potential new resident. Who's available?"

Cathy popped her hand up in the air.

Sam looked a bit surprised.

"OK, but we'll need someone to man the front desk in your absence."

Cathy grinned.

"I think Brad can handle my normal morning routine. He's hung around long enough to know how the volunteer sign in goes, and he's familiar with the rest of the staff."

Sam saw Brad standing near the front door holding a cup of coffee.

"What say ye, young Brad?"

Brad nodded.

"I'm good with it if you're up to her driving."

Cathy laughed.

"Let me grab a set of keys."

She stepped into the workroom behind her and took a set of keys from the lockbox. Sam looked at Brad, who had made his way behind the counter.

"You're in charge, Brad."

Brad chuckled at the idea of being in charge.

Cathy and Sam got into one of the community vans parked at the entrance of the community and headed into the city.

After almost an hour, they reached Grant Park, and Sam called Howard's phone. Howard answered, and they set a meeting spot. Cathy pulled into the parking lot inside one of the park entrances. Sam crawled out of the van and surveyed the horizon. As he strained to focus his eyes, he caught movement to his right. After a few minutes, the approaching figure waved his hand at Sam. When Howard reached where Sam was standing, Sam threw his hand out and shook his hand while simultaneously pulling him in for a hug.

"I know this seems like a big step but relax and know you haven't committed to anything at this point. We're just going to give you a tour and some lunch, and then you can decide what the next steps are. OK?"

Howard nodded in agreement.

"Alright."

When they reached the van, Sam introduced Howard and Cathy.

"Howard, this is Cathy. She normally works the front desk in our office building. All the residents in our community know her, and so do the volunteers. If you ever have any questions, you can call our main phone line and reach her. She is a wealth of information on how everything works, what's going on, who lives where, and anything else you want to know."

Cathy chuckled as she handed Howard a business card.

"He makes me sound like an internet search engine with tennis shoes. But in all seriousness, here is one of our cards with our phone number and email. Anytime you have a question or just need to talk, call us or email us. We have a lot going on, and we can help in a number of ways, from getting your Social Security benefits, Medicare, transportation to a doctor, counselor, or therapist, grocery shopping, bus passes, or even job opportunities."

As they began the ride back to The Home Place, Howard slipped the card into his shirt pocket. He couldn't remember the last time someone gave him a business card.

"Give me the skinny on your community. I've heard it mentioned on the street, but I'm not sure I completely understand it all. How's it different than a shelter?"

Cathy smiled.

"First of all, you have your own home. You don't have to share it with anyone. We have several different sizes to choose from, and each has a monthly rental rate. Before you ask, our staff will work with you on establishing income to afford your rent, groceries, and any medication you need. We have a lot of job opportunities within the community so you can check them out and pick out something you want to do. We have a bus stop, so you can work outside the community if you choose, or you can transfer to the MARTA system and ride anywhere in Atlanta that there is a train or bus stop. We have a medical facility where doctors, nurses, and dentists volunteer. A lot of times, you don't even have to leave the community for routine appointments. We also have counselors and therapists who volunteer at our counseling and addiction center. We have a huge garden, and we raise chickens. Every week, we have a farmer's market where you can get free, fresh vegetables and farm-fresh eggs. We have a library that offers books and videos on loan. We have a carpentry shop and an artist shop where some of our neighbors create items that we sell in our gift shop and for local merchants."

Howard looked out the window at the passing traffic.

"This doesn't sound like any shelter I've ever been to before. This sounds like a small town."

Sam smiled.

"Precisely. It's a small community of people who have been where you are and have chosen to live in a safe and comfortable environment. Some of our volunteers and staff have elected to buy a tiny home or an RV and live in the community as

296 | ALLEN MADDING

well. I have a tiny home on a small cul-de-sac with four neighbors who were formerly homeless. They regularly check on me, and I regularly check on them."

Howard nodded.

"So, is it like a church shelter where you gotta be clean and sober before you can stay there?"

Sam shook his head from side to side.

"Not at all. We have no expectations that anyone can kick an addiction while living on the streets. You're invited to live in our community, and you can work with the staff at the counseling and addiction center for overcoming any addiction."

Howard's raised his eyebrows.

"Wow! Alright."

When they arrived at The Home Place and drove in under the archway, Sam could see Howard straining his neck to try and take in everything he was seeing.

"Wow, this is amazing! It really is a small town. How many homes are in here?"

Cathy piped up.

"We presently have 85 occupied homes, and there are 12 under construction. There are another 10 RVs on order."

Cathy parked the van and led them to one of the golf carts with two forward-facing bench seats.

"Howard, I'm going to drive us around the community and give you an overview. At any time if you want to stop and walk around, just say the word. I'm not on any timeline. There are five different models of homes, including the RVs, and the rental rate on each are different. I'm going to first show you one of each of the different models and point out the major differences. Don't worry yourself with the rental rates right now. If you decide you want to live in our community, our staff will work with you to get you connected to your benefits and to find a job that suits your needs. Some of our neighbors started out in the smallest of our homes and later decided to upgrade. That's always an option, as well as going the other direction."

Sam pointed toward a large building on one side.

"Howard, that is the convenience store and gift shop. It has some basic groceries and items like a convenience store on the street. Next to the store is a small post office, and next to it is a laundromat."

They rode a little farther and stopped in front of a group of large canvas tents set up around a stone fire pit.

"This is our community tent section," Cathy pointed out. "Originally, we did not have tents, but some of our neighbors said they weren't comfortable moving into a tiny house. They had spent several years in tents and sleeping in the open, and they were struggling with the adjustment. We created the tent community. Some of the original people who chose the tents went on to a tiny house, and a couple are still in the tents. They each have a raised wooden floor, a queen size mattress, electricity and lighting, a small refrigerator, a small dresser, and a table and chairs. They don't have stoves in them, but there is a community kitchen right over there with a restroom and shower facility on the backside of it."

They stepped off the golf cart, and Cathy led them to one of the tents. They stepped up on the porch, which had two camping chairs and a small wooden table. She opened the canvas front door of the tent to reveal the interior. There was a large rug in the center of the wooden floor and a bed complete with linens and blankets against the back wall. On one side was a small bedside table and lamp. On the other, a chest of drawers. To one side sat a table and two chairs beside a small refrigerator with a microwave on top of it. On the other side was a re-cliner and a reading lamp.

"Wow!" Howard remarked. "This is downright nice right here. This is a huge upgrade to my tent. It's only got enough room to get my backpack and sleeping bag inside. And I really like that front porch! Sam knows I like the fire in the burn barrel under the bridge, and that fire pit seems familiar."

They continued on, looking at one of the RVs and three of the different-size tiny homes. Next, they saw the chapel, the main office building, the medical center, and the counseling and treatment center. They concluded their tour at the pavilion.

"Lunch is ready," Sam noted.

Howard looked amazed at the crowd lining up to be served.

"Howard, we have several volunteers working here today building tiny houses, while others are helping in the garden and working on landscaping. We serve a community lunch for all our neighbors in the community, the volunteers, and our staff. This can be a pretty big crowd at times. But the tables only seat 8 people, which brings it all back down to where you can have a conversation and not feel like you've been lost in the crowd."

They made their way through the serving line, got plates, and found a table. Once seated, a group of four people wearing matching T-shirts joined them at the table. As they ate, Sam and Cathy made conversation with the group and discovered they worked for a local insurance company that was volunteering on the construction of one of the tiny homes.

"It's really nice of y'all to take time away from your family and lives and come out here and work," Howard said meekly between bites of food.

One of the volunteers smiled. "We're thrilled to be here!" she said. "I think this is an amazing community that provides wonderful opportunities for people who have struggled with homelessness."

Howard finished eating and sat contemplating for some time while the rest of the table chit-chatted. Finally, he looked up at Cathy.

"Miss Cathy," he said quietly.

"Yes, Howard?" she answered.

"What would I have to do to be able to move into one of them tents? I really took a liking to them."

A huge toothy smile broke across Cathy's face.

"Well, buddy, we can walk over to the office and put your application in now if you like."

Howard nodded.

"I'd like that."

CHAPTER 52

On Friday morning, Brad and Gladys were busy preparing the new tiny house for their newest resident, Ronnie. Brad learned on the overnight that Ronnie was an Atlanta Falcons fan, so he picked up a few items to decorate his new home.

Gladys made the bed up with red and black sheets, pillowcases and a comforter. Brad hung a Falcons" Rise Up!" banner above the headboard. He tucked a red and white football with the Falcons logo printed on it on one of the bookshelves in the main living area and draped a Falcons blanket over the arm of the recliner. Gladys hung a wooden sign that said "HOME" over the small dining table. Brad packed the cupboard with canned goods and the refrigerator with meat, fresh vegetables, and bottled water. Gladys put two boxes of coffee and two mugs on a shelf over the coffee maker. Brad stocked the small bathroom cabinet with shampoo, soap, toothpaste, shaving cream, and a safety razor. Gladys followed behind him to stack bath towels, hand towels, and washcloths on the shelf over the toilet.

While they were completing their work decorating the tiny house, Sam and Lewis were pulling up to the familiar overpass where Ronnie stood with his backpack slung over his shoulder. Lewis rolled the passenger window down and called out to him.

"Hey buddy, you need a ride somewhere?"

Ronnie laughed.

"As a matter of fact, I need a ride home," he said with a grin.

Sam smiled from behind the wheel of the van.

"Funny, that just happens to be where we're headed."

Lewis opened the side doors and helped Ronnie with his backpack while he climbed in one of the rear bench seats.

"It's kinda odd, I guess. But I've been out here long enough I will almost miss the daily routine. At the same time though, I am not going to miss sleeping on the ground and worrying if my belongings will still be there when I wake up."

Lewis nodded knowingly.

"I understand where you're coming from with that, but after a couple of weeks adjusting to your new routine, it will be a lot easier. A warm, comfortable bed every night and a shower helped me adjust kinda quickly."

When they arrived at The Home Place, Ronnie looked up at the archway over the entrance. On both sides of the archway were posters that read: "Welcome home, Ronnie!" He was speechless.

Sam parked the van, and they packed into one of the golf carts. Sam drove them to Ronnie's new home. Gladys and Brad were sitting in rocking chairs on the tiny home's front porch as they approached.

Brad popped up out of the rocker and helped Gladys to her feet.

"Welcome home, Ronnie!" Gladys greeted him. She reached out her hand, which held a door key.

Ronnie took the key and stared at it in his hand for several minutes and finally looked up at her, "It's really mine, isn't it?"

Brad smiled.

"Yeah, it is. Walk on in and take a look around."

Ronnie opened the door and stepped inside. He gradually gazed around the main living area with a table and two chairs, a recliner, and a bookcase with several books lining the shelves, and his eyes stopped. He reached and picked up the football.

"Falcons! Heck yeah!" he said with a huge grin.

Brad stepped past him and opened the pantry cabinet door.

"We've stocked you up on some groceries to get you settled."

He opened the refrigerator door.

Ronnie was speechless.

Brad closed the cabinet and the refrigerator.

"Over here is your bathroom," he said, opening the bathroom door, "complete with a nice-size shower, towels, and toiletries."

Ronnie was stunned.

"And back here is your bedroom," Brad said, guiding Ronnie to see the freshly decorated area.

"Man!" Ronnie declared. "It's like y'all fixed this place up with everything I like!"

Gladys and Brad made their way back out to the front porch and down to where Sam, Cathy, and Lewis were waiting outside. After a few moments, Ronnie appeared on the front porch.

"Ronnie, we are pleased to welcome you to our community and as our newest neighbor," Cathy said. "If you need anything, members of our staff and I are available at the front office right over there," she said, pointing to the large office building. "The office is open 8 a.m. till 6 p.m., Monday through Saturday."

Lewis cleared his throat.

"And I live in the tiny house directly behind us. When you walk out on your front porch, you're looking at my front porch. If you need anything, feel free to come over. I'm happy to help."

Ronnie wiped the corner of his eyes while trying to keep from making any eye contact with anyone.

Sam walked up on the porch and gave him a hug.

"You're home now, and your neighbors are here to support you. There is going to be a lunch celebration at noon in the pavilion, and you are the guest of honor. We're going to let you settle in, and we'll be back over to escort you to lunch after bit."

Gladys gave Ronnie a moment to compose himself.

"I know you have a load of clothes that you'd like to have washed. If you'll give me your laundry, I'll carry it over to the laundromat and get 'em all washed up for you."

Ronnie looked her eye to eye.

"You don't need to do that. Y'all have already done so much for me."

Gladys shook her head.

"I won't take no for an answer. It's a tradition that we do your first load of laundry, so hand it over."

Ronnie stepped back in the door of his new home and started to dig dirty clothes out of his backpack. Gladys stepped up on the porch and handed him a large duffle bag that had his name embroidered on it.

"Here is your new laundry bag."

Ronnie looked up.

"Wow! Thank you!"

He quickly filled the laundry bag with all the clothes from his backpack. Gladys grabbed it up and carried it to the golf cart.

"I'll get all this back to you later this afternoon."

She drove away in the golf cart toward the laundry mat.

Ronnie stepped back inside his tiny home. He wiped the corners of his eyes with his shirt sleeve. He opened the cabinet above the coffee maker and pulled out a mug that had his name printed on it and a small cup that held premeasured coffee. He stared at it for a couple of moments.

"Ain't that fancy?" he said to himself.

He stared at the coffee maker for a minute before he figured out how to open it and put the coffee in the machine. He placed his mug under the spout and pressed the power button.

"This is the fanciest coffee maker I think I've ever seen. It beats having to shake grounds into a percolator."

After several minutes of noises, three buttons on the machine flashed in blue. Ronnie leaned over the top of the machine and noticed each button had the picture of a coffee cup next to it. He pushed the one that appeared to be the largest. Hot coffee began dripping into his mug.

"I guess I've mastered the coffee maker. Wonder what else I will learn today."

After finishing his cup of coffee, Ronnie opened the door of the bathroom and looked it all over again. He decided a shower would certainly be nice. He pulled off his work boots and clothes, adjusted the water temperature, and crawled under the flowing water.

"Wow, I can take a shower anytime I want to. This is freaking awesome!"

When he finished showering, he grabbed a large, fluffy towel and dried off. A thought instantly ran through his mind. He didn't want to put his dirty street clothes back on after taking a shower and smelling good for the first time in weeks. He stepped out of the bathroom wrapped in a towel and walked into the bedroom. He opened the small closet at one end of the bed to find several clean pair of underwear and socks in small cubbies down one side. To his surprise and delight, on one shelf was what looked like a brand-new pair of blue jeans, and on the shelf below it was a red Atlanta Falcons sweatshirt. He quickly dressed in clean clothes and returned to the bathroom to look at himself in the mirror. He picked up a comb from a mug on the vanity countertop and combed his hair.

After dressing, Ronnie sat down in his recliner and slowly looked around his home, taking in every detail. After several minutes, there was a knock on the door. Ronnie scrambled to his feet and opened the door to greet Gladys and Brad.

"How's it going, Ronnie?" Brad asked.

A huge beaming smile broke across Ronnie's face.

"It's like Christmas when I was a kid – only on steroids!"

Gladys grinned.

"Pretty nifty shirt you got there."

Ronnie continued to beam.

"Somebody really did their detective work. All the clothes in here are my size!"

Gladys nodded while casting a glance in Brad's direction.

"Santa's li'l helpers have been busy lately, Ronnie."

Ronnie chuckled.

"I guess so."

Brad looked at his phone and then looked up to Ronnie.

"Are you hungry?"

Ronnie nodded.

"Yeah I am."

Gladys patted his shoulder.

"Well, let's get you over to the pavilion. I 'spect lunch should be about ready."

The three loaded onto an awaiting golf cart and drove to the pavilion where Ronnie estimated there were over 100 people milling around.

As they stepped off the golf cart, Ronnie heard a voice over the PA system.

"Lunch is ready to be served. Thank you to everyone who has come out to volunteer today. I want to welcome our guest of honor and the newest neighbor in our community. Please give a round of applause for Ronnie!"

Ronnie felt himself blush. He threw a hand up in the air and waved.

"As guest of honor, we would like you to be first in the serving line for lunch, Ronnie."

Ronnie looked down at his feet, not wanting a bunch of attention. He felt someone grab his elbow. He looked up to see Gladys.

"Come on, let's get up front before they get all the good stuff."

Ronnie went along without argument knowing it wasn't wise to argue with a woman – especially a strong-willed, older woman like Gladys.

As they moved to the front, Ronnie recognized Sam Mathews voice.

"Let us pray. God thank you for another beautiful day at The Home Place. Please bless our friend and neighbor, Ronnie, as he gets adjusted to living with us. Thank you for everyone here that has made today possible and is laboring to make a day like this possible for many more of our homeless friends. Thank you for this wonderful-smelling hot meal. May you bless it to our nourishment and bless our conversations to bless our neighbors. Amen."

Ronnie lifted his eyes.

"Amen."

A volunteer behind the table greeted him.

"Hi, Ronnie. Would you like a sloppy joe?"

Ronnie nodded.

"Any chance I can have two?"

The volunteer smiled.

"Sure you can!"

He placed two buns on a plate, filled them with sloppy joe meat, and topped them with a bun. He handed Ronnie the plate.

"They've got a lot more choices. Fill that plate the way you want it."

Ronnie nodded.

"Thank you."

The three navigated through the serving line, with Ronnie's plate gradually stacking higher and higher. When they reached the end of the serving line, Brad led them to one of the picnic tables where Sam was sitting with a travel mug of coffee.

Sam scrambled to his feet as Ronnie sat his plate down on the table. Ronnie grabbed him and hugged him with all his might.

"Thank you for everything you've done for me over the years. I love you, Sam."

A tear trickled down Sam's cheek.

"I love you too, buddy. It's my greatest honor to call you my friend, and friends look out for each other."

They sat down and began eating. A volunteer came to their table and got their drink requests.

"Don't get too spoiled by this, Ronnie," Gladys advised.

"Tomorrow, you'll have to get your own drink from the tables on the far wall."

Ronnie chuckled.

After regaining his composure, Sam looked up.

"Are you getting settled into your home alright? Is there anything you need?"

Ronnie swallowed a bite of food, wiped his mouth with a napkin, and looked up.

"So far, I've managed to figure out that fancy coffee maker that uses the tiny cups of premeasured coffee, and I had one of the most relaxing showers I've had in years. I think I'm doing alright."

He flashed a big grin and took another bite of food.

Sam smiled back.

"Good deal. After lunch, Brad is going to bring you over to the office. Our staff will help you get your mailbox, apply for Social Security and Medicare, get a bus pass, and set you up for any appointments you want with the barber shop, dentist, doctors, or counselors. None of it is required. Whatever you want or need, we're happy to help you get set up. Ask them anything you have questions about, and they'll point you in the right direction."

CHAPTER 53

After a couple of months living in his tiny home at The Home Place, Ronnie was working his job cleaning the laundromat and the adjoining bath house when Sam walked into the laundromat.

"Good morning, Ronnie!"

Ronnie looked up and greeted him with a smile.

"Good morning, Sam! What's going on?"

Sam set his coffee mug on top of one of the dryers.

"Well, tomorrow night, three of us are going to your old stomping grounds to spend the night on the street with some of our homeless friends. I wanted to see if you were interested in going with us."

Ronnie paused and stared off into the distance. After a moment, he looked back up into Sam's gaze.

"Ya know, ever since I moved in here, I been thinking I wish some of the guys I knew on the street could have this. Just be given a chance to have a better life, get help with their addictions, and have a dry place to sleep. I'll go with y'all. Can we stop and get some chili dogs to take with us?"

Sam chuckled.

"Brother, it's a tradition. We eat at The Varsity, and we carry a couple trays with us for the community out there on the street."

Ronnie smiled.

"I kinda liked that part. That and those popcorn pans you guys have."

Sam chuckled again.

"Jiffy Pop. You know when I was a kid, my folks would get a couple of those, and we would pop popcorn on the stove. I thought it was the greatest thing ever. Several years ago, I saw them in a grocery store and thought that would be neat to carry on the street when we went out. Now we stock them in the li'l market here, and we have them for carrying on the street."

Ronnie nodded.

"I never saw them growing up, but they sure make a pretty good snack over a burn barrel."

Sam smiled.

"How are you liking this job?"

Ronnie looked up.

"I like it a lot, Sam. I tried for a long time on the street to get a job – any job, really – but no one wanted to hire someone who didn't have a home address or hadn't bathed in a week or so. Now, this is my laundromat. Once in a while, I got to use one on the street, but they were always dirty and dark. I keep this place shining and keep all the lights working. I know a little bit about working on appliances and plumbing, so if something were to break, chances are I could fix it. And I'm earning enough to pay my rent and have a li'l spending money for the first time in a very long time."

Sam nodded.

"Well, don't let me keep you. We'll meet up at my old car Saturday around 5 p.m. I'll bring your sleeping bag and pillow."

Ronnie nodded in confirmation.

"Sounds good."

Ronnie returned his attention to making the laundromat shine like a new penny for his neighbors.

CHAPTER 54

When Saturday afternoon rolled around, Ronnie made his way to the parking lot and to Sam's old car. Ronnie leaned himself against the rear of the car and quietly drank in his surroundings. It was a beautiful landscape: trees, shrubs, the garden in one direction, the farm animals close by, and the tiny houses each uniquely designed and tastefully decorated.

Just before 5 p.m., Sam and Brad came walking up.

"Good afternoon, Ronnie," Sam called out.

"Good afternoon, y'all," Ronnie responded.

"Been waiting long for us?" Sam asked.

"Nah, nah. Just enjoying the weather and taking in the scenery. This is a really nice place to live," Ronnie replied.

Lewis joined the group, and they piled in the old car. The doors squeaked open and closed.

"We've got a trunk full of socks, shoes, blankets, drinks, and Jiffy Pop," Brad reported with a smile.

"Who's ready for some Varsity hot dogs and Frosted Oranges?" Sam asked as he started the car.

Ronnie piped up, "As always! I've been eating good here since I moved in, but I still get a hankerin' for some chili dogs and onion rings."

Everyone in the car laughed.

"They're one addiction I haven't kicked since I left the streets," Lewis volunteered.

Sam laughed.

"Probably because you don't want to kick that addiction."

Lewis chuckled.

"You have a point, Preacher. You have a point."

As per their tradition, after they finished eating, they carried several trays of hot dogs, chili dogs, french fries, and onion rings to the tired, old car.

Ronnie sported a huge smile.

"I have to admit, it makes my heart happy to carry this meal up to the camp under the overpass. I won't ever forget where I came from, and I like giving back to the folks that are still out there. I wonder if Miss Kendra would like a few hot dogs while she's waiting for the train tonight."

When they arrived at the overpass, Ronnie quickly got out of the car and headed up the embankment while everyone else set out the food. When he reached the camp at the top of the embankment, he greeted those seated around the burn barrel and searched the surroundings. He soon located Howard.

"Howard! I hear you've been approved for one of the big canvas tents at The Home Place."

Howard looked up from where he had been sitting on one side of a tent out of the direct line of sight of those at the burn barrel.

"Say what?"

Ronnie repeated himself.

Howard dropped the metal cup in his hand trying to scramble to his feet.

"You can't be serious. Don't kid me about something like this, Ronnie."

Ronnie shook his head.

"Nah, nah. I wouldn't joke about something like this, Howard. I talked with Miss Gladys and Miss Cathy this morning. They said you've been approved. You're gonna be my neighbor again!"

Howard's eyes grew big.

"You think I can manage not to get thrown out? I'm still drinking and all."

Ronnie shook his head again.

"Nah, man. Look, we've all come from the same place. We're all dealing with our past and with addictions. When you are ready to try to work through all that, they have folks in the community to help. As long as you don't get into a fight with someone or something like that, you'll be fine. Thing is, at night, it's so quiet and peaceful. I didn't realize how much I missed peace and quiet till I moved out there. I've slept better than I have in years. You're gonna love it!"

Howard grinned a cautious grin.

"It's a big step. I hope I don't mess nothing up."

Ronnie shook his head again.

"Howard, you're going to be surrounded by neighbors in a community that want the best for you and care about you. It's a lot to comprehend. I've been there for six weeks now, and I'm still getting used to it, but it's so nice to have a dry bed, clean clothes, food to eat, and access to a bathroom and showers."

Howard nodded.

"That does sound pretty good."

Ronnie motioned toward the group gathered at the burn barrel.

"Let's get these folks down to the car and get 'em fed."

Howard nodded again.

"Sounds like a plan."

They walked up to the community gathered around the barrel. Ronnie recognized several, but there were three or four he didn't. He cleared his throat.

"Hey y'all, we got a load of chili dogs, hot dogs, slaw dogs, cheeseburgers, french fries, and onion rings down at the car at the bottom of this hill. Got a bunch of cold drinks, coffee, tea, and hot chocolate, too. Anybody hungry?"

Dust kicked up as people jumped to their feet from sitting on the ground and concrete blocks and lying in the tents nearby. Soon, a little over a dozen homeless men and women were descending the hill toward the car.

Brad looked up from where he had just finished organizing the spread of food across the hood of the old car.

"Looks like someone rang the dinner bell."

The crowd filled plates and grabbed drinks and scattered along the curb to eat. Sam spotted Howard and made his way to where he sat eating a plate of hot dogs and cheeseburgers.

"Howard, my friend. How are you doing?"

Howard wiped his mouth on the shoulder of his shirt.

"I'm still above ground, Preacher. How about you?"

Sam smiled.

"I'm better than I deserve for sure."

Howard nodded while taking another bite of food.

"Preacher Sam, can you confirm a rumor I heard?"

Sam raised an eyebrow.

"Depends on the rumor, I guess."

Howard swallowed hard.

"I hear tell that I've been approved for one of these big tents I took a shining to when I was out there."

Sam nodded and smiled.

"Not a rumor at all. That's a fact. When do you think you'd be ready to move in with us?"

Howard looked directly into Sam's eyes.

"I'm ready right now, if you think I won't get kicked out."

Sam engaged Howard's stare.

"Howard, my friend, you're not gonna get kicked out unless you get in a fist fight. We have very few rules. I have spent the night here with you before, and I've seen how you interact with the community. I'm confident you'll be just fine. We're a community of people struggling to free ourselves from addictions and encouraging one another."

Howard nodded.

"Well then, I guess I'm ready when y'all are."

Sam smiled.

"Excellent. I'll let Cathy know. She'll give you a call Monday and get things planned for when and where we can pick you up to bring you to your new home."

Howard smiled, revealing a couple missing teeth.

"Cool."

Sam saw Jacob sitting just a few feet down the curb and walked over to greet him.

"Good evening, Jacob. Get enough to eat?"

Jacob looked up with a grin.

"I sure did, Preacher. I sure like them chili dogs. You doin' alright?"

Sam patted his shoulder.

"Better than I deserve, Jacob."

Jacob finished mopping the remains of his plate with a piece of hotdog bun and looked up at Sam as he popped it in his mouth.

"Make sure you put your bed roll up there by my tent, so I can look out for you tonight."

Sam nodded.

"I'll do that. Thank you."

Brad banged his knuckles on the fender of Sam's old car.

"Folks, there's clean blankets, socks, and coats in these shopping buggies here by the car. When you've finished eating, come see me and let's get you fixed up. We've got a couple pair of work boots as well, if anyone is needing to replace their shoes."

A line soon formed at the shopping carts, and Sam and Brad began handing out clothing and blankets. While they did, Ronnie and Lewis bagged up garbage. Soon, the shopping carts were empty, and the community had reconvened around the burn barrel at the top of the embankment. Sam filled the percolator and set it on the metal grate over the edge of the fire. Not long after, several were shaking Jiffy Pop pans over the barrel.

A little before midnight, Sam spread his bed roll near Jacob's tent and laid down. Brad sat conversing with a small group at the burn barrel, while Ronnie eased down the embankment with a paper bag under one arm. He quietly walked down to the corner where Kendra stood pacing, waiting for a train that never would arrive.

"Evening, Miss Kendra."

Kendra stopped her pacing for a moment and looked up at Ronnie.

"Would you like a couple hot dogs and a bottle of water while you're waiting on your train?"

Kendra eyed the bag in Ronnie's arm.

"Sure," she said shifting her eyes from the bag to his eyes and back again.

Ronnie stepped forward and held the bag out to her. She took a cautious step toward him, grabbed the bag, and stepped back quickly. She opened that bag and peered into it seeming surprised the contents were as described.

"Thank ya," she said.

Ronnie nodded.

"You're welcome. Have a good night and stay safe."

He turned and headed back toward where Sam's old car was parked, all while feeling her stare at the back of his head. He didn't turn around to engage her, knowing she was wondering why one homeless guy would be giving her a sack of food. Once he reached the car, he turned and made his way up the embankment toward the group under the overpass. He casually glanced back in Kendra's direction. He could see her pacing again while eating a hot dog. He smiled and made his way to the circle of community at the burn barrel.

Around midnight, the conversations quieted, and most had stretched out to sleep.

CHAPTER 55

Somewhere in the early hours of morning, Sam woke with an intense, crushing pain in his chest. He realized he was sweating profusely. He instantly thought about a nitro-glycerin pill. He didn't have one with him. He knew there were a couple stashed in the glove box of the old Crown Vic down the hill, but he couldn't seem to overcome the pain enough to even sit up, let alone walk down to the car. He closed his eyes and tried to slow his breathing. The pain wouldn't subside. He quietly began praying while struggling to breathe. Soon the pain seemed to ease, and he felt a rush of cool air. His arthritis-ravaged back and joints stopped aching, and his chest didn't hurt anymore. He could hear singing and felt light as a feather. After several minutes, he felt himself stand up, and he heard a deep voice call out to him:

"Well done, my good and faithful servant."

"The world is a dangerous place, not because of those who do evil, but because of those who look on and do nothing!"

ALBERT EINSTEIN

Epilogue

While fictional, this story is loosely based on events that occurred while I lived and worked in Metro Atlanta. Many of the characters are based on individuals I have encountered in the area around 14th and Peachtree Streets.

On January 7, 2014, Charlie Perkins, a 70-year-old homeless man was found dead on the streets of Atlanta.v It had reached 5°F the night before, and the medical examiner reported his cause of death as hypothermia. In other words, Mr. Perkins had frozen to death.

There really was a snow and ice storm that shut down traffic in Atlanta. It happened a couple of weeks after Mr. Perkins death. The local meteorologists predicted snow around 10 a.m. on Tuesday, January 28, 2014. The Georgia Department of Transportation (DOT), Atlanta city government, and surrounding counties did not think much would happen, so roads were not treated. School systems, government offices, and businesses did not announce plans for closing. Snow began falling around noon. Temperatures dropped rapidly, and ice began forming. Schools and offices quickly announced 1 p.m. closings. Millions of people hurriedly headed for the interstate system and surface streets, causing them to be quickly overwhelmed. Everyone trying to leave at 1 p.m. was simply more than the Atlanta roadways could accommodate. Semi-trucks and other automobiles slid sideways on ice, and soon, interstates were blocked.

While there we many stories of 14-hour commutes, thousands of people were stuck on the roadways and forced to spend the night in their cars. Many children slept in school gymnasiums and cafeterias. Compassionate Atlantans opened their homes to complete strangers and carried peanut butter and jelly sandwiches, water, and coffee to stranded travelers.

The issues of homelessness and hunger are extremely significant in the United States. While homelessness is more prevalent with people living under bridges and in parks in large cities, homelessness exists in smaller communities with people living in tents and cars. The hunger issue is even more widespread. There is no area within the United States that is not touched by hunger. These are not issues that exist due to a failure of government programs. These are issues that are due to a failure of "We the people." Our first reaction is to claim ignorance: "I don't know anyone who is homeless. I don't know anyone who is hungry." But if we stop and think about it, we all know someone who is a single parent living on a minimum wage job. Just by knowing the minimum wage in our area and the average rent, we can put two and two together and surmise that they are struggling with poverty. With poverty comes hunger and homelessness. They might be doing OK now, but one significant illness or accident, and they will be struggling to put a roof over their heads and food on their table. We all know seniors who have retired on limited incomes, some living only on their Social Security check. Expensive prescriptions not fully covered by Medicaid/Medicare and high rent quickly cause seniors to struggle with decisions of weighing their prescriptions against groceries, rent, and utilities. Neighbors struggling with terminal diseases or living with disability from accidents are all candidates for hunger and homelessness.

Our children often see more of it that we do. They go to school and see other children receiving free or reduced lunch. Whether they completely realize it or not, they see children that are struggling with hunger and possibly homelessness.

These are the children whose family moves from one relative's house to another. And, these are the children who, more often than not, get their only meal each day at school for lunch. When school closes for a snow day or when school closes for the summer, these children do not know if they will have anything to eat.

I urge you to familiarize yourself with the level of homelessness and hunger in your community and to investigate how you can help make a difference in your own backyard. I am not suggesting that you go out and launch a food pantry or homeless shelter. Instead, I am suggesting that you research the organizations that are already working to address these issues in your local community and consider volunteering with one. Local nonprofit organizations are working with limited budgets and struggling to meet huge challenges with limited resources. They desperately need volunteers who can catch the vision, help with fundraising, collect canned goods, pickup surplus food from local restaurants, and a host of other things. Around the country, there are hundreds of thousands of these organizations that are working tirelessly to make a positive difference in their corner of the world. I urge you to find one and invest some of your time and maybe even some of your money to aid them in their mission.

Finally, I challenge you to consider serving not because it is a good thing to do and not because it will make you feel good about yourself. I challenge you to serve because it reflects the Spirit of God. He calls us to love those he loved, to care about the things he cares about, and to be heartbroken for the things that break His heart. Through serving, we do not necessarily change the world, but we are changed more into His likeness. And by doing so, others can see Him in us.

Just outside of Austin, Texas sits a community called Community First! Village. It is a model for the world on how to address homelessness. Alan Graham, Founder/President/CEO, Mobile Loaves & Fishes has done an excellent job of listening and addressing the needs of those struggling with homelessness. I highly encourage you to purchase and read his book, *Welcome Homeless: One Man's Journey of Discovering the Meaning of Home.*

What Can I Do?

1. Volunteer at a local food pantry, homeless shelter, or cold night shelter in your area. Ask questions, meet struggling families, and hear their stories.
2. Sit down with a homeless person, buy them a meal, and ask them to share their story.
3. Read Alan Graham's book, *Welcome Homeless: One Man's Journey of Discovering the Meaning of Home*, available on Amazon.com
4. Volunteer to work on a Habitat for Humanity home build and encourage your employer to sponsor a build.
5. Encourage local leaders to address the issues causing homelessness, instead of trying to sweep it out of sight.
6. Own a rental property? Consider providing housing for a homeless family.
7. Consider donating land or property to a homeless organization or leave an estate to them in a will.
8. Visit Community First! Village in Austin, TX and study what they are doing in partnership with corporations and private citizens.
9. Consider starting a "Building Beds" program in your community. Bridgepoint Church in Saint Petersburg, Florida became aware of numerous children in their community that did not have beds. They began working with guidance counselors who identify children who are struggling in school and determine that they do not have a bed to sleep on. Parents are connected with the program, and Building Beds provides them a twin-size bed, new mattress, sheets, a pillow, a stuffed animal, a night light, pajamas, and toiletries.

Questions for Reflection

1. If I was homeless, what would I desire the most?
2. What lengths would I go to if I learned my child was homeless and living on the street?
3. What are my attitudes toward homeless people when I see them? Do I cast judgment on homeless people without knowing their story?
4. Should my excess (income, time, and energies) be focused on me or on those around me? What could I change in my spending habits to allow me to financially support ending homelessness in my community?
5. How can I provide a hand up and not just a handout?
6. What could I do for one that I wish I could do for all?
7. How can I serve those who are in need financially, physically, mentally, and/or spiritually?
8. Where can I volunteer that will bring me in contact with homeless in my community? Could I teach a trade or craft to a homeless person that they could use to become self-sufficient?
9. How can I be an advocate for the homeless in my community?
10. Who do I know who needs to read this book in order to stir their awareness of the plight of the homeless?

326 | ALLEN MADDING

Appendix

The Point-in-Time (PIT) Count is an annual effort led by the U.S. Department of Housing and Urban Development (HUD) to estimate the number of Americans without safe, stable housing. Conducted annually in late January, HUD staff and volunteers attempt to count the number of homeless individuals on a single night across the United States. As one can imagine, locating and counting unsheltered homeless individuals is a daunting task and it is assumed the numbers are possibly low.

On a single night in January 2016, the Point-in-Time count identified 355,212 homeless nationwide of those 157,204 were unsheltered.

In the country's largest cities, the Point-in-Time count identified:

73,523 homeless in New York City, NY

43,854 homeless in Los Angeles City & County, CA

10,730 homeless in Seattle/King County, WA

8,669 homeless in San Diego City and County, CA

8,350 homeless in our nation's capital - District of Columbia

6,996 homeless in San Francisco, CA

6,524 homeless in San Jose/Santa Clara City & County, CA

6,240 homeless in Boston, MA

6,208 homeless in Las Vegas/Clark County, NV

6,112 homeless in Philadelphia, PA

5,889 homeless in Chicago, IL [vi]

4,063 homeless in Atlanta, GA [vii]

Smaller cities also included in the report were Honolulu, HI with 2,797 homeless and St. Petersburg/Clearwater/ Largo/Pinellas County, FL with 2,383 homeless.

373,571 people (68%) were staying in emergency shelters, transitional housing programs, or safe havens, while 176,357 people were staying in unsheltered locations. There were 194,716 people in families with children experiencing homelessness, representing 35 percent of the homeless population. 330,890 people experiencing homelessness were men, while 217,268 people were women, and 1,770 people were transgender. Women experiencing homelessness were more likely to be sheltered than either men or transgender people. More than three-quarters of women experiencing homelessness 165,780 people were staying in emergency shelters, transitional housing programs, or safe havens, compared to 206,999 men, and 792 transgender people.

39,471 veterans were experiencing homelessness and there were 35,686 unaccompanied homeless youth.[viii]

These seem like staggering numbers, and one might find themselves asking how one person can make a difference. What could I do to change the tide of homelessness in my community? My suggestion is to begin by looking around your community. Does your community have a homeless population? Where are they? How many are there? What organizations are seeking to end homelessness? You can get a lot of answers to these types of questions by seeking out places to volunteer and serve in your community.

Other Books by Allen Madding

Volunteer Management 101: How to Recruit and Retain Volunteers
by Allen Madding and Dan King

An employee needs the paycheck to pay the rent, the mortgage, the car payment, student debt, the credit card bill, the utilities, and a host of other bills. Volunteers, on the other hand are not motivated by a paycheck to stick it out when the manger is chewing someone out or things get uncomfortable.

The volunteer is simply motivated by making a difference and being a part of the organization. Their commitment hinges on how vested they are with the vision and purpose of the organization. When it gets to be too much of a hassle to serve, when they feel unappreciated, or when they feel the commitment is too demanding, they will walk away – usually without any warning or explanation.

With several decades of experience between them, Madding and King share insights on how to manage these valuable resources in your organization.

About the Author

Allen Madding is an advocate for families, children, the hungry and the homeless. He is a follower of The Way, author, grant writer, blogger, guitar player, Harley Davidson motorcycle rider, hiker, traveler, Atlanta Braves and Dallas Cowboys fan, and an information technology professional who lives with his wife Allison in St. Petersburg, Florida.

A graduate of Georgia Southern University with a Bachelors of Business Administration - Management Information Systems and Keller Graduate School of DeVry University with a Masters of Business Administration, he grew up in rural South Georgia where he developed a love for hunting, fishing, and racing cars. He raced short track stock cars for nine years while operating a local computer store in his hometown and served as a volunteer fireman and EMT. He moved to Atlanta in 2000 taking a full-time job in Information Technology management, and began writing weekly contributions for Speedway Media and then Insider Racing News.

He has actively supported Habitat for Humanity participating in over 14 home builds. After a short-term mission trip to Venezuela in 2011, he became keenly aware of the level of hunger in his community and began seeking a way to contribute. Allen and Allison launched Feed the Hungry Forsyth, Inc., a nonprofit food rescue organization in Cumming, Georgia, in December 2011 to collect unsold food from area restaurants and delivering to community food pantries.

---

[i] Bible passage from the New International Version

[ii] HomeAidAtlanta.com

[iii] HomelessTaskForce.org

[iv] "I Know a Little" - written by Steve Gaines, recorded by Lynyrd Skynyrd, MCA,1978

[v] Man, 70, Freezes to Death in Atlanta, AJC.com, http://www.ajc.com/news/news/homeless-man-freezes-to-death-in-atlanta/ncfjj/

[vi] City of Chicago 2016 Homeless Point-in-Time Count & Survey Report (Prepared by the Voorhees Center for Neighborhood & Community Improvement, University of Illinois at Chicago)

[vii] 2016 Homeless Point in Time Count by Partners for Home

[viii] The 2016 Annual Homeless Assessment Report to Congress Part 1: Point-in-Time Estimates of Homelessness, The U.S. Department of Housing and Urban Development, Office Of Community Planning And Development, November 2016

www.ingramcontent.com/pod-product-compliance
Lightning Source LLC
Chambersburg PA
CBHW030416180626
46812CB00005B/2036